# THE ACCIDENT

Lori Miller Kase

# The Accident

Lori Miller Kase

Woodhall Press | Norwalk, CT

Woodhall Press, Norwalk, CT 06855
WoodhallPress.com


Cover design: LJ Mucci
Layout artist: LJ Mucci

**Library of Congress Cataloging-in-Publication Data available**
ISBN 978-1-960456-33-5 (paper: alk paper)
ISBN 978-1-960456-34-2 (electronic)

First Edition
Distributed by Independent Publishers Group
(800) 888-4741

Printed in the United States of America

For Danny, Brandon and Sara

# Prologue

The accident is all over the news.

Dads wave the papers in front of their teenage kids—a cautionary tale.

Moms speak about it in hushed tones while standing with their children at the bus stop. They whisper about it over coffee at Village Bagels and while waiting for their yoga classes to start.

Kids talk about it while crowded around lockers, huddled in stairwells, leaning over homeroom desks. They talk about it on the bus, in the cafeteria, and behind the bleachers, where people are leaving flowers and footballs by the photo someone stuck onto a metal pole.

But I don't say anything. Because of what I know.

# Chapter One

I stare at Tyler's profile picture. His blue eyes seem even bluer above the black grease smeared below them. He's smiling, giving a thumbs-up. He'd probably just won a game.

Switching screens, I click on the photo that had been shared from phone to phone at school—the one of his body under a sheet. I study the silhouette outlined by the white fabric, the protrusions where the nose, the shoulders, the feet would be. So still. How could this be the same person?

I zoom in, searching for proof that he's under there—someone I know. Someone I knew. To see a piece of his clothing? A glimpse of his blue and white practice jersey? His jet-black hair? The front door slams and jolts me away from my screen. Finally. Rob.

I hear feet on the stairs. My brother's door squeaks open, then shut. It's always shut. But I *need* to talk to him. Maybe he knows something. After all, he and Tyler are—*were*—in the same grade. I'm about to get up and find out when I hear Rob talking to someone.

His room is next to mine and the wall between us is very thin. I know this because whenever I practice guitar or sing along with the radio, Rob shouts at me to shut up. Or punches the wall.

"Shit, what are we going to do?" I freeze when I realize the other voice belongs to Zach.

Rob mumbles something, but I can't make out what he's saying. I lean forward on my beanbag chair, toward our shared wall, but still can't decipher his words. I hear footsteps, which I assume belong to Zach. They get softer and then louder.

"Shit, shit, *shit*." Zach's voice too, gets louder as he paces toward the wall, quieter as he walks away. His voice sounds different. Scared. My stomach tightens.

Their words are muffled, but I can make out some of what they say. "...shouldn't have....too high to drive..." *What?!* They couldn't be talking about the accident, could they? *Not Zach. Please don't let it be Zach.*

"Zach, calm down," Rob says, his voice rising so that he doesn't sound calm either. "...just think..." What is he saying? I want to hear, and I don't want to hear.

"Rob, he's dead. Jesus."

My heart stops for a second. My hands close into fists and the computer teeters on my lap. I grab it just before it falls to the floor. At that moment, Rob's Phish song ringtone interrupts their conversation.

"Yeah, he's here," Rob says. "Uh huh. Yeah. OK." More mumbling. And then they're gone. I don't move. I glance down at the computer screen, which has gone dark. And slowly close my laptop. Yet, even as part of my brain is engaged in the mechanical act of shutting my computer, the other part is racing. *Is it* their *fault Tyler is dead?*

The light overhead is bright, too bright. I toss my laptop on my bed, jump up, start pacing, clenching and unclenching my fists. Back and forth, back and forth. Just like Zach. I stop in my tracks. What do I do with these words I've just heard? My stomach tightens again, my breathing gets more shallow, the breaths come quicker. My heart is racing—I seriously might have a heart attack. I bend forward, hands on my knees, try to take deeper breaths. I stare hard at the white fibers of my shag rug, just to focus on something concrete, familiar, then plop back down into my beanbag. I have to calm down.

I reach onto my bookshelf and retrieve the guitar pick I'd stashed behind my music books that day I first bumped into Zach at The Music Shoppe. Before the accident. I let myself sink further into the beanbag and twirl the tortoise shell pick he gave me around in my fingers. I rub my thumb along the smooth edges of the pick, study its swirls of black and brown. Close my hand over the pick and press it, hard, into my palm. It's surprisingly sharp.

# Chapter Two

Who even knew Zach played guitar? A few weeks earlier, I'd discovered that he had the lesson slot right before mine. As he was leaving the lesson room and I was entering, we had that kind of awkward moment you have when meeting someone out of context.

"Oh hi, Rob's sister," he said, looking slightly puzzled to find me there.

"Oh hi, Rob's friend," I said back, my face getting warm, which was weird, because why would I be blushing in front of Zach, who'd been my brother's friend since elementary school?

"I didn't know you were a musician," he said, nodding toward the guitar case slung over my left shoulder. I liked that he called me a musician.

"I didn't know you were a musician either," I said with a half-smile, thinking to myself how ridiculous this conversation was, but at the same time, kind of enjoying it. When he smiled back, he smiled as if something was just dawning on him, like I was not only his friend's sister, but a girl—a girl who might be slightly more interesting.

Eric stuck his head out of the music room.

"You two know each other?" he asked. "Well, your friend Zachary just had one of his best lessons ever, so let's hope his juju rubs off on you today."

Zach smiled again, and handed me the guitar pick he'd been holding.

"It's my lucky pick," he said. "If you use it, you're guaranteed to bring down the house. Or at least, to impress Eric."

"Get out of here," Eric said to Zach, shooing him from the room. "Hannah and I have music to make."

It wasn't my best lesson. Zach's smile. I'd never seen it like that. I left The Music Shoppe feeling strange. Wondering if I'd see him there again the following week. Hoping I would.

I started looking for Zach at school. But he was a junior, so he had classes in a separate wing of the high school from me. I didn't see Zach—or Rob—in the hallways like I used to when we overlapped in middle school.

A couple of days after the guitar lesson encounter, I convinced my best friend Alex to sneak out for lunch—technically, only juniors and seniors are permitted to leave school grounds. And Zach was there. At Frank's Pizza. With my brother and the rest of their crew, of course. Rob barely acknowledged me, but Zach nodded his head in my direction, grinned. A dimple flashed on one side when he smiled. My stomach did a flip.

"He SO likes you," Alex whispered as we waited in line to order. "He definitely wants to *tap that.*" She pointed her finger at me and I swatted it away.

"Right, Alex." I rolled my eyes. I know I'm inexperienced for my age. We're both behind in that department. But Alex loves to *talk about* boys—though who she's in love with changes practically every week. She's on a mission to lose her v-card before we graduate. I just want a boyfriend, to be part of a couple.

I snuck another glance at Zach, and found him watching me. I turned back, embarrassed. But at the same time—*he was watching me*. I wondered what might happen next.

Zach appeared at our house more often. Instead of going straight to the basement to play video games like Rob's friends usually did, he stopped to talk to me first.

"He came over again today," I reported to Alex more and more frequently.

"What a surprise."

But Alex *was* surprised when I told her what happened the last time Zach came over.

I was sitting on the front porch swing scrolling through my phone, pushing off the planked wood floor with the toe of my sneaker, mindlessly swinging, when the porch step creaked, startling me. I looked up—and there he stood.

"That looks like fun," he said, pausing at the front door. "May I?"

I wasn't sure what he meant until he started walking toward the swing. Toward me. Something fluttered in my stomach as he picked up my guitar case, which had been propped up beside me, moved it to the floor, and sat down. Right next to me. Like, really close.

"Um, yeah," I said after the fact, flustered, feeling my face getting warm, not sure where to look because if I turned toward him I knew his face would be *right* there. I peeked at him sideways, without turning my head, and he grinned—showed that dimple again.

"Were you going to play?" he asked, nodding toward the guitar.

"Yeah, in a bit." My right hand automatically flew up to my hair, which I played with as I tried to come up with what to say next. But all I could think about was how near his leg was to my leg.

"We should play together some time." I was so surprised by the suggestion that I turned toward him to see if he was serious. And there he was—those hazel eyes smiling right along with his mouth. Which was just inches away from my mouth.

"I'd like that," I whispered, my voice lost somewhere deep in my throat.

Zach's phone buzzed in his lap, interrupting the moment. He glanced down.

"Uh," he said, hesitating for a second. "Rob's waiting for me..." He rose from the swing. Then locked eyes with me. "To be continued." He grinned, and then disappeared inside the house.

*To be continued?*

I've been thinking about that encounter all week. About what might have happened if Rob hadn't texted from the basement. I've been impatient for the "to be continued" part to happen, but at the same time, I've loved the feeling that something might.

But this was all before the accident, before I overhead Zach and Rob talking.

Now I don't know how to feel about Zach.

# Chapter Three

"Hannah, come down for dinner." I know Mom will call again, more impatiently, if I take too long to respond. Nothing makes her crazier than when she "works so hard" to make a "special" meal for her family, and then we "ruin" it by waiting until it gets cold to show up at the table. After what I just heard, I don't really feel like eating. But I pull myself off my beanbag and head downstairs.

The smell of my mom's marinara sauce wafts up the stairway. I swallow hard. Try to put on a neutral face as I enter the kitchen.

Everyone else is already seated—Mom and Dad at the ends of the table, Rob slumped in his chair, his back to the wall. I didn't hear him come back in. I slip into my seat across from my brother. I always sit on the outer side of the table to be closer to Felix, our cockapoo. Who—as if on cue—inches his way toward the table and lies down expectantly beside my chair. But tonight, I barely glance at Felix. Tonight I'm more interested in Rob.

"So nice of you to grace us with your presence," Mom says, passing a bowl filled with spaghetti Bolognese. Stray pieces of spaghetti, dripping with red sauce, dangle from the side of the bowl. I suppress a wave of nausea and use the tongs to drop a tangle of pasta and meat sauce onto my plate.

"I was doing homework," I lie, glancing over at Rob. He looks sullenly at his food, moving the spaghetti around on his plate.

"Rob, how about eating your food instead of playing with it," Dad says, twirling his fork in his dish several times, then transferring a giant ball of noodles into his mouth. Rob rolls his eyes and puts a forkful of spaghetti into his mouth with an exaggerated motion.

"So, I heard Dr. Finnely spoke to the students today about Tyler Miller," Mom says. "How was that?"

My heart sinks. After what I've just overheard—not to mention the nonstop talk about the hit and run at school—I can't bear having to talk about Tyler Miller at the dinner table. Having to act normal in front of our parents, having to make sure I don't give anything away. I shrug. And look to Rob, who runs his hand through his hair.

"How *was* that?" Rob asks.

"I mean, it's so sad, and I know this has hit a lot of the kids and teachers hard." Mom speaks slowly, like she's choosing her words carefully. "You know, if either of you ever want to talk to someone about it—"

"No, Mom, we don't need to see a shrink, if that's what you're implying" Rob says, then glances up at me and adds, "Well, speaking for myself, of course. Hannah's always been a little psycho."

I scowl at my brother. And purposely don't look at my parents.

Would he say that kind of thing if he knew that I know? It's almost as if his fate—not to mention Zach's—lies in my hands. I wish I'd never heard them talking. I'm not good at lying.

"Rob!" Mom says. Dad just gives him a look.

"Me neither," I mumble, digging into my pasta. The last thing I need is to meet with some therapist, to have yet another person trying to talk to me about what happened. I'll protect Rob, even if he doesn't deserve it. And of course I'll protect Zach.

Mom sighs. "How could someone just drive away?" she says to no one in particular.

"I know," Dad says, shaking his head. I'm struggling with the same question. What if Tyler hadn't died right away? What if they could have saved him?

"Whoever did this will get what's coming to them—those cops'll figure it out," Dad adds. We all know "those cops"—neighbors, classmates' parents. Will they soon become the enemy?

"People are saying there might have been a drunk driver involved," Mom says.

*Not drunk*, I think. *High*.

"*People* are idiots," Rob snaps. He emphasizes the word "people" as if putting it into quotes. I glance up at him. His forehead is furrowed, his lips pressed into a straight line. He looks mad, not scared. "Nobody knows anything. People just make shit up."

I want to tell my brother to shut up. Why on earth would he choose this particular day to suddenly break his usual dinnertime silence? Why can't he just focus on shoveling the food in, like he typically does, acting as if he's just tolerating our mother's attempts to engage us in meaningful conversation?

"Rob," Mom says sharply. Then she pauses, and changes her tone. "Look, I know this is upsetting..."

"Mom, I hardly knew the kid. I played with him when I was ten. Can we just drop it? This is all anyone's talked about all day long. Can't we just eat dinner?"

So much for keeping a low profile. Mom gives Dad a look. I shift uncomfortably in my seat.

"Yes, we can just eat dinner," Dad says. Felix whimpers beside my chair. I slip him a chunk of meat from the edge of my plate, and leave my hand hanging beside my chair so that he can lick the remaining sauce off my fingers.

I retreat to my room immediately after dinner, giving the homework excuse, but once behind my closed door, I bypass my backpack—and desk—and fall back into the beanbag chair. Tyler Miller is dead. *Dead*! It's hard enough to wrap my head around that, much less the possibility that Rob and Zach might have had anything to do with it.

I scroll through my phone. The story, of course, is trending on social media, an endless slide show of the hit and run's aftermath playing on repeat. There's the chaotic accident scene, lit by the red and blue lights of emergency vehicles. Policemen trying to hold back the crowd gathering in the early morning mist. Trucks painted with the call letters of the different news stations, scattered randomly around the periphery, at awkward angles, as if their drivers parked hastily in a rush to join the fray. Camera people, holding their cameras above their heads and angling them down toward what lay at the center of the commotion. That silhouette of a human figure. Still, beneath the sheet.

We hadn't been friends, exactly. But Tyler used to come to our house when we were all in elementary school. He and Rob were in the same fourth and fifth grade classes and used to hang out. The friendship faded once they started middle school, and Tyler didn't come around anymore. But he still nodded hello toward me in the halls when I got to the middle school. Or when I'd pass him jogging through town. He was friendly like that.

Everyone in town knew who Tyler was. He was a football legend—held the state record for most touchdowns scored in a season. Everyone talked about how colleges were already trying to lure him with athletic scholarships. And all the girls had crushes on him, including me and Alex, though mostly we admired him from afar. He was only one year ahead of us.

I know I will continue to see these photos in my head, even when I'm not looking at my computer. Especially at night, when I try to sleep. But even that horrible image, the body beneath the sheet, isn't as bad as the videos. In the videos, the cacophony of voices and sirens add to the chaos, intensifies the panicky feeling that has taken permanent residence inside my gut. What if I could rewind those videos? What—or more importantly, *who*—would I see?

# Chapter Four

"What is with you, Hannah-Ban?" Alex used to call me Hannah Banana, but dropped the extra syllables somewhere between elementary school and high school.

It's been three days since the accident. Alex and I walk from English to Social Studies, practically being carried along by the throng of students changing from one class to another. Locker doors clang open and bang shut, and students' voices fill the hallway around us.

"What do you mean?" I answer, not bothering to turn my head.

When I realize Alex has stopped walking, I stop too, and glance over at her. She puts her hands on her hips and stares into my face. Students continue to move around us, some throwing us dirty looks for blocking traffic.

"Really?" she says. Alex and I have known each other since first grade—she knows when something is up with me. "You're, like, on some other planet this week." I shrug. We continue in silence down the hallway, then turn left toward the Social Studies wing.

"Ohhh..." Alex says, as if something is just dawning on her. "The hit and run...." She nods. I tense, but don't feel the need to respond.

"We didn't *really* know him," Alex blurts out. "I mean, it's sad and everything, but it's not like we hung out with him." She's right, we didn't, but I suddenly flash back about a decade to a younger version of Tyler having a snack at the kitchen table with me and Rob. I see Tyler holding a bag of chips out to me across the old pine table—something Rob would never have done. I remember taking notice. Yes, he was already cuter than most of the boys at school, but it wasn't just his jet-black hair and bright blue eyes that drew my attention. He was kind. Even back then he had a sort of magnetism about him.

"I know, but it's so weird to know someone close to our age who's dead," I whisper. "And that anyone could have done it. Even someone at this school." I regret the words as soon as they leave my lips, but am especially sickened by the way Alex's eyes widen.

"Do you think it's someone from our school?" An aspiring journalist, Alex loves drama and intrigue.

"No, of course not," I say quickly. "If it was, they wouldn't have driven away."

"True..." Alex pauses and tilts her head to one side, squinting her eyes a little, as if she's watching thoughts scroll through her mind. "But then again, if the person thought he had killed Tyler, and stopped, he would have gone to jail. Imagine someone we know going to jail..." Alex stops for a second. I have no choice but to listen.

"On the other hand," she says, "if they kept driving, they wouldn't actually *know* that they killed him, and no one else would either. Or, if they knew, what would be the point of stopping, since they couldn't save him, and they'd just end up getting arrested for murder?" *Murder*. I feel sick.

Just then, our friend Kei comes up from behind us and tries to insinuate herself into the conversation. "Who? Do you know something about the hit and run?"

"No," I say, maybe a bit *too* quickly. "We're just coming up with theories..."

"Well," says Kei, "I hear there was a huge party at Kevin Russo's that night—he doesn't live that far from where Tyler was hit. Anyway, his parents were away, and like half the senior class was there. And it went *really* late. And people got *really* wasted..."

Did Zach and Rob go to that party? They aren't seniors—but some of their friends are. My stomach twists into knots. Fortunately, at that moment, we arrive at our classroom. I won't have to talk about the accident anymore. But that doesn't mean I won't have to think about it.

*Too high to drive*. They didn't say *they* were too high to drive, did they? Maybe they were talking about someone else. Maybe they knew who did it and were feeling guilty. There's no way Rob, who'd gotten into trouble that other time with the car, would take any chances when it came to driving.

He'd just gotten his license and wasn't supposed to drive with anyone else in the car—aside from our parents—for at least six months. At that point, according to Connecticut law, he could drive a sibling, and I'd hoped Mom would make Rob drive me places. I imagined it as a new stage in our relationship, in which I would arrive places with him, sans parents. Maybe we'd start talking about stuff, have actual conversations. He wouldn't be allowed to drive his friends for a year, so I'd have him to myself for at least six months. He was bound to talk to me if I was the only one in the car. Right?

He'd only had the license for a month when he took the second car one Saturday night. Mom and Dad were out. Three of his friends—Zach included—were with him.

"Where are you going?" I asked when I noticed Rob grabbing the car keys off the kitchen counter and heading with his friends toward the garage door. Alex and I were watching a movie in the family room, which is separated from the kitchen by only a dining table.

"Out," he answered dismissively.

"But you can't drive other people yet," I said.

"What are you—the driving police?" he asked. I remember his friends laughing. "We'll be back before Mom and Dad. We're just running out to get some food and stuff."

I was pretty sure that Mom and Dad would approve of the "stuff" they were getting even less than they would approve of the idea of him breaking the law and driving his friends. They were always getting mad at Rob about something. And he usually deserved it. But I didn't want to seem uncool, so I dropped it.

"What they don't know won't hurt them," he said, waiting for an acknowledgement of some kind from me.

"I know nothing," I answered. I would say anything to make Rob like me. Alex just laughed.

Thanks to a nosy neighbor, who reported to our mother the next morning that she had been "shocked" to see Rob drive by with "a car full of teenagers," Rob was grounded for the next two weekends—and had to listen to repeated lectures about driving being a *serious* responsibility, and how part of that responsibility involved obeying the laws that had been created to protect not only him, but also other drivers and pedestrians, and that he'd *better* be damn sure that meant no drinking and driving *ever* or you will have your license taken away. Dad's voice always reached a crescendo at this point in the lecture, even though our parents never did find the "stuff" Rob and his friends brought back from that excursion. No, he would never drive high, especially after that. Would he?

I tune out as Ms. Herman drones on about the nuclear arms race and glance out the classroom window at the empty athletic fields. Well, not entirely empty. The district has moved gym classes indoors and suspended after-school activities, but the TV crews who'd set up camp the day after Tyler was killed seem to be in no hurry to leave. The thought of having to pass by all those media people again at the end of the school day makes my stomach churn. Maybe I'll even take the dreaded bus.

A buzzer sounds from the school's PA system, startling me back into the classroom.

"Ms. Herman, please report to Dr. Finnely's office."

Ms. Herman glances at the loudspeaker, two grooves forming between her eyebrows. She's old-school—and old—and spends most of our 45-minute classes giving boring lectures. She does *not* like to be interrupted.

Ms. Herman sighs loudly. "Okay, class. Take out your books and start reading Chapter Seven—The Cold War—I'll be back in ten." She pauses in the doorway. "Read—don't talk," she adds sternly. She cups a hand to her ear. "I'll be listening."

Pages rustle as everyone opens their books, but the minute Ms. Herman exits, the phones come out and the room erupts in whispers.

"Hannah!" Alex turns around from the seat in front of mine. "Look at this." I brace myself as Alex holds her phone to my face. It's Tyler's Facebook page. A picture of the accident site is now his cover photo: Someone has stuck a sign in the ground—*RIP Tyler*—and people have left flowers and footballs and teddy bears (why teddy bears?) on the ground around the sign.

Goosebumps form beneath the sleeves of my sweatshirt. "Who do you think changed his cover photo?" I whisper. Surely not his parents. Would his brother, a freshman, have taken the time to do that? His teammates? How would his friends even know his password?

"I don't know," Alex says, shaking her head. "It's kind of creepy."

I nod. And wonder who's supposed to take charge of a dead person's Facebook page.

# Chapter Five

We meet up at our lockers after the endless morning classes.

"Do you want to go to Frank's for lunch?" Alex asks. The idea of running into Zach and Rob gives me a stomach ache but it will seem suspect if I say no. I never say no to *any* opportunity to run into Zach.

A blast of heat from the pizza ovens—along with the sounds of cashiers shouting orders and noisy tables—hit us as soon as we open the door to Frank's. The place is packed, as usual, but I immediately spot Zach by the counter, balancing a slice of pizza on a paper plate in one hand, a red "Coca-Cola" cup in the other, his signature plaid flannel hanging open to reveal a gray tee. I feel Alex's elbow jab my side, and give her a warning look before shifting my eyes back to Zach. Is he more somber than usual, or am I just imagining it?

I study the way his dark brown hair looks tousled, as if he never combs it, how it's so long it almost touches his shoulders. I notice the dimple, and realize he's smiling at me. *Oh my God, he caught me staring. How humiliating.* I give him a half wave—and quickly look away.

"I'm so embarrassed," I whisper to Alex. "He saw me looking."

"You guys are adorable," Alex says as we inch forward in line. "I wish you'd just hook up already."

I try to elbow Alex but she side-steps and I swing at the air. I would never tell Alex this, but the truth is, I don't know if I'm ready for *hooking up*, per se. As far as my friends are concerned, I'm as eager as they are to lose that V-card. But really, I would be fine with a kiss.

Ever since that afternoon on my porch, I've been imagining kissing Zach. Thinking about that *To be continued*. I want things to progress, but I'm also scared for them to. Am I crazy to want this, to want *him*? Maybe Zach isn't the kind of person I thought he was. Maybe he has a dark side. I try to ignore the feeling of dread that starts to rise in my stomach when I think of what he might have done.

"I'll get the drinks?" I say fake-cheerfully, my voice stepping up an extra octave. I grab two cups without waiting for Alex to answer, head to the soda fountain. I keep my eyes focused in front of me and away from Zach, Rob, and their friends. I start filling the first cup with Dr. Pepper when I'm startled by Zach's voice.

"Hey," he says, reaching his cup under the Coca-Cola spigot, lightly tapping my arm with his.

"Hey," I say back, trying to sound casual. But inside I'm dying: This is the closest I've been to him since the porch swing. I hope he can't hear my heart beating quickly against the inside of my chest. I attempt to switch cups gracefully to fill the second one, but flustered by Zach's nearness, I spill half the contents of the first cup onto his extended arm.

"Whoa," he says, pulling his arm away and stepping back from the soda machine. The brown liquid stains the edge of his sleeve and drips down his arm. He puts down the cup, holds his arm away from the machine—and me—and shakes his hand, spraying drops of soda into the airspace behind us. "You're dangerous."

"I'm s-so sorry," I stammer, putting down the cups, thinking that this whole thing with Zach could become something dangerous. "I can't believe I just did that." I reach toward the napkin dispenser, but he reaches at the same time and our hands collide. I pull mine away quickly.

"I'll live," he says, blotting his sleeve with a fistful of bunched up napkins, looking amused. He must think I'm crazy. Not knowing what to do next, I pick up my and Alex's drinks. Thankfully, Alex shows up at that moment with our pizza.

"Come on, klutz," she says as she passes. I hurry behind her, mortified. And very conscious of the part of my hand that came into contact with his.

That afternoon, the Woodfield Chief of Police holds a press conference, announcing that the department has launched a "high-priority" investigation into the hit and run and insisting they will find those responsible. Everyone watches on their phones between classes.

"Don't drive recklessly in Woodfield," the police chief warns viewers. "And *don't* leave the scene of an accident. We will hunt you down and arrest you."

"Wow," whispers Kei.

"Yeah, pretty intense," says Alex.

I wonder if Rob and Zach are watching and feel nauseous.

For the rest of the day, wherever I go, students are talking about it, debating the likelihood of the perpetrator being someone from our town or just someone passing through. Kei brings up the party again. "I mean there were probably lots of drunk drivers on the road, even people we know," she whispers to me and Alex as we walk to our next class. I jump right in, can't help myself.

"Kei, we have no idea what happened. Let's not start any rumors."

"Yeah," mumbles Alex, "we can't make assumptions without having facts." But I can see her reporter wheels spinning, and my stress level rises. "I mean, for all we know," she adds, "it could have been football players from a rival team just intending to cause a minor injury ...." We both give her the side-eye—sports are competitive in our town, but not *that* competitive. We continue down the hall. "The point is," she says knowingly, "it could have been *anyone*."

The constant speculation about what happened weighs on me—by the end of the day, I just want to be alone. I'm tired of feigning interest in Alex and Kei's theories, tired of worrying about my brother, tired of the swirl of emotions that clog my chest whenever I think of Zach. I'm just plain tired. After school I skip the bus, hurrying past the WTNH reporters.

Cars speed past as I walk along Elm Avenue toward home. It's pretty warm for late September, but I can tell from the yellowing leaves on some of the trees that fall has arrived. Usually my favorite season. Now I long for summer, wish I could go back to the days *before*. Before the accident, before everything became so complicated.

I take a deep breath. It even smells like fall—there's a certain crispness to the air, mixed with the earthy scent of what I can only imagine are decomposing leaves. I focus on the sidewalk, taking care not to step on the lines between squares. Tell myself that if I make it all the way home without touching any lines, it will turn out that I'd misheard what Zach and Rob were saying. That they weren't to blame. If I can just count to 100 squares before hitting another red light—just 100 squares—the police will find the *real* culprit. But part of me knows. Part of me keeps coming back to the same questions over and over. Why would Rob and Zach sound so freaked out if they weren't involved? And if they were in the car, how could they not stop after hitting someone? Rob couldn't do that. I know he couldn't. Could Zach?

By the time I walk up my leaf-littered driveway and pull open the door, I'm so caught up in my spiraling thoughts that it takes me a minute to notice Mom standing in front of me. Even with her sleeves rolled up and her shoes off, she looks perfectly coiffed, as always—flawless makeup, polished nails, not a fly-away hair in sight. It's annoying.

"What's wrong?" she asks. She has a built in worry detector, always knows when I've got something on my mind. Usually, I tell her what I'm worrying about, and she knows just what to say to make me worry less. Not this time.

"Oh, nothing. Just tired. Why are you home?"

"My last client cancelled." Mom's a speech therapist. She helps people to make their words come out the way they mean them to. But sometimes her vocation makes her annoyingly persistent in trying to get her own children to voice things that we have no desire to.

Case in point: "Are you sure there isn't anything you want to talk about?" she asks.

"Yup." I drop my backpack on the counter.

"You want something to eat?"

"Nah," I say. Still, I walk straight to the fridge and open the door. "I *am* kind of thirsty though." I grab a bottle of water.

"So any news in school today about the hit and run?" Mom says, sitting down at the island to go through a pile of mail. She throws out the question in a nonchalant way. I know she's anything but. And I'm sure she's seen the news conference.

"No," I answer, scooping up my backpack. "I have to go do homework."

"I heard something interesting," Mom says, as if I hadn't just announced my exit. I turn slowly back around to face her.

"What?"

"Wel-l-l-l," Mom says, as if she's about to say something earth-shattering. "Linda's nephew is a police officer, and he says that they already have some leads and that he wouldn't be surprised if they begin questioning suspects as early as the end of this week." She concludes this announcement in a triumphant way, as if proud to possess knowledge about the investigation that only a select few are privy to. Mom is clueless that she might be gossiping about her own son.

"Wow," I say half-heartedly. But my heart starts racing again. I pause for a second, then throw my backpack over my shoulder and make my exit. "Gotta go." I hide my panic as best I can, but feel Mom's puzzled gaze on my back.

I shut my door and sink into my beanbag chair. What am I going to do? Are the police planning to question kids who'd been at that party? Had Rob and Zach been there? Part of me doesn't want to know what really happened. But I have to find out.

*Hey* I text Alex.

*Hi. Where r u*

*Home. I've been thinking. How do we find out who was at that party?* Alex knows how to find out anything. It's the reporter in her.

*Yeah, you're right. Maybe Kei was onto something...I'm on it.*

I don't ask her how she's going to do it. And I ignore the uneasy feeling that settles into my stomach when I think about Alex digging around for clues. Instead, I focus on what *I* can do. I have to warn Rob.

# Chapter Six

I don't hear Rob come in until it's almost dinnertime. The clanking of pots and the buzz of the fan above the stove tells me that Mom's still downstairs, cooking. I've been trying all afternoon to figure out what to say to Rob, whether I should reveal what I've heard or just innocently mention what Mom said about the police and see how he reacts. But the truth is, it's not natural for me to walk into Rob's room—or even knock on his door. That space has always been off limits. And it isn't as if Rob and I ever really talk, unless the family happens to be having a conversation at dinner. The "next stage" in our relationship that I thought would coincide with his learning to drive never happened. He rarely drives me anywhere.

The fact that my brother and I don't have much of a relationship always bums me out. It doesn't help that I'm the "good one" in the family, that my parents are always using me as an example of how Rob should buckle down and put some effort into his work. *Like your sister.* Still, I'm kind of envious of friends like Kei who are close with their siblings. Maybe when we get older, Rob will show more interest in my life, in me. At this point, to be honest, the only time he ever really talks to me is when he's high.

I can usually tell when he's high because his movements are slightly slower, but more fluid somehow. And he's more—mellow. But even though everything else about him seems more relaxed, he becomes more talkative, in a frenetic kind of way. It's as if there are two dials on him, and the one controlling his speech is turned up, while the one that controls almost everything else about his body is turned down. It's not that weed heightens his interest in me, per se. But if I'm there, in front of him, he draws me into his philosophizing.

"Don't you think it's interesting that certain foods evolved to be considered appropriate for breakfast, but you would never really think of having them at other times of the day?" he said to me one afternoon when I came into the kitchen after a couple of his friends had left. Rob stood in the pantry doorway, eating a bag of Cheetos. Our parents weren't home from work yet, and I'd come down for a snack. I looked at him skeptically.

"I mean, you would never eat these for breakfast," he said, holding up the red Cheetos bag and then licking the orange powder off his fingers. He reached into the closet and pulled out a packet of instant oatmeal. "But you would never have this for snack."

"Breakfasts are culturally-determined," I said, recalling a social studies unit from the previous year on food culture around the world. "Like, people in Japan eat miso soup and rice and fish for breakfast..." I reached over him to grab a bag of Smartfood off the shelf. Rob rolled his eyes at me and continued as if I hadn't spoken.

"And when you think about it, what makes certain things food, and other things not? Like take that apple over there," he said, nodding his head toward the bowl of apples our mother kept out on the counter in the hopes we would choose to eat one for a snack instead of raiding the pantry for what she called "fake food"—like Cheetos and Smartfood.

"Who decided that you just eat the fruit part, and not the leaves and the stems?" I thought about how Rob could turn an apple into a pot-smoking implement. I'd once run down to the basement to look for some old music, not realizing that Rob and his friends were there, and saw Rob stuffing weed into a hole cut into the top of an apple.

"Sister alert," his friend Nick had said, and Rob had leaned over the table and blocked my view of the apple-pipe with his back, but not before I'd caught a glimpse.

"Actually, I think apple leaves make you sick," I say with a mouth full of popcorn. "I mean, I know the seeds are poisonous..." I reached into the bag for another fistful of cheddar-cheese-coated kernels.

Rob killed a tiny sugar ant with his finger, ending its march up the inside of the pantry door. He held out the crushed ant to me. "And why do some cultures consider this a delicacy, while others consider it a pest deserving of extermination?"

"Ew," I said, stepping back from his insect-sullied finger. The whites of Rob's eyes were laced with fine red lines. I breathed in through my nose, subtly, to see if I could detect the sweet scent of weed that sometimes wafted off Rob's clothes when he emerged from a video-game session with his friends. I knew he'd be showered and changed by the time we sat down to dinner with our parents, his Febreze-spritzed clothes tossed haphazardly into the laundry room hamper.

I wondered what being high felt like. The worst thing I've ever done was try e-cigarettes with Alex and one of her newspaper friends behind the bleachers at school. I hated the taste, and vaping made me cough uncontrollably for ten minutes. I had no desire to vape—or smoke—anything else anytime soon.

"It's been real," he said, wiping the dead bug from his hand with the crumpled up Cheetos bag and saluting me with his orange-stained fingers on his way out of the kitchen.

I never let on to Rob that I knew he was getting high—I savored the few moments of camaraderie I shared with this version of my brother. But now I can't help wondering if maybe I should have. The accident changed everything, of course. Now I can't bear to think about Rob getting high.

*Too high to drive.* I can't stop hearing those words. And I can't stop asking myself the question that has been burning a hole in my stomach ever since I heard them for the first time. *Who* was too high to drive? Was it Zach? Was it Rob?

# Chapter Seven

I've been pacing back and forth across my room, but when the screen door slams, I stand suddenly still. I decide I'll wait for Rob to come upstairs and then follow him into his room.

I hear his backpack land with a thud on his bedroom floor. I run my hand through my hair, pulling it around the back of my head and over one shoulder. Rubbing the ends of my hair between my fingers, I listen for any sounds coming out of Rob's room. Silence. My stomach tenses as I tiptoe toward my door.

What should I say, I wonder. *I heard you and Zach talking*? I don't want to sound like I'm holding something over him. *Did you hear anything about the hit and run?* That would make me sound like my mother. I make myself walk into the hallway, hoping that I'll figure out what to say once I see Rob. But his door is closed. Should I knock, or would that be too formal? Just peek my head in? He'll be pissed if I just open his door. What if I walk in on him doing something—private? I knock.

"Rob?" I say his name quietly. I don't want to attract Mom's attention.

"What?"

"Can I open the door?"

"Why?"

"I want to ask you something."

"So ask."

I sigh. He's not going to make this easy. I open the door a crack, and see that he's just sitting on the edge of his bed, probably right where he dropped the backpack, which remains unopened, next to his foot. It scares me that he hasn't moved since he walked into his room, that he isn't even reclining on his bed or leaning against the wall behind it. Just sitting up straight on the edge. His look says "Why are you bothering me?" but he says nothing. Just turns up a hand as if to say "Well?"

I open the door just enough that I can squeeze my body through. Then shut it behind me.

"Did you and Zach go to that party at Kevin Russo's?" I blurt.

"What? Why the fuck is it any of your business what parties I go to?"

I shift in place, look down at my feet.

"Well, I'm just asking because—"

"Because what, Hannah?" He slowly gets up and starts walking toward me. This isn't going as I planned. Though, what did I expect? I grab the ends of my hair and start rubbing it between my fingers again. I came in to warn him, so I might as well get it over with. I swallow, and start again.

"Well, I hear they're going to start questioning people," I say, lowering my voice, "and I heard you and Zach talking—"

Suddenly Rob is right in front of me, up in my personal space, pointing a finger at my face. "YOU. Don't. Know. Anything. I don't know what you think you heard—" Rob's fierce whispers are interrupted by the sound of Mom's footsteps on the stairs.

"Where is everyone?" she calls.

I slide out from between Rob and the door and put my hand on the knob.

"I'd better go," I say quietly.

"Yeah, you'd better."

# Chapter Eight

I sit outside the lesson room at The Music Shoppe the next afternoon, thumbing through a songbook I grabbed off the shelf on the way in. If I don't have something to look at while I wait for my lesson, I'll spend the whole time worrying about Rob. Wishing I'd approached him differently. Or not at all. I open the music book. A compilation of songs by Sara Bareilles. Mom played the *Kaleidoscope Heart* CD over and over when I was little—it was like the soundtrack to my childhood. Maybe I'll try to learn some of her songs.

I flip through the first few pages of the songbook, but can't concentrate. Instead, I wonder if Rob is still pissed. Or maybe he's nervous? He barely looked at me during dinner. And I didn't see him this morning either—though I never see him in the mornings, since he has a "free" first period.

I close the book and look around. A little boy sits on a piano bench outside the other lesson room—the one with the keyboard.

He can't be more than seven. His feet, which dangle from the bench, swing back and forth in time to the music coming from behind the closed door.

*Rhapsody in Blue*. The name of the song pops into my head. I studied piano for a few years in elementary and middle school before switching to guitar. My piano teacher, an old guy named Mr. Nowakowski who had hairs growing out of his ears (a trait I found both fascinating and disturbing), pulled out *Rhapsody* when I announced that I wanted to learn how to play jazz. As he demonstrated the piece, he explained that it was a good piece with which to transition from classical to jazz, since it combined elements of both. I remember liking the exuberance of the music, its ragged rhythms and modern-feeling tempo.

I struggled with it for two weeks before deciding to spend the third week perfecting the classical piece we'd been working on previously—Mozart's Concerto in C—instead. When Mr. Nowakowski asked me to play "Rhapsody in Blue" at my next lesson, I informed him that I preferred classical and played what I considered to be a near perfect rendition of Mozart's Concerto. What I really preferred was to be good at things.

I watch the boy's feet—and his little iridescent green and black sneakers—swinging to the beat of "Rhapsody in Blue" and am struck that the song doesn't seem to evoke the same sense of exuberance I remember. Maybe it's the sad, almost listless expression on the boy's face, but I'm picking up more of a blues note in the piece. The boy sits next to a pretty college-aged girl, who's reading something on her phone.

"You're going to stay here, right?" he says, tugging on the girl's sleeve.

"Yup, not going anywhere." She doesn't look up from her phone. She pats his leg for a second, but then needs her hand to type something. The boy follows her hand with his gaze.

I check my own phone to see the time—two minutes until my lesson—then flip it over to check the mirror I've affixed to the back. It's also two minutes until I see Zach, who seems to have permanently shifted into the lesson slot before mine.

I pull out my lip gloss and swipe it over my lips, pressing them together to even out the shine. I hold the phone further away so that I can see my hair. Ugh. I put the phone back in my backpack and use my hand to sweep my hair around the back of my head and over my shoulder. I glance back at the boy and find him watching me. I smile, but he just looks back down at his swinging legs. I turn to the door and watch for Zach.

# Chapter Nine

"Hey, be back in a minute," Eric says as he emerges from the lesson room. I nod, collect my stuff.

"Hey, Jared," Eric says, tousling the little boy's hair as he walks by. The boy lifts his hand in a pseudo-wave, but his expression stays the same. Eric looks like he's about to say something to the boy but changes his mind. Instead, he heads to the front of the store. I pick up my guitar and peek into the lesson room.

Zach's packing his guitar, with its faded wood and frayed strings, into a well-worn case covered with half-peeling stickers. Along with a psychedelic-colored Phish sticker (the word Phish contorted to fit into the shape of a fish), the decals on Zach's case pay homage to the Grateful Dead (with dancing bears), The Beatles (with the words "Let It Be"), and, to my surprise, Jason Mraz. If I were to place even a single sticker on my pristine leather case, it would be that one, with *love* spelled out in bold, primary-colored letters that look like shapes (rectangle, circle, triangle, square) and Jason Mraz's name in small letters underneath, like a postscript. Seeing my favorite singer's name on Zach's case brightens my mood a bit. Something else we have in common.

"What's up?" Zach says with a playful grin. He's so cute that for a minute I forget my worries. I smile back and try to think of something clever to say. But then I remember what I *really* want to talk to him about and the worry resurfaces, darkening my mood like a veil.

"What's wrong, Hannah?" Zach comes closer and puts his hands on my arms. "Are you okay?"

"Oh, I'm fine...Just a little out of it. I, uh, went to sleep really late last night." I'm flustered. And acutely aware of the feel of his skin on my skin where his hands and my arms touch. His hand is firm, and warm, and it almost feels like there's an electric current running between us.

Part of me just wants to blurt it all out—ask him, outright, about his involvement, tell him what I overheard. But I don't want to ruin this thing with Zach, whatever this *thing* is. Maybe I misunderstood. Maybe Zach and Rob are not to blame.

His face is close to my face, almost as close as it was that day on the porch. He smells like Ivory soap and spearmint gum and Axe deodorant—I know it's Axe, because Rob always leaves his opened on the counter next to our sink, and its distinctive scent wafts up into my nostrils every morning as I brush my teeth. I think about the way Zach said *To be continued* and something flutters in my stomach.

"Well, have a good lesson," he says, moving away suddenly and turning to pick up his instrument as Eric returns to the lesson room. I busy myself removing my guitar from its case, hope I'm not blushing. But Eric isn't looking at me—instead, he's glancing back over his shoulder, then shaking his head.

"So sad about that kid's brother," he mutters.

"About who?" I ask, looking up from my guitar.

"That boy out there," Eric says quietly. "His brother is the one who was killed in the hit and run—Tyler Miller." When he says Tyler's name, he lowers his voice to a whisper. It gives me the chills.

"No," I say, confused. "His brother's in ninth grade." I notice out of the corner of my eye that Zach has grown still, frozen in place above his guitar case.

Eric shuts the door. "That's his other brother," he says, his voice still quiet. "There are—were—three of them. Jared's the youngest. Guess their mom thought he'd be better off getting out of the house and resuming his normal activities, but I don't know..." Eric's voice trails off.

My insides churn. I had no idea about the existence of this other brother. This innocent little kid, whose life had just been turned upside down. Possibly because of my brother and his friend. I can hardly bear to look at Zach—yet I do. And my stomach sinks, because he looks pale. And for the first time, unsure of himself.

"Anyway." Eric seems to suddenly realize that Zach is still there. "I know there's no place you'd rather be, Kirkland, but you need to move your butt out of here so that your friend and I can get down to business."

Zach stands. "Uh, yeah, of course." He tries to assume a casual air, but I can tell by his expression that he's shaken. "I'm outta here." He fumbles as he picks up his guitar case, almost dropping it. "See ya," he says, nodding at me on his way out. But his voice is so quiet that even Eric looks at him strangely.

"Bye," I say, watching him leave. I notice, as he passes, that the knuckles on the hand that holds his instrument case are white.

"So," says Eric. "Shall we?"

I close my eyes for a second and try to get the image of Zach's white knuckles out of my head, then shuffle through the sheets of music strewn across the bottom of my case until I find the song we've been working on. I set the music on the stand, so that the first and second page rest side by side, the remainder of the pages stacked behind them.

"How did you find the piece? Any problems?"

I stare at the title of the song, printed in bold upper case letters at the top of the first page: **I'M YOURS**. I think of Zach.

"Hello? Anyone in there?"

"Oh, sorry. What? "

"What's with everyone today?" Eric says. 'I asked you how you did with the piece."

"Oh, um, good. I'll show you."

I reach into my case for my capo and attach it to the fourth fret. I arrange my fingers so that my third finger is on the top string, the low E, the second on the A, and my ring finger is curled up to cover the high E. The G chord is one of the first chords I learned, so I let muscle memory direct my fingers while my mind returns to the moment before Zach left. His expression. It told me everything I needed to know.

# Chapter Ten

"That's right, go ahead," says Eric, bringing me back to the lesson. I shake my head, trying to shake away my troubling thoughts, and begin to play.

When I first started taking guitar lessons, I was embarrassed to sing in front of Eric—or in front of anyone, for that matter. I didn't think my voice was good enough. But now, sometimes, I become so absorbed in the song I'm playing that the words just come out without me even realizing it. I love the reggae-ish feel of this one, and while it doesn't take me to the usual calm, serene place, I try to push Zach and Tyler and his little brother out of my mind so that I can focus on the music.

*Before the cool done run out, I'll be giving it my bestest*
*And nothing's gonna stop me but divine intervention*
*I reckon it's again my turn*
*To win some or lose some*

I sing quietly, plucking the strings rather than strumming them, because I think plucking is more suited to the staccato-like notes in the song's chorus.

*But I won't hes-i-tate no more*
*no more*
*It cannot wait*
*I'm yours*

At first, I feel like I'm killing it—connecting to the song in a way I haven't before. Yet even as I play, and *feel* the words I'm singing, my mind flits back to Zach. Maybe he needs someone to talk to about all of this, someone who wasn't involved. *Someone like me.*

Suddenly I've lost my concentration, I stumble on the words, play the wrong chord. I stop, drop my hand from the strings.

"Sorry," I say.

"You were going so strong," says Eric. "What happened?"

I shrug. But inside I'm mad at myself. Because I actually practiced this week. A lot. I know this song backward and forward.

"Can I start over?"

"Sure," says Eric.

I force my eyes to focus on the lyrics in front of me, even though I know the words by heart. But I can't find my way back into the song. First I drop my wrist, causing my fingers to lie flat on the neck of the guitar, so I end up muting the adjacent strings. A classic beginner mistake—but I'm not a beginner.

"Curve those fingers," says Eric. "You know better than that."

I lift my fingers, start again. But when I open my mouth to sing, I lose my place on the page and my mind goes blank. I drop my hand from the strings again, and feel my shoulders droop. It's hopeless. All I can think about is Zach, the boy, Tyler Miller.

"Sorry," I say again. "I don't know why I keep messing it up." Even though I do know why.

"How about working on that one again this week, and we can move on to another song?"

"Okay."

I pull out my next song. And attempt to concentrate on my guitar-playing for the rest of the hour. It's not my most stellar lesson.

"Why don't you continue to work on that Jason Mraz song for next Thursday," Eric reminds me as I'm leaving. "And the Ed Sheeran one too."

"Yeah, I will." As I open the door, the piano room door opens at the same time. The little boy—Jared Miller—and I step into the waiting area simultaneously.

I offer a weak smile, but he doesn't notice. Instead, his eyes scan the empty chairs outside the lesson room, and he looks frantically around the music store until his eyes land on the girl who was sitting with him earlier. She rushes toward him from the front of the store. "I'm here, Jared, sorry..."

"You said you would stay."

"I stayed, I just went up front for a sec." She's slightly breathless. She brushes his hair off his forehead and takes his music from him. "So how was your lesson?"

He shrugs. He looks so small as he reaches for the babysitter's hand. She looks down at his hand, then at him, and kisses his hand before they walk out. The tender gesture makes me want to cry. Realizing I've become immobilized, watching them, I make myself follow them out of the music shop. I barely notice my guitar case knocking against the racks of music on my way out.

A cold burst of air greets me outside. Winter's still months away, but it feels like the transition to the cooler days ahead has already begun. The chill cuts through my jean jacket and makes me shiver. It's one thing to think of Tyler, a boy I hardly knew, being gone. But it's another thing entirely to see this sad little boy, his brother, almost a week later, and to understand that his life is irrevocably changed. I stand outside The Music Shoppe and stare after the boy and his babysitter long after they disappear from view. Then I walk home and cry. For the boy, for Tyler, for all their family has lost.

# Chapter Eleven

I stop short when I see the police car parked in front of my house. I've just turned the corner onto my street and am still half a block away. My heartbeat quickens. Are they onto Rob? Is he being questioned?

I don't know whether to turn around or continue home. I wish I could call Zach, ask him what to do. But he doesn't even know I know anything. And we don't call each other. Usually, I'd call Alex, but I can't talk to her about this.

I bend down to tie my shoe, in case anyone's watching. I know I'm being paranoid. Who would be watching? Still, I remain kneeling on the leaf-covered sidewalk, fingers on my laces, trying to figure out what to do.

I randomly think of my first few weeks at sleep-away camp, back when I was eleven. I lived in a bunk with a group of girls I didn't know, strangers really. Lots of the other girls were from New York City and seemed more sophisticated than me, older than their age, and I hadn't really connected with anyone yet. So I stood on the periphery and tried to look like I fit in. I tiptoed, like the others, into the bathroom with my flashlight after lights out, listened more than participated in their illicit late-night conversations.

One of my bunkmates had an older brother who worked as a cook in the mess hall, and she confided one night that he was going to get us a bottle of vodka. I'd never tried any kind of alcohol—unless you count a sip of Maneschevitz wine at Passover, which is more like grape juice—and drinking was grounds for getting kicked out of camp. So the knowledge that this was going to happen, that I was going to either have to participate in this strictly-forbidden activity or risk being an outcast for the rest of the summer, filled me with dread. I was allowed only one phone call home before visiting day. And that was scheduled a few weeks out. Not that I necessarily would have discussed this dilemma with my parents. But the fact that I had no one with whom to share my doubts, my fears—and this secret—made me feel even more alone.

This same feeling overwhelms me as I stand up. I sigh and swing my backpack off my back and onto the ground, unzip it, and shuffle around inside, pretending to look for something. Mom usually beats me home from guitar lessons—it's almost dinnertime after all—so she's probably home too.

It occurs to me that if the police start questioning Rob, Mom and Dad will know. And maybe that wouldn't be *so* terrible. Like me, they have Rob's best interests in mind. They would know what to do.

I zip my backpack, stand up, and sling the pack over one shoulder. I start walking, slowly, toward my house. I've got to see what's going on. But as I approach my house, I feel a rising sense of dread. What if the police officer starts questioning *me*? What if he asks me if Rob went to the party? Of course, I don't know if Rob went to the party, but I know I'm guilty by association. I know *something,* even if I'm not exactly clear on what that something is. What if he asks me if I have "any information" about the hit and run? I'd have to lie to protect Rob and Zach. To a police officer.

I try not to think of Tyler's little brother. His face when he thought his babysitter left him. I try not to think about Zach's expression at the guitar lesson. Or of Rob's anger when I asked him about the party. I try not to think about anything at all, but by the time I reach my yard, I've worked myself into a panic.

Just as I get to the driveway, the front door opens and I see Mr. Scarelli from a couple of streets over—a neighbor who also happens to be a police officer. He says something to Mom, who remains at the door. He nods in my direction as he gets into his car, and I offer a feeble wave in response. I look to Mom for a clue. My heart beats wildly.

"Hi Han," she says, holding the door open. "I got a flat on the way home from work. Thank God, Paul Scarelli was driving by, put on the temporary tire, and dropped me home after I left the car at the gas station."

I debate whether I should be relieved as Mom follows me into the kitchen, talking non-stop. "I have no clue how to put that thing on so his timing was impeccable." Is she hiding something? Surely, if Officer Scarelli told her that Rob was a suspect, she would be too upset to be babbling to me about her car. "That could have been a complete disaster."

Having your son or brother killed in a hit and run is a disaster. Having your son or brother sent to jail for doing the hitting and running is also a disaster. But having a flat tire? I find my mom's melodrama even more annoying than usual.

"How was guitar?"

"Fine," I say, opening the fridge. I stare blankly at the array of organic fresh-pressed juices, the neatly stacked Tupperware containers filled with assorted fruits, raw carrots, celery sticks. One more attempt by Mom to make up for the Cheetos and other assorted junk food in the pantry.

"Sooo, did Officer Scarelli say anything about the hit and run?" I don't look at her as I ask. I don't want her to see how unnerved I am to even have uttered this question.

"No, but they can't talk about an ongoing investigation, so I'm not surprised. But you know how there's a memorial service for Tyler Miller on Saturday, before the game?"

Yes, I knew. How could I not? There have been flyers plastered all over the school hallways, not to mention on every telephone pole in Woodfield. Tyler *had* been a mythical figure in our football-loving town, after all. But I've been trying not to think about it, trying not to wonder if Rob and Zach are planning to show up; trying not to think about what it's going to be like to watch Tyler's family, especially little Jared, as members of the faculty and the football team talk in the past tense about his brother.

"Yeah," I say, studying the unappealing snack choices in the refrigerator, still not looking at my mother.

"Well, Paul told me that Principal Finnely—along with the police department—have decided to hold an assembly for parents on Friday afternoon. Apparently so many parents have been calling in with questions about what to tell their younger kids about the accident, and with concerns about how their kids are reacting to Tyler's death, and some kids are falling behind in their work, and parents are wondering about the school's policy—"

I realize that if I don't cut my mom off, she's never going to stop talking. "So, are you and Dad going?" I force myself to look over my shoulder. But Mom's looking down at a pile of produce on the granite countertop in front of her, pulling vegetables out of the grocery store plastic as she speaks. I can't read her expression.

"Well, of course," she answers, pausing to roll up the sleeves of her perfectly-pressed white button-down shirt. "And what Paul suggested, was that we talk to our kids about whether they have anything they'd like to bring up, or any questions they would like answered, or any concerns..." Maybe my mother is purposely not looking at *me,* straining to be casual as she fishes for information.

"No, I don't," I say, a little too quickly, turning back to the fridge and settling on a baggie filled with a stack of sliced American cheese. "I mean, what is there to say?" I peel away one of the thin squares of cheese, and put the rest of the stack back on the shelf. I fold the piece of cheese in half, and then in half again.

"Well... Paul also suggested that we talk to our kids about that night—see if there is anything they want to share?" Now Mom is studying me a bit too intently, her dark brown eyes nearly piercing my composure.

I look her directly in the face and shrug. "There's nothing really to tell." I take a bite out of the pile of cheese in my hand, not tasting it. It sticks in my throat and I have to swallow hard. But my fake air of nonchalance must be convincing enough, because Mom turns on the faucet and starts washing the vegetables. Who knew I could be such a good liar?

"OK, just checking," my mother adds as she returns to the counter and starts chopping the carrots. "I told him we were very close and that you guys would have told us anything if you had anything to tell us, but I figured I'd let you know what he said..." I wonder if this is a sincere statement of what she believes to be true, or if she is trying to guilt me into confessing something. I feel myself starting to sweat and it's not even hot.

"Is Rob home?" I ask suddenly, wondering whether Mom has already gone through this whole dialogue with him—or whether that future encounter is just another thing for me to worry about.

"No, he's having dinner with his friends. It's just us three tonight." Great. Mom turns on the gas, dumps the vegetables she has been cutting into a big cast-iron pan set on one of the front burners. Even the sizzle of the vegetables hitting the oil in the pan frays my nerves. There's no way I can sit through another dinner—alone!—with my parents tonight.

"Actually, I might be having dinner with Alex—I think we're going to the movies."

"On a school night?"

"Yeah, I finished my homework in study hall."

"Well, that would have been a nice thing to mention to me before I bought the food for dinner."

"Sorry, we just talked about it right before guitar, and I didn't have a chance to call you. I'll go call her and see what our plans are." I slip out of the kitchen before Mom can respond. The scent of garlic, onion, and the other simmering vegetables follows me up the stairs. I feel slightly guilty. Still, I pause in the middle of the stairwell and pull out my phone to text Alex.

*MOVIE & DINNER TONIGHT?*

I run up the rest of the steps, willing Alex to respond.

While I'm waiting, scrolling through my phone, a Channel 3 news flash catches my attention. *Police ask for help in identifying vehicle and driver in hit-and-run crash that killed local teen.* Oh no. As if it wasn't stressful enough having Reporter-Alex on the case, wondering what *she* might find. I reluctantly read on.

*Woodfield Police are asking the public for help identifying cars that were in the area during a deadly hit and run early Sunday morning. Police found Tyler Miller, 17, unresponsive near a blind curve on Willet Rd at 5:32am. The victim is thought to have been jogging when he was struck by a vehicle that left the scene.*

*Local police report that they have called in an accident re-construction team from CT State Police to aid in the investigation. They are also asking residents or business owners in the area with Ring-camera or surveillance videos, and anyone with any information about the incident, to call the Woodfield Police at (475)555-1319.* Ring cameras? Surveillance videos? My nerves are once again on high alert.

My phone buzzes in my hand, making me jump. I realize Alex has texted back.

*Yes! Where should we get dinner*

*You pick,* I type. Though I've lost my appetite.

# Chapter Twelve

No one says much in the car on the way to the memorial service. I steal glances at Rob, next to me in the back, but he's slumped against the opposite door, staring wordlessly out the window. He keeps pulling at the knot of his tie as if it's choking him. I'm sure he's just as thrilled as I am to be in this car with our parents.

"I'm going to head over with Zach," he argued this morning, but Mom and Dad were strangely united on this front, insisting that we should drive over to the memorial service as a family. They also made Rob change from his jeans and hoodie, "out of respect for the Miller family," Mom said.

"But there's a game," he said, clearly irritated.

Dad just pointed his finger upstairs. "Go."

"Well, I'm sitting with Zach and my friends for the game." Rob always had to get in the last word. I was listening from the top of the stairs. I looked down at my jeans, then headed back to my room to change into a skirt.

I wondered if the other girls would be wearing skirts or whether they'd just be dressed in jeans, like for a regular game, in which case I'd look stupid. I assessed my outfit in the full-length mirror on the inside of my closet door, turning to the side, and then back to the front again, and decided that the slightly flouncy maroon skirt that peeked out from under my chunky grey sweater was sufficiently short—and revealed just enough leg — to be sexy. In a subtle way.

"This is so stupid," Rob had muttered under his breath as he passed me in the hallway. The sound of his voice startled me—he hadn't said a word to me since our encounter in his room several days earlier. I guess I'd kind of been avoiding him. Before I could respond to his comment—agree with him, maybe, to show solidarity—he was already down the stairs.

Cars are backed up all the way around the circle and up to the turn-off from the main road, where Dad idles, unable to move forward. I crane my head to see what's ahead and can see multiple TV news vans clogging the entrance to the school parking lot. "I guess we know what's going to be on the 5 o-clock news today," I mumble.

"You'd think they'd give the family a break, today of all days," Mom says, shaking her head.

"Yeah, right," says Dad. "Anything for a story." Mom sighs.

"At least the police are here to keep the order," she says, watching through the window as several police officers direct cars and people through the lot. Rob remains quiet, but I can see that he's becoming more and more agitated. He shifts around in his seat, and his eyes dart around the crowd as if he's looking for someone. Zach?

"Why don't I get out of the car with the kids and get us seats while you park?" Mom suggests.

"What's the rush?" Rob snaps.

Dad ignores his tone and says, "Good idea."

Rob rolls his eyes and opens his door. I open mine too.

"Hannah!" Alex runs up to me, out of breath. "Can you believe this scene—all the reporters—I bet the whole town is here..." Alex leans close to my ear. "Including Zach." My pulse quickens when I hear his name. Of course he's here.

"Come on, Hannah," Mom says, walking ahead. "Let's get seats and you can talk to Alex later." Never one to be rude, she turns for a second, throws out a "Hi Alex," and flashes a pseudo-sincere smile in her direction before continuing to the bleachers. I roll my eyes at Alex. Rob walks ahead of us, his hands shoved in his pockets, his head down.

"Gotta go," I say to Alex, shrugging.

"OK, come find me after the service. I'm sitting by the side of the bleachers where all the flowers—" Suddenly, Alex stops talking and her whole expression changes. I follow her eyes and see two police officers escorting the Miller family through the crowd, which has abruptly quieted. It's like the wake of a boat, but in reverse—the family causing the crowd to part. They hold hands in a row: the father, the two remaining sons, and the mother, all dressed in black. The mother's eyes are red; the father's expression, blank. Kevin—the brother who's the freshman — wears sunglasses, and Jared, who stares at his feet as he walks, just looks small. Small and lost. My heart hurts for him. The crowd closes up behind the family.

"That's so sad," whispers Alex.

"I know." I fight to hold back tears. I notice my mother's eyes welling up—and I don't want to be like her. When I turn to gauge Rob's reaction, I realize he's no longer there.

"I'll see you later," says Alex, pressing my arm as she disappears into the crowd. I look around. Rob is nowhere to be seen.

"Mom, what happened to Rob?"

She too, scans the area.

“Oh, he is so infuriating,” she says. “Let’s just get seats and he and Dad can find us.” I follow Mom, knowing Rob won’t be finding us.

The bleachers are packed—Alex was right—the whole town probably *is* here. As soon as I confirm that neither Rob nor Zach are in the bleachers, I turn to focus on the somber scene playing out on the field. Lindsay Orner, the school’s resident diva, starts singing “Amazing Grace.”

The players, in uniform and wearing matching black armbands, stand in a line, staring solemnly ahead. Behind the players, up on a makeshift platform that has been erected for the service, Tyler’s family—minus one—silently faces the crowd. The coach and the principal position themselves on either side of the family like bookends, and the town selectman, who I assume is a friend of the Millers, behind them, his hands resting protectively on Mr. and Mrs. Miller’s shoulders. I’m almost relieved that I can’t really see their expressions from where we sit—high up—in the bleachers.

I wonder what it must be like for Tyler’s parents, so used to proudly watching their son shine on the field from these bleachers, to be standing on the field in his absence. What must it be like for their family to be at the dinner table and have an empty chair where Tyler used to sit? How could they bear that empty seat? I try to imagine Rob’s seat empty, and know I wouldn’t be able to take having to stare across the table at that empty space if he was gone forever. Even though he barely speaks to me, his presence rounds out our family. I pick up bits and pieces of his life from the short answers he gives to our parents’ constant questions, and every once in a while, he even makes us all laugh.

Of course, Tyler's seat wouldn't be empty if it weren't for... I block that train of thought. And then my stomach is in knots again, because *all* of this—the whole town, the reporters, the mourning team members and classmates, the grieving family—all of this wouldn't be happening if it weren't for Rob. And Zach. Or one of their friends. How could I be on their side? How could they be watching this? How could they live with themselves? I don't even know if I can live with *myself*.

I realize that Lindsay has stopped singing and now the coach is talking. "...not only a commendable student/athlete, but also a good person, a loving brother and son, a beloved teammate and classmate and friend to so many here at Woodfield High. Tyler was taken from us abruptly, and too soon, and we will never forget him. We play today's game in his honor. His indomitable spirit will be a guiding force..." I tune out the coach and focus back on the family. The father and brother seemed to be holding up the mother, while Jared clings to his brother's other arm.

I look away. And force myself, once again, to pay attention to what the coach is saying.

"Please join me, Tyler's team, and his family, in a moment of silence. Let us all remember not only what this bright young man meant to this team, and to this town, but also what he meant to each of those who were lucky enough to know him." I bend my head down, in unison with most of the others in the bleachers, and am surprised by the extreme quality of the quiet that ensues. I hadn't even noticed the low hum of conversation that must have been going on even as the coach spoke, the sounds of spectators shifting in their seats, the creaking of the bleachers. But now, even the wind has stopped blowing.

All is still.

Keeping my head down, I sneak a peek at those around me. Some dab at their eyes or noses with tissues. Mom, of course, cries at everything, so I expect to see *her* eyes welling up. Dad's eyes even glisten a little. Halfway into the moment of silence, a chorus of sniffling comes from the front of the bleachers, where the cheerleaders sit. And then Tyler's mother shatters the silence with a single, heart-piercing sob.

The guilt is suddenly overwhelming. How is it fair for me to keep what I know a secret? Tyler is *gone. Forever.* He will never grow up, never play college football, never have a life, a family, a career. How can I protect the ones who may have erased his whole future? And caused this family so much pain? I've never felt so burdened by a secret. A secret I never wanted and now don't know what to do with. I watch as Tyler's father and brothers all crowd in on the sobbing mother, though they're all crying now, and look like they're all sort of holding one another up.

I glance at Mom again, and see that she isn't even watching this heart-breaking scene on the football field; instead, her head is turned and she's looking at something—or someone—all the way to the right of the bleachers. I follow her gaze and am surprised when my eyes land on Officer Scarelli, who quickly turns away and looks down. When I look back at Mom, she has her head down and her eyes closed. It happened in such a fraction of a second, that I wonder whether I imagined the whole interaction. Still, something about it leaves me feeling weird.

The coach is talking again. They're going to retire Tyler's jersey. Number 48—we all know it well. How many times have we all seen that number on the back of the player running toward the goal post to score the winning touchdown? How many times have we seen that number—held up high above the shoulders of the other team members—as they celebrated one of their many wins and acknowledged their most valuable player? Of course nobody else could ever wear that number again. The coach hands the folded jersey to Jared. As Tyler's little brother steps forward solemnly and puts out his hands to receive it, I cry silently.

Now the band marches—without playing—onto the field. Half of the band members march to one side of the platform, the other half to the other side, until the platform holding up Tyler's family seems to be floating in a sea of blue and white, the school colors, and the hue of the band members' uniforms. They too wear the black armbands. The players, some wiping their eyes or noses on the sleeves of their jerseys, stand at attention, and place their hands on their hearts as the band starts playing the national anthem. I too, put my hand on my heart. It's beating so fast. I'm strangely comforted by the feeling of Dad's hand resting gently on my back, though I worry that he'll be able to feel my pounding heart. *Please ask me,* I silently beg my father. *Please ask me right now what I know*. But he doesn't say anything, just stands there, with his left hand on my back, and his right hand on his heart.

I feel like I might burst. I just have to know what happened the night Tyler was killed. I have to know how Rob and Zach were involved. I need to tell them that I know. Because I can't stand to be alone with the knowledge any longer.

# Chapter Thirteen

I ditch my parents after the service and try to find Alex. Hundreds of people descend from the seats at the same time—the game isn't going to start for another 20 minutes—so the area in front of the bleachers is a mass of bodies. I decide it will be quicker to go in the opposite direction.

Heading around the back of the bleachers, I see Tyler's photo tacked to one of the bleacher support pillars and my heart skips a beat. The photo curls up at the edges, and the pile of flowers and footballs beneath it reminds me of Tyler's Facebook cover photo. I force myself to turn away. That's when I spot my brother and Zach standing near the edge of the woods that border the other athletic field.

They're talking to someone I don't recognize, partly because his back is to me and partly because I'm an entire soccer field away. Rob's back is to me too, but I could identify his messy dark brown curls anywhere, not to mention the way he stands with his thumbs stuck into his back pockets, crumpling up the edges of his jacket. Zach is facing in my direction, but his head is down. His arms are crossed—he's all closed up.

Maybe, just maybe, this mystery guy is to blame for Tyler's death. Maybe what I heard through my bedroom wall was Rob and Zach freaking out because they knew the person responsible. They're probably discussing it now—I mean, they must all be pretty shaken up seeing the whole town gathered to honor Tyler, seeing the family, hearing the coach...

I try to move a bit closer so that I can see who Rob and Zach are talking to, but really, I can't take my eyes off of Zach. I don't know him at all, do I? I don't think he could leave another person to die, but maybe there's a hard edge to his personality that he's kept hidden from me. Maybe it was even his idea to keep driving. What kind of person am I attracted to?

I barely realize that I've stopped moving, that I'm just standing there, staring at Zach, when he looks up and meets my eyes from across the field. It's so unexpected that I don't even think to avert my gaze. How long would we have stood there, eyes locked, if Alex hadn't come along at that moment? I'm startled when I feel her hand on my arm, notice her other hand waving back and forth in front of my face.

"Hello, Earth to Hannah. Does Zach have you under a spell or something?" I feel my face get warm.

"Sorry, I was zoning out..."

"Oh, is that what we're calling it now?" Alex loops her arm in mine and half drags me toward the concession stand. I can't help but take one last glance over my shoulder, and am not surprised to see that Zach is still watching me. I walk self-consciously beside Alex, part of me savoring the feeling of being watched by a boy, this boy—and part of me wondering what I'm getting myself into.

"I wish you two would just hook up already," Alex says, rolling her eyes.

"Me too," I whisper. Alex raises an eyebrow.

"Um, really?" She looks at me all wide-eyed.

I shrug, raising my eyebrows back at her. Of course her idea of hooking up and *my* idea of hooking up are definitely different, but I let her think what she wants.

"Aww, my little Hannah is growing up." As if she's so experienced. I roll my eyes. "But enough about you two lovebirds," she says. "Let's see if we can find Jake. I'm sure he's here somewhere with his soccer crew." Jake Kramer is the latest object of Alex's affection. She sits behind him in Spanish, and after every class, she sends me the "Jake Report" via text: a detailed account of what he was wearing, every word he'd uttered, and every move he'd made during class.

The mixed aromas of hot dogs, popcorn and nachos hang in the air above students gathered in packs around the concession stand. The groups of kids stand in a line-like formation, and we plant ourselves at what appears to be the end of the line. We survey the crowd, looking for familiar faces, friends, Jake's friends, Jake. I note, with relief, that most of the other girls are also wearing skirts.

It's amazing to me how quickly things have reverted to normal. We've just sat through a memorial service for Tyler, yet it could almost be any football game, on any Saturday—not the first game where Tyler is gone.

"So, Alex," I say quietly, suddenly remembering our discussion from a few days earlier. "Have you found out anything about who was at that party?"

"Not yet, but I will...." Alex looks at me sideways. "Why? Did you hear something?"

"No, no....just being here, with the memorial and everything... it reminded me...."

Our friends find us at that moment, interrupting our exchange.

"Hannah! Alex!" Kei shoulders her way through the crowd, our other friend, Ami, in tow. "Hey!" We form a small circle. I smile at my friends—I like being part of my own little pack. Safety in numbers.

"How sad was that?" says Kei.

"So sad," Alex says, looking around for Jake. "Hey, did you guys by any chance see Jake in your travels?"

"You have such a one-track mind," Ami says, laughing. "And yes—he's behind the bleachers with the other soccer guys."

Alex cranes her head toward the bleachers, trying to see above the crowd. "Um, we need an excuse to walk by the bleachers again..."

"I'm starving," says Ami who is always supposedly on some healthy eating kick, but has no qualms about getting hot dogs at football games. "Let's get food and then we can take the long way to our seats. Because that won't be at all obvious." They all laugh. I force myself to smile.

I wonder if Zach, Rob, and the mystery guy are still by the woods. Will they be making their way toward the bleachers by the time we head in that direction? That might be my only chance to bump into Zach before the end of the game—unless they get up during half time. Obviously, we won't be sitting near one another during the game: It's an unspoken rule that the older kids sit higher up, toward the back of the bleachers, while freshmen and sophomores stay closer to the bottom.

I turn my attention back to the concession stand and wait impatiently as the throng of students between us and the counter slowly shrinks. I halfway listen to Ami and Alex and Kei as they chatter at one another while scoping the crowd. But my mind lingers on the soccer field, and I wish really hard that at some point today I find myself alone with Zach. I *will* find an opportunity to be alone with Zach.

# Chapter Fourteen

*Be careful what you wish for.* One of Mom's stock phrases. I hear her voice in my head, dispensing this particular piece of wisdom as I emerge from the girls' bathroom and practically bump into Zach. My head is turned as I say hi to Kalina from French class—his head must have been turned too. We both stop just as we are about to collide.

"Oh, hi," he says.

"Oh, hi." *Wow, great response Hannah.* We stand uncomfortably close, but for some reason, I don't want to be the one to step back. He doesn't step back either. He hooks this thumbs into his front jean pockets, and stands, rocking back slightly on his heels and looking at me. I can't tell what he's thinking.

This is awkward—isn't this awkward? My right hand wants to fly up and touch my hair, to smooth it down and pull it around the front of my shoulder, but I hold it still with my left. I search my brain for something to say. I wonder what it would be like to touch his hair—to gently brush aside that loose wave that hangs over his right eye. Time seems to slow as we watch each other—I'm not sure if five minutes go by or just five seconds.

"Great minds think alike," he says, finally, smiling slightly. I laugh, nervously, but feel my body relax a little. He nods his head toward the soccer field.

"Wanna walk?" he asks. *Walk?* My stomach flutters, but I nod.

"I don't think the game is going to start for a while," he adds, as if reassuring me. His voice sounds a bit more subdued than usual.

He moves his body so that he's right next to me, close enough that our sleeves brush together as we walk. He's way taller than me, so when our arms touch, my shoulder only reaches to just above his elbow. "Nah, I don't think so either," I hear myself say.

I'm acutely aware of the sound of the leaves crunching into the grass as we walk, and of the soft rustle of our jacket sleeves as they make contact. The voices of the other people at the game quickly become background noise. It's as if Zach and I are miked, and only the sound immediately surrounding us is amplified.

"I was hoping I'd run into you today," he says. "Though not literally." I smile. *Did he want to be alone with me too?* Zach kicks at the leaves as he walks, setting them noisily aloft, and I watch, mesmerized, as they flutter back down to the ground around his black Vans.

As we cross the soccer field, I notice that there are fewer and fewer people around. Even the small clusters of students that dotted the field earlier have gravitated toward the game. I look ahead at the pines on the opposite side of the soccer green. The tall evergreens are interspersed with more colorful trees—maples and birches that haven't yet completely shed their leaves. I follow the bare trunks with my eyes up toward the sky; they stretch through the leafy canopy and then disappear beneath a thick layer of pine needles. I bring my gaze back down to the fiery color straight ahead and think about how my line of vision is different from Zach's, because of the difference in our heights. I wonder where his gaze lands. Does he see things differently than I do?

I feel more daring than I really am, walking with Zach toward those woods, toward those trails where I know certain kids hang out to smoke—and do other things. And maybe I *do* want to do those other things with Zach. But I'm not the kind of girl who goes into the woods. And I *really* don't know what kind of boy Zach is. Sure, he's been coming to our house and playing video games with Rob for years—yet, until I first ran into him at The Music Shoppe, I had no idea he was even into music. And though I'm majorly crushing on the Zach I think I know, I wonder if the version of him that lives in my head is just my own invention. I just can't see him leaving another person to die.

Then again, despite Rob's failings as a brother, I would never have expected him to be party to a hit and run, either. Could anyone ever know how they might react in a situation like that until they are actually in it? Still, I remind myself, I don't know for sure that they were even directly involved.

My pulse thrums in my ears. I glance over at Zach, but he's looking down at the leaves he disrupts with each step. Okay, let's say he *was* involved. This can't be easy for him, being here, at this game, seeing the family, having to act normal, innocent. Will he ever confide in me? Should I bring it up? How could we not talk about why we're both here, on this day? How could we talk about anything else?

We reach the edge of the woods, but Zach keeps walking, so I do too. A trail appears as soon as we pass between two birches and enter the woods. The path is littered with yellow leaves and dark green pine needles, which make it blend into the rest of the forest floor, but Zach seems to know where he's going. I like the feel of his arm touching mine, the way he adjusts his stride so that I can keep up. We just walk together quietly, and somehow it doesn't feel weird or awkward.

We walk deeper into the woods, and without really meaning to, I make a decision. I don't know exactly what's going to happen when we get to wherever we're going, but I'm going to ask him for the truth.

"Hey," he says, interrupting my thoughts. I turn toward him and realize he has stopped walking. Now's my chance...I open my mouth to speak, but before I can say anything, Zach takes a step closer, and rests his hands gently on my arms, just below my shoulders.

"Can I kiss you?" he asks quietly, his hazel eyes boring into mine. My resolve to confront him dissolves, just like that. I nod. He bends his head toward mine, and kisses me. And kisses me. And kisses me.

I've always worried that I wouldn't know how to kiss right—that I wouldn't know how to hold my head, or how to arrange my lips, or what to do with my hands. But I didn't need to worry. Kissing Zach came naturally.

"I've been wanting to do that for a long time," he says, when we finally stop. If you could smile on the inside, I think, this is what it would feel like.

"Me too," I say, surprising myself. Then I stand on my tippy-toes and kiss him back. I won't be bringing up the accident today. I don't want this to stop. We press into each other and I am electric, charged, aware of every spot on my body that touches his. *Who am I?* I've always been "good." But maybe being a good girl isn't all it's cracked up to be.

# Chapter Fifteen

My lips tingle from kissing him. We keep peeking sideways at each other, smiling, as we walk out of the woods and back toward the football field.

"So who are you, Hannah Greene?" he says after a little while. "And how has it taken me this long to notice you?"

"You were too busy playing video games...I've been right upstairs, all these years." We both laugh. He wasn't ever on my radar either—and he knows it.

We don't say much on our way back to the football field, but we walk even closer together, as if there are magnets in our limbs. I think we both walk slowly on purpose, wanting to prolong whatever this is, not wanting to return to reality.

Maybe I jumped to conclusions about Zach. It's possible I misunderstood what I overheard. When I replay the conversation between Zach and Rob in my head, I fixate now on what they *didn't* say. They didn't actually say they were involved. Yes, Zach was clearly upset about *something* to do with Tyler's being dead, but he never actually said he was there. Neither did Rob. Someone was *too high to drive*—but maybe it was one of their friends, and like me, they were just feeling burdened with information they wished they didn't have.

Zach's hand brushes mine and I return to the moment. Suddenly, I hear the voices, the cheering, the sounds of other people, like someone has flicked a switch and un-muted these sounds. The game must be underway. How long were we in the woods? It feels like we've been gone for a long time.

As we get closer to the football field, I feel Zach move slightly away from me. My heart sinks, just a little, and I glance sideways again. Something has shifted in Zach's expression— like a shadow has passed over him. I must sigh more loudly than I mean to, because Zach turns toward me.

"I've got to find my friends—"

"Oh, yeah, me too," I say, trying not to look too disappointed. "They must be wondering what happened to me."

"But, hey, you're going to be at guitar Thursday, right?"

I nod, trying to seem chill. He is reassuring me.

"Cool," he says. And then a little more quietly: "And maybe I'll see you on the porch before that..." He looks down at the ground as he says it, suppressing a smile. I catch sight of the dimple just as he turns and heads toward the other end of the bleachers. I head toward my friends, feeling lighter.

The second row is packed, but Alex has saved a space for me.

"Oh my God, did you get lost or something?" Alex asks after I sit down. "I was about to send out a search party." The other girls huddle together watching something on Kei's cell phone.

I lean toward Alex and whisper into her ear, "I ran into Zach." Alex's eyebrows go up, and I raise my own in response. I press my lips together to stifle a smile, and Alex's eyes widen.

"Really?" she whispers.

"Really."

"And?"

I shrug, and give her a mysterious grin. I think about Zach's lips—so soft—and how they tasted faintly of Tic Tacs. I know I'm making her crazy. But I want to keep this for myself, at least for now.

"Hey, Hannah —look! We're on the news!" Kei tilts her phone toward me, and I see that the news camera has been panning the bleachers—there we all are, the students of Woodfield High, the residents of our boring suburban town, staring solemnly past the camera. Then the lens switches directions, and focuses in on the Millers, huddled together on that platform in the field.

It was hard enough to watch Tyler's family standing there, grieving in front of an audience, the first time. Now, to have to see it played back again—I feel like a reluctant passenger in a time machine, being carried back to those excruciating minutes before the game.

The Millers must have left right after the ceremony—I watch on Kei's screen as the news cameras trail them while they're escorted off the field. I think about these reporters, how they come out and feed on other people's sorrow. Would Alex do that one day? I could never.

"I forgot I told my parents I would check back in with them," I hear myself saying as I rise to leave my friends. Alex gives me a funny look, but the others are pinned to the screen. "Look, there's Harrison, and Kurt Johnson..." Ami points to the phone, calling out names of the football players as the news cameras captures glimpses of their grief.

"I'll meet up with you again at half time," I assure Alex. Alex shrugs in a "suit-yourself" kind of way, and turns her attention back to Kei's phone.

I walk around the back of the bleachers to get to my parents. I glance around at the crowd, and realize I'm looking for Zach. And Rob. No sign of either. I don't really want to be with my parents, but I just couldn't sit for another second with my friends looking at that stupid phone and that stupid video of the memorial.

I kick the ground with the toe of my bootie. I stop by the photo of Tyler as I pass it again and stare at it. I stare right into Tyler's eyes. I feel guilty that he's dead, and that my friends are watching themselves on the news, and that I kissed Zach at his memorial. I'm sorry, I say silently to his photo.

# Chapter Sixteen

"Hannah, there you are," Mom says when I get back to our seats in the bleachers. Dad stares at the field with his lips pressed together. He seems angry. I look at him, then back at Mom, for some explanation. But Mom just chats on, like she does whenever there's tension in the family.

"We're thinking of taking off during half time," she says. "Half a football game is more than enough for me, and we've got so much to do in the house and the yard and everything." Then, lowering her voice, she adds, "Besides, it's too sad to watch this game without Tyler in it." I don't engage—for some reason, her comment annoys me. Instead, I glance over at Dad, and see that he too, looks irritated.

"Maybe I'll go home too," I say. Both of my parents raise their eyebrows in surprise. "I have cramps," I add, an explanation they won't question. I just had my period a week ago, but the excuse seems to work, since they both look back toward the field, and the scoreboard. So do I.

There are only 30 seconds left on the board—it's the fourth down in the second quarter. The score is still 0-0. As if on cue, our eyes drop simultaneously from the board to the players on the field below. Number 17—it looks like Justin Rubin—has the ball under his arm and is sprinting across the field with most of the opposing team on his tail. Justin and Tyler had been almost inseparable, yet here he is, running across that football field as if his life depends on it. Could I do that, if it had been Alex? Just go on? What is it like to have your best friend die?

The cheerleaders, lined up on the edge of the field, are going crazy, jumping up and down, waving their blue and white pom-poms and chanting something—I strain to hear what— above the increasing noise of the crowd. "Just-In...Just-In....Just-In..." Suddenly, most of the people around me are standing and craning their necks to follow number 17 as he tears across the field. The people around us join in the chanting, and soon, swept up in the excitement, we do too. "Just-In, Just-In, Just-In." The bleachers shake as the fans stomp to the beat of the chant.

When Justin crosses the goal line and throws the football down onto the ground, the crowd goes wild. The halftime buzzer goes off at almost the same moment, adding to the clamor. It isn't until the sound of the buzzer fades that I realize the chant has morphed into something else. "Ty-Ler, Ty-Ler, Ty-Ler..." My eyes fill with tears as I see Justin reach into his waistband and pull out a jersey. Number 48. He holds Tyler's jersey high above his head as the rest of the team swarms around him.

"Come on," Dad says. His voice cracks slightly. My mother follows as he makes his way to the aisle and down the rickety aluminum steps of the stands, discreetly wiping her eyes with one hand as she grabs the railing with the other. I imagine there are lots of wet eyes around us, but I purposely keep my eyes on the steps below me as I follow my parents out.

The three of us don't say anything as we push through the crowds and head toward the far parking lot. I scan the crowd one more time for Zach. I think about kissing him in the woods.

Before the accident, I didn't really keep secrets from my parents. I didn't have any. Now I have two. It wouldn't even occur to my parents that while they sat on the bleachers, watching the football game, their daughter had been making out with someone in the woods. Especially with Rob's friend. Especially with the person who might be responsible...Not that Rob would be thrilled if me and Zach become a thing either. He'd see it as the crossing of some boundary.

I'm startled out of my thoughts by someone's hand on my arm. I turn to find a reporter, standing too close, sticking a microphone in my face. I pull my arm away.

"What's it like to be here, today, at the first football game without Tyler Miller?" he demands. Flustered, I look around for my parents. A cameraman moves close, pointing his lens right at me. The reporter touches my arm more gently this time, taking it down a notch. "I know it must be difficult here, today," he says softly. "Did you know Tyler Miller?"

I step backwards, but bump into another reporter. I'm surrounded, trapped. I look for an escape route. But there's nowhere to go. Can the reporters hear how hard my heart is beating?

"Do you know anything about the hit and run?" asks the person attached to the microphone. I freeze. Why are they asking me that? Why are they asking *me* anything?

"I don't know anything," I blurt out. I feel my heart beating in my ears, my breaths coming more quickly. I can see my parents, who must have finally realized that I am no longer behind them, trying to get around the camera crew. I feel another hand on my shoulder, and am on the verge of panic when I turn and see the uniform.

"That's enough," Officer Scarelli shouts, pulling me to safety, and holding up his other arm to signal to the reporters and cameramen to stay back. "You should all be ashamed of yourselves, preying on kids like that. Now get out of my sight before I charge you with disturbing the peace—or assault!"

And just like that, it's over. The reporters move away, shaking their heads, mumbling— looking for someone else to hound with their questions—and my parents are there, standing on either side of me with their arms wrapped protectively around my shoulders.

"I can't thank you enough for rescuing her, Paul," Mom says to Officer Scarelli. She touches his arm while she says it, which, when I think back to it later, will strike me as overly familiar. But I'm just thankful to be with my parents and away from the reporters, so I don't think much about it in the moment.

"Yeah, thanks Paul," Dad adds gruffly, as he abruptly whisks me away.

*Are you still there?* I pull my laptop out from under my nightstand and sit propped against a pillow on my bed. I feel bad that I left without saying goodbye to Alex.

*Yah. Where r u*

*Home. Sorry I missed you—my parents wanted to beat the crowds*

The text sounds lame, even to me. But Alex is chill.

*Now we know why we don't take our parents to games*

*I was practically assaulted by reporters on the way out!* Even typing the words makes me feel claustrophobic and slightly panicked.

*Oo, maybe you'll be on the news...*

Not the response I was looking for. I change the subject.

*Did you see Jake?*
*Yessssss*
*Did you see Zach?*
*You have a one track mind*
*Sigh. I know*
*I didn't. But gotta go. Meeting Jake at concessions*
*Go for it*
*Bye Hannah-ban*
*Bye Lex*

I find myself clicking over to Facebook on my phone and searching *Tyler Miller*. There's an announcement about today's memorial on his page. A chill runs through my body. Again, I wonder who is keeping Tyler's Facebook page up to date.

Even though he's dead, there are literally hundreds of comments on his timeline. Lots of people have just written *RIP*. One of his teammates has written *Miss you dude.* I swallow hard when I read that one. Tara Birch, who went out with Tyler last year, has practically written a novel. Followed by two blue hearts. I can't imagine Zach dying.

Someone has posted a trio of photos: There's Tyler in his football uniform, one arm draped around Justin, the other around John Dougherty, another teammate. They all grin at the camera. There's a fuzzy photo that shows him running across the field with a football tucked under his arm during a game. Probably about to score a touchdown. In the last photo, Tyler is with his baby brother. They are both holding up their arms, showing off their muscles. Jared looks up at Tyler with a wide smile on his face. He looks at his big brother as if he worships the ground he walks on. The images on the screen blur and I quickly close my laptop.

# Chapter Seventeen

On Monday, I race home after school to do my homework out on the porch. Just in case. No Zach. *It's just Monday*, I tell myself.

On Tuesday, I dawdle by the lockers with Alex after school and take my time walking home. Again, even though it's a cool day, I put on a sweatshirt and settle on the porch swing to brainstorm an English essay that's due on Friday. I brainstorm and brainstorm, looking up from my notes about every five seconds to check for signs of life on my street. No Zach.

*He said* maybe *he'd see me on the porch,* I remind myself. But the disappointment sits in my stomach like a physical weight.

On Wednesday, I purposely don't rush home after school. I grab a coffee with Alex and Kei at Beans, the little coffee shop near school, though I can't stop wondering, as I sip my pumpkin spice latte and listen to them talk about Jake and his teammate Mike, who Kei is crushing on, if Zach is going to show up at my house while I'm gone.

"I've got to go," I tell Alex when Kei gets up to go to the bathroom. "Zach said he might stop by this week..."

"Stop by?" Alex raises an eyebrow.

"Exactly," I say, collecting my stuff. "Tell Kei I had an appointment or something."

I pause before I go. "Any info on the party?"

Alex tilts her head to the side. "I'm working on it..." She eyes me suspiciously—I don't usually fish for gossip.

"Cool," I say casually, then change the subject. "Hopefully I'll have something to tell you later." I wink at her before heading for the door.

"Yeah, I hope your *appointment* goes well," Alex says as I push the café door open with my butt, and we both laugh.

At home, I listen by the basement door for Rob and Zach—no voices—grab my guitar from the family room, and bring it out to the porch. I practice out there for an hour, my mood plunging as the minutes tick by. No Zach.

I go inside, dejected.

Maybe I made too big a deal out of what happened on Saturday. Maybe it wasn't that big a deal for Zach. Maybe he's kissed a lot of girls in those woods.

My phone pings. I pick it up immediately, a tiny kernel of hope forming in my gut. But it's just Alex.

*So?*

*He didn't come :(*

*That doesn't mean anything. He's prob just busy with something*

*I guess...*

*Hannah-ban, trust me, he likes you. You'll see*

When I wake up in the morning and check my phone, I see that Zach texted me late at night.

*Sorry I haven't been by – crazy week! See you tomorrow*

And I am hopeful once again.

"I've got a lead" Alex whispers to me at our lockers before homeroom.

"A lead?"

"Yeah—remember you said we had to figure out who was at that party?" I feel my regret in the pit of my stomach.

"Um, yeah..."

"Well, I was thinking," she says. "It could have been anyone at that party who hit Tyler. Not to mention anyone not at that party. So the question isn't who was at the party. The question, is who would *not* turn back after hitting Tyler?" I want to remind her that just a couple of weeks ago, she said it wouldn't have made sense for them to go back. But I don't say anything. I just listen, feeling vaguely nauseous.

"Well, I found out that Jeremy Clark—you know, the football player who Tara Birch broke up with to go out with Tyler? Well, he was at the party and supposedly was drinking *a lot*...and he *hated* Tyler."

"Hmm," I say, wanting to believe her theory. "He does sound like a plausible suspect." Rob is somewhat friendly with Jeremy. They played squash together freshman year—it was my brother's one-time foray into sports. It's entirely conceivable that Rob and Zach still hung with Jeremy, entirely conceivable that they would be hanging out and getting high together at a party. Maybe Jeremy was the one who was "too high to drive."

But the more I continue with this line of thought, the more I realize that having a possible suspect that isn't Rob or Zach isn't as much of a relief as I thought it would be. Because it's also entirely possible that Rob and Zach could have been the ones to supply Jeremy with the weed that got him high. Which could explain why they would freak out if they somehow knew that Jeremy was driving the car that killed Tyler.

I'm not surprised when Tyler's little brother is not at The Music Shoppe that afternoon. I know people grieve and then, eventually, go on with their lives. But I don't really get it. How can you be overwhelmingly sad every day—and then one day decide, okay, it's time for me to go back to real life? Who decides when it's time to act normal again? Maybe the meaning of "real life" changes after such a huge loss. Maybe real life just becomes trying to get through the day-to-day.

Still, Jared's a little kid. He has hundreds, thousands of days left in his life. Will he get used to his brother being gone? Or will having a dead brother be the thing that defines his childhood and becomes part of his hidden self? Alex makes fun of me, but I'm convinced that everyone has a hidden self, one that's tucked away behind the self he or she presents to the world. Part of this hidden self consists of what is actually there, and part of it is just wishful thinking. It's who you really are, and who you want to be.

My hidden self is mysterious, and confident, and always knows what to say at parties or with people I don't know that well. My hidden self is a little bit silly, and still likes to do kid-like things like dressing up for Halloween and lip synching to the radio with a fake microphone while dancing around my bedroom. My hidden self is an artist who writes deep, meaningful songs full of truth and beauty and musical integrity—songs that will someday play on Coffee House and other singer/songwriter radio stations.

I wonder if I'll ever get to know Zach's hidden self.

The door to the lesson room creaks open, and I look up to see the front of Zach's guitar case—and then Zach—emerging from his lesson.

"Hey," he says, grinning just enough that his cheeks dimple.

"Hey." I grin back as I pick up my case.

"Careful—Eric is being a hard-ass today," he says lightly, nodding toward the lesson room.

"I heard that." Eric's disembodied voice floats in from behind the cracked door.

"I'll keep that in mind," I say, swinging my guitar strap onto my shoulder, feeling an instant mood boost.

"Hey Greene, " Eric calls. "The clock is ticking...."

I shrug apologetically at Zach and squeeze past him to get into the lesson room. Our arms brush as I pass by, and I think about the woods. My skin continues to tingle where our arms touched as I walk into my lesson.

At the end of the hour, when I make my way toward the front of the store, my stomach does a little dance. Zach stands at the edge of one of the rows of shelves, shuffling through sheet music. Still here. I come up behind him and see that he's looking at a classical guitar piece.

"You play classical?" He looks up from the music, not at all surprised to see *me*, and nods his head slowly and deliberately.

"I do." He's grinning at me again. *He waited for me to finish.*

"I'd love to learn how to do that," I say, "but I'm *just* at the point where the chords are starting to come naturally to me—if I start trying to do fancy picking stuff with my fingers, I'm doomed...."

"Doomed?" He says it in an exaggerated way. He's making fun of me.

"Yes, doomed!" I answer dramatically, liking that he already feels familiar enough around me to do that.

He absentmindedly ruffles through the pages in his hands, and I put my stuff down and start to look through the sheet music beside him. We stand side by side like that for several minutes, picking up different songs, thumbing through the pages. It's nice. Every now and then he leans slightly toward me so that our arms touch. I barely notice what's on the music sheets in my hands.

"Um, do you have to go right home?" he asks finally.

"Nooo...." I say slowly, looking up from the music.

"Wanna go to the arboretum? I'll teach you a little classical if you want..." Rob and Zach and their friends often hang out at the arboretum. I'm pretty sure that's where they go to get high. And where couples go to make out. I wouldn't know for sure, since I've never been. Alex and I both have a plan to become more experienced. I'm clearly making progress toward that goal.

"Sure," I answer. If only I felt as casual as I sound.

By getting into Zach's car, I am breaking one of my parents' rules: I'm not supposed to drive with another teenager without asking. But instead of feeling guilty, I feel brazen, reckless, carefree. Zach lowers the windows so that the autumn wind blows through the car as we drive. I turn toward the open window and watch the reds and oranges and yellows of the trees pass by in a blur. The wind whips around us as Zach presses on the gas, making my hair fly into my face. I pull it away from my mouth and steal a glance at Zach—his hair too, is blowing across his face, but he ignores it.

He reaches his right hand toward a knob on the dashboard and turns on the radio. I smile when I recognize the notes from "Hey Love," an old Jason Mraz song and one of my favorites.

"Oh, I love this song," I say.

"Yeah, me too." Instead of putting his hand back on the wheel, he rests it on the console between us, all the way on the edge closest to my leg. The closeness of his hand makes me suddenly aware of every nerve ending in my thigh. *Hey, love*. I subtly press my leg against the console, so that it's closer to his hand. He lets his fingers graze my thigh. It's the lightest, barely-there touch, yet the heat of it penetrates my jeans and makes my pulse go crazy.

Neither of us speak; instead, we listen together.

*Hey love, where you going to*
*You're not sleeping anymore, you're just trying to.*
*Stay love, where you running to*

When I realize that I've started singing along to the music, I stop abruptly and peek over at Zach. He glances at me at the same time, and we both crack up.

"I can't help myself—I love Jason Mraz!"

"I get it," he says, nodding his head and shifting his focus back to the road. I'm smiling as I turn back to the window. But as I listen more carefully to the lyrics, my smile fades.

*Well in case you never noticed*
*the path you never chose has chosen you*
*Don't be afraid to face and break it,*
*your secrets...*

Again, the weight of what I know—or rather, what I *think* I know—sits heavy in my stomach.

As we drive down the winding road leading into the arboretum, a former estate turned nature preserve, I take in our surroundings. Inside the gates of the property, the trees that line the access road meet high above it, forming a tunnel-like canopy and blocking out all but patches of sunlight. I'm sure this will soon change, as the leaves that still cling stubbornly to the branches drop to the ground. But today, it feels like we've left the entire world behind. We're surrounded by woods—and quiet. I make a conscious decision to leave my worries behind as well.

Soon we reach a clearing, and huge expanses of perfectly-manicured lawn, dotted with perfect specimens of different kinds of trees, sprawl before us. The leaves on the trees range from various shades of yellow-golds to fiery orange-reds.

"Wow," I say.

"I know, pretty spectacular, right? You've never been here?"

"No," I say, slightly embarrassed that I haven't had any reason to. "It's so beautiful. The whole place looks like a painting."

"Yeah, I love this place." Zach maneuvers the car onto the side of the road and parks it.

"You can just leave the car here?" I say, realizing as I ask the question that of course we can leave the car here—we haven't seen a sign of another person since we drove in.

"I don't see anyone around that's going to stop us," Zach says. He grins, opens his door and climbs out, so I do the same. He opens the back door, grabs his guitar case—and mine—and then goes around back, pops the trunk, and pulls out a red plaid blanket.

"Here, let me take my guitar at least," I say, reaching out my hand. He hands me the blanket, instead, and nods his head at a massive, blazing red sugar maple, a few hundred yards away.

"Let's go over there, and you can spread out the blanket for us," he says. I hug the blanket to my chest, a jumble of nervousness and anticipation knotting my stomach as we walk away from the road and even further away from civilization—and other people.

When we've almost reached the tree, I stop and look over at Zach. "Here?"

"Yeah." I take the blanket by two corners, and then whip it out so it catches some air and settles down flat on the grass.

"Done with such finesse," he says, teasing me.

"I have talents," I answer.

"Yes, I've noticed," he says, raising his eyebrows, and I feel my face get hot. I bend over my guitar case and start taking out my guitar to hide my fluster. Does he think I'm a good kisser? I peer at him sideways, without lifting my head, and see him suppressing a smile as he does the same.

"I'm going to teach you how to play classical guitar," he announces, as he sits down and arranges his guitar in his lap. I sit across from him, placing my own guitar on my lap, and watch with awe as he starts to pick at his strings. He plays a Spanish-sounding piece, and I'm amazed at how his right hand plucks one pattern on the strings, while the fingers on his left hand jump from fret to fret and string to string in a completely different pattern.

"This is 'Malaguena,'" he says without taking his eyes off the strings. Without even a hiccup in their movement, his fingers flit about the guitar strings as if they have a mind of their own. I twirl the edges of my hair as my eyes travel from his fingers to his face. He's completely absorbed in his playing—I become absorbed in studying his face.

I see how it relaxes when he plays. I notice the lock of hair that hangs down over his right eye. I note that his lashes are long—almost as long as a girl's—and that his eyes are sort of hooded, so that he looks perpetually sleepy. In a sexy way.

He suddenly stops playing, and looks back at me, catching me studying him. He smiles, leans over his guitar, brings his face right up to mine, and kisses me before I even have time to be embarrassed. He kisses me so intensely that I feel the kiss pass through my entire body.

I've closed my eyes, and when the kiss finishes, and we pull apart, I open them slowly and see Zach watching me intently. I smile, widely—I can't help it—and then he does too. Not only does he get dimples when he smiles, but also crinkles at the outer corners of his eyes, so it's like his whole face is smiling. I've never had a boy's attention so wholly focused on me in this way—and I like it. A lot.

"Okay, stop distracting me," he says, laughing, and puts his guitar down on the blanket.

"I'm distracting *you*?" I've never been more distracted by anyone in my life. I sit up stick straight, pick up my guitar, and put on a serious face. "OK, I'm ready to learn, Maestro." He grins, then scooches around me on his knees so that he's kneeling behind me.

"Now, with classical, it helps if you put your left leg a tiny bit higher than your right, to hold the guitar up at an angle," he says, putting his hand under my left thigh to lift it slightly. A current runs through my leg. He takes my right arm and places it so that my elbow leans on top of the body of the guitar, kind of holding it in place, and my fingers dangle down above the strings. Chills. He takes my left hand and places it under the neck of the guitar, so that it wraps around the fretboard. More chills. He then takes each finger—one finger at a time—and places it on a different fret along the E string. I've never experienced such heightened awareness of my own body. My mind travels with his hands, focused on wherever he touches.

"Now, you know how Eric always tells us to make sure we keep that curve in our fingers—and that only the fingertips touch the strings—that most of each finger should be held away from the fretboard? This is even more important with classical." Instead of listening to his words, I focus on the warmth of his breath on my neck. As he curls his left hand around mine to demonstrate what he means, I feel myself pressing the back of my hand into his. I lean my body back, slightly, so that my back and his front touch too.

"You're distracting me again," he whispers into the back of my hair. At this rate, it will be a while before I master classical guitar. But I have a feeling I'm going to learn other things from Zach.

# Chapter Eighteen

The long lashes. The lock of hair hanging over one eye. His long fingers strumming the guitar. That grin. I think about Zach when I wake in the mornings, and when I go to bed at night. I daydream about him during classes, and when I walk between classes. I think about the feel of his hands on my hands as he showed me how to position my fingers and the whisper of his breath on my neck when he spoke. I think about the guitar sliding off my lap, and of his hands on other parts of me. I think about kissing him, in the woods, and of our bodies intertwined on the grass in the arboretum.

And I think about him every time I hear Rob come home from school, because there's always the chance that Zach will be with him.

He has started texting me. Every now and then, in the middle of the day, my phone pings and there's a "hi" or a silly emoji or a random "where r u." We're usually on opposite ends of the school, but I love that he thinks about me when we aren't together. No boy has ever texted me before.

Late one afternoon, I'm in my room doing homework when a text makes my phone ding. I smile at the phone when I see it's from him.

*i'm downstairs, you here?*

*yes*

*meet me on front porch*

*k*

I pop up from my bed, grab my guitar, quietly make my way down the stairs, slip out of the house, and close the door softly behind me. Zach sits on our porch swing, grinning, his guitar case and backpack on the seat beside him, one arm draped along the back of the swing.

"Hey," he says.

"Hey." I smile back, and sit on the rocking chair across from the swing. "Rob's still downstairs?" He rarely emerges from the basement until dinner.

"Yeah." He makes a "come here" motion with his finger. I lean toward him and he kisses me softly on the lips. *Swoon.*

"I love that I make you blush," he whispers, before sitting back on the swing and picking up his guitar. Which makes me blush more. I feel the heat start at my neck and spread up my face.

He nods over at my guitar. "You want to play?"

"Mm-hmm." I lift my guitar out of its case.

"What are you working on this week?"

I take a breath, then set up my fingers on the second and third strings, second fret, to play the opening chord. A power D. I start playing the intro to "Hey There, Delilah." I play slowly, haltingly, since I'm new to finger-style technique, but he joins in, playing at my pace. We play other songs too—he lets me pick which ones. He always joins in, effortlessly, no matter what I play. He's that good.

"How do you do that?" I ask him after.

"Do what?"

"Just play—anything."

"I don't know. I've been playing for as long as I can remember. My dad taught me when I was like 5 or 6. He could play by ear."

"So, it's in your genes..."

He shrugs. Changes the subject.

"Is it true that you and Rob used to write rap songs together?" He raises an eyebrow. I laugh.

"I can't believe he told you that. That was like a million years ago."

"I wouldn't have pegged you as a rapper."

I tilt my head to the side and meet his eyes. "There are lots of things you don't know about me." *Am I actually flirting?* He looks at me so intently then that I feel his gaze in my whole body. I shift in my seat.

"Do you still write?"

"Not rap...and not really. I mean, I've only written parts of songs..."

"Maybe you'll show me sometime."

"Hmm...we'll see." I can't imagine showing anyone the stuff I've written. I would feel so... exposed. Now it's my turn to change the subject. I leaf through the music in my case and pull out another song.

"Let's play this one."

He starts texting me whenever he leaves Rob. Sometimes when I come outside, I sit next to him on the swing and we kiss. I pause every now and then to glance at the street, to make sure nobody's around. The porch swing is partially obscured by overgrown shrubs, but still, it would be weird for my mom to come home and see me kissing Zach. I don't ask if my brother knows Zach's hanging out with me. It feels like a secret liaison.

I haven't yet figured out a way to bring up the accident with Zach. I don't want to ruin things between us. But even as I grow more and more comfortable in his company—and stop worrying that I won't know what to say or do when I'm with him—I also get more and more anxious about the secret we share. And the fact that he doesn't know we share it. Not to mention that I don't exactly know what it is that I know.

I can tell, sometimes, that it weighs on Zach's mind—or at least I assume that's what he's thinking about. Suddenly his brow furrows as if he's momentarily distracted by a disturbing thought.

"What's wrong?" I asked when I caught that look on his face as I sat down across from him on the porch a couple of days ago.

"Nothing," he said, and he kissed me, and laughed when I was momentarily flustered from the unexpected greeting. I dropped it, knowing it probably had to do with the accident, but not wanting to push him into talking about it if he didn't want to. In a way, I feel like distracting him from the heavy weight he must be carrying is like a gift that only I can offer.

Yet his secret—even though I'm not entirely clear on the details of that secret—is also a heavy weight for me to carry. When I'm not with him, I constantly try to find ways to justify what he and Rob may have done. If they gave Jeremy weed, and he got high, and they let him get into a car? Maybe what Zach really said was they *didn't know* he was *too high to drive*? What if they were in the car with him? Maybe it was dark, and they heard the car hit something, but didn't realize it was a person. Deer run rampant around our corner of Connecticut, and I've heard my parents talking about friends' cars colliding with random deer that suddenly appeared out of nowhere. Mom's co-worker's car was totaled after one materialized on the road in front of his car as he drove to work in the early hours of the morning.

If they heard or felt a thump, but didn't see anything in the predawn darkness—wouldn't they have just assumed they'd swiped a deer? Especially if they were high? In which case, what would have been the point of stopping?

# Chapter Nineteen

We sit next to each other in the town library, our notebooks and textbooks mingling on the table we share. Zach arranges himself in his chair so that his left leg touches my right leg. When we're together, he always manages to have some part of his body touching mine. There's something intimate—and thrilling—about it, to be physically connected in some way even when we're out in public.

It's almost midterms, and we're both swamped with work. I'm reading excerpts from *Les Liaisons Dangereuses*—Dangerous Liaisons—for French. How ironic. I only vaguely understand what's going on in the passages, since my French isn't advanced enough to comprehend all the details and subtext—or even the entire plot for that matter—but I frequently refer to an English copy of the book, which lies open next to the sheet with the excerpt.

*Les Liaisons* is a book written in letters, and I know it's a love story, and that there are two sets of lovers, but I don't quite grasp how they're all related to one another. Especially because every time I successfully translate a sentence, I get distracted by Zach's leg against mine.

Zach has a test the next day, so he's supposed to be studying the chapters in his American History book on the Civil War, but I notice that he's spending more time doodling in the margins of his notebook than he is taking or reading notes. I become fascinated with his doodles, which I realize are intricately connected to one another like a complex and fantastical laboratory machine.

At the top corner of the notebook, he's sketched a ball perched on the precipice of a sort of chute, or track. The track, which is propped up by narrow stilts, winds decoratively across the top of the page, and even through some of the text, then arrives at a cliff—or rather, the edge of a table, on the other side of the page. Then there's a drop where the ball should roll off the edge and into a bucket that is sketched in (with all the proper shading) at the bottom right corner of the page. I assume the ball is then meant to fall over and knock into a series of tiles or dominoes that march across the bottom of the page.

"Wow," I say, startling Zach out of his artistic trance. He covers his notebook with his arm. And looks embarrassed.

"What is that?" I ask, fascinated at this new aspect of Zach revealing itself in the pages of his notebook. He's like a many-layered dessert, appealing from the moment you look at it, but as you dig deeper, you realize that there's so much more to it than you originally thought.

"Oh, nothing, I'm just doodling," he says, his face reddening. I've never seen him get embarrassed—it's usually me blushing. I'm both charmed by his embarrassment and amazed that I have the power to elicit it.

"That is *not* just doodling," I say. "That is so—" I search for the right word. "So....elaborate. It's so cool."

"It's a Rube Goldberg," he says shyly.

"A what?"

"A Rube Goldberg—he was this cartoonist who was also an inventor. He would always draw these crazy invention cartoons. I've been doing it since I was a kid."

"Do you have a lot of these?"

He shrugs. "Yeah, I guess..." He pauses for a minute, and seems to assess me.

"Notebooks-full," he admits.

"Can I see them?"

He shrugs again. "If you really want to." He sounds skeptical.

"I want to."

"OK," he says. He grins—showing his dimple—then turns back to his notes. I do the same.

That night, when I open my French notebook, a small, folded note falls out of its pages. I open it to one of Zach's intricate drawings. At the top of the page, there's a marble emblazoned with a question mark, and the beginning of a track for the marble to roll along. The track ends in the middle of the page. There, that same marble is drawn in lighter pencil, floating down the page while suspended from a striped parachute, and poised to land at the end of the sentence – *Come over after school tomorrow*—that Zach has scribbled in his chicken scratch handwriting at the bottom of the page.

I pick up my phone from my desk and text him.

*OK.*

"Do you think his mom will be home? Am I going to have to meet his mom? Do you think he wants to introduce me?"

"Well—" Alex and I sit on the stone wall in front of the school's entrance, in our usual pre-morning bell spot, legs dangling above the sidewalk a few feet below. I lean in close to Alex, so that she—and no one else—can hear me above the swirl of voices and activity as other students arrive and congregate on the nearby steps.

"And if she's not home, then we are going to be *alone* in the house... do you think he's *trying* to get me alone in his house?"

Alex raises her eyebrows.

"I mean, things got kind of hot and heavy in the arboretum, you don't think...."

"Oh my God Hannah, will you calm down! He asked you to come over, he didn't ask you to sleep with—" I put my hand over Alex's mouth.

"Shush," I say, laughing, looking around to make sure there's nobody within earshot of our conversation. Alex ducks her way out of my grasp and places her hands on my shoulder like a wise old relative.

"Hannah-Ban," she says. "Life is not an emergency." This is Alex's favorite bit of advice, one that she imparts to me often—whenever I'm "freaking out" about something. I, of course, never characterize my own—okay, slightly frenetic—outbursts, in which I verbalize whatever worry is preoccupying my brain, as "freaking out." But Alex, who likes to think she is wise and mature and more laid back than I am, acts like it's her job to keep me on an even keel.

Of course, Alex also freaks out about boys on a semi-daily basis, but that's beside the point. The morning bell interrupts our conversation.

"Ughhhh," I say, resigning myself to two more hours of worrying until I can discuss my dilemma again with Alex at lunch. Which, of course, we do.

As soon as the final bell rings, Zach and I meet by the front wall and walk together toward his neighborhood. We walk with our arms brushing against each other, our steps kind of in sync, our short bursts of conversation alternating with comfortable silence. Yet when I think about actually being at Zach's house, my heart beats hard against the inside of my chest. I think about how I used to drive by and stare longingly at other couples who looked like me and Zach probably do right now, and how you can never really know what is going on with people—in their heads, in their relationships.

"So, how's that Jason Mraz song going?" he asks.

"Which one? *93 Million Miles*?"

"Yeah."

"Good, I guess. I mean, it doesn't really make sense for me to sing it, since I'm a teenage girl, and the lyrics are addressed to someone's son. But I really like the song."

"I don't know—I don't think it matters, really. I mean, women authors write books from the point of view of male characters. You're just telling someone's story."

"Hmmm. I never thought of it that way."

I like talking to Zach about music. I don't really have anyone else who I can talk with about playing guitar. And certainly nobody else has ever talked to me about the "art" of music like Zach does. He's constantly surprising me. I'd never have imagined that this boy who sat with Rob and their other friends in front of a big TV screen (or two) playing video games for hours at a time actually thought about other things, like music, so deeply.

Sometimes, when we sit together on my front porch, we share a set of earphones to listen to new songs—he wears the left ear bud, me the right—and we dissect the songs. What the musician does with the chords, how the switch to minor key changes the mood. He asks me questions, like why did I think the songwriter picked that title, and would I have called the song something else?

I usually go back to my music notebook after these talks, the one I keep hidden in my desk drawer, and look back at the partially-written songs I've scribbled in there over the years, to see whether I placed minor chords in the right places, and whether the music effectively conveys the mood I'm trying to express.

"What are you thinking?" he says, bringing me back to earth.

"Nothing – what are you thinking?"

"I'm thinking that you are very hot when you're thinking about 'nothing.'"

I feel myself blushing, and elbow him in the side to distract him so he won't notice. He laughs.

We turn off the main road that runs through town and into a neighborhood that is marked by two grey stone posts. Wrought iron letters spell out the words Meadow Farms on the low wall to the right of one post.

"Welcome to Meadow Fahms," Zach says with a flourish of his hand and a fake British accent. The modest homes that line Zach's street don't quite match the official entryway or Zach's formal introduction into the neighborhood. The shingled, split level structures, fronted by small patches of lawn and the requisite ornamental trees, wear varying shades of blue, grey, yellow and white. They have black or white shutters, and blacktop driveways, and display their house numbers on black or white tin mailboxes affixed to wooden posts.

Number 17, Zach's house, is slightly more disheveled than its neighbors—the house numbers painted on the mailbox are partially rubbed off, and like Zach, the lawn looks like it could use a good haircut. I find the less-manicured state of his lawn just as charming as I find his slightly-tousled, shoulder-length hair. I follow Zach up the driveway and inside.

Nobody greets us at the door or calls out to acknowledge our presence. My stomach does a nervous flip. We have the house to ourselves.

"You want a snack? I'm starving." Zach leads me into the kitchen, without waiting for an answer. He pulls a bag of Oreos out of the pantry and tilts the bag toward me, grinning.

"Very funny," I say, but I help myself.

Rob and Zach came into the kitchen once when I'd been mindlessly eating Oreos while studying for a test. I didn't notice them watching me stuffing my face with cookie after cookie until the two of them started cracking up. I was mortified.

"This is why we never have any Oreos in the house," Rob said before heading to the pantry to snag a bag of chips for him and Zach. Zach loved to tease me about this incident. But I have no way to defend myself. Oreos are my weakness.

Zach waits until I finish my cookie, and then comes closer, so that I'm pressed against the kitchen island. We kiss, for a long time. "Mmm," he says as he finally pulls away. "Oreos."

I push him toward the kitchen door so he won't see me blushing again. "Let's go see your drawings."

"Yes, ma'am."

I follow him up the stairs, curious to see his room, yet at the same time nervous to be alone with him while nobody else is in the house. Not because I'm afraid of him. I'm more afraid of the situation. And of myself, and what I might be willing to do.

His bedroom walls are plastered with music posters and vintage album covers. They cover almost every inch of three walls. Music sheets and partial compositions of songs are tacked haphazardly on a bulletin board above his desk, and the desk is book-ended with two tall bookcases brimming with music CDs—*CDs*— and vintage cassettes. I recognize the guitar case propped against the side of his bed, but there's also a slightly smaller guitar, caseless, nestled in a stand in the corner of the room, and beside it, a little blue ukulele.

"You play the ukulele?" I ask.

"Sort of."

I survey his bedroom walls, in awe, then wander closer to the bookshelves. I run my hand along the edges of the CD cases, which appear to be grouped by genre: Jason Mraz with Ed Sheeran, John Mayer, and other singer/songwriters; a really old-school grouping comprised of artists like Crosby, Stills and Nash, Simon and Garfunkel, Neil Young, and Joni Mitchell; a whole section devoted to the Beatles. The cassettes have musician and album names or concert dates written in block ink lettering on the edges of the cases. I feel like I'm in a museum looking at an exhibit. The Zach exhibit.

I move from the bookcases to the bulletin board, admiring his music annotations and studying what I assume are original song lyrics. I notice that he, in turn, watches me studying his things. But I'm too intrigued to feel self-conscious. It fascinates me to see the objects that live in Zach's personal space, all the things he chooses to keep and display, though I imagine some of the items are simply relics from his childhood that he hasn't bothered to get rid of. I'm getting a glimpse of Zach's hidden self.

I wander over toward his bed—*his bed! Stomach flip*—to examine the oversized map that covers the wall behind it in place of a headboard. The map is studded with different colored pins. Most are blue, but I notice a few green ones scattered throughout New England—and one stuck on Denver, Colorado. I look at him questioningly and he says, "Blue is where I want to go—green is where I've been."

"What's in Denver?"

"My dad."

"Oh." I can't imagine my dad moving that far away if my parents ever got divorced. I look back at the map, curious about where Zach *wants* to go, and notice a red pin stuck into England. "What does red mean?" I ask, touching it, and moving my face closer to the map, as if that would give me the answer.

"Beatles' country," he says, as if stating the obvious. "I've always wanted to go to the real Abbey Road in London. Actually, I had this idea that someday I'd drag Rob and Ben and Nick there so that we could do that pose that the Beatles do on the cover of the Abbey Road album." He motions with his head toward an album cover on the wall to the left of his bed, where John, Ringo, Paul and George stride across the thoroughfare that has been made famous by this iconic photograph.

I have an "aha" moment. I notice that George Harrison, in that photo, looks kind of like Rob's friend Nick, especially since Nick has started to grow out his straight brown hair. "Ohhhh, so that's why you guys call Nick, George..." I say.

"You got it," he says, looking at me in a proud sort of way. I feel silly for how good this makes me feel.

I notice that while I've been exploring his room, Zach has closed the bedroom door—heart flutter—but I also notice that a huge poster covers the inside of the door, a poster of what looks like an even more elaborate version of one of Zach's doodled contraptions.

I walk over to the poster and see that it's actually a blown-up version of a New Yorker magazine cover. Pipes and funnels and meters and light bulbs and all kinds of intricate machine parts take up almost the entire cover, except in the bottom right hand corner, a professorial-looking guy stands with a coffee cup extended under a spout at the bottom to receive a drip of coffee that is apparently produced by the wacky invention.

"Ah—I take it this is an original?"

"Yup, an official Rube Goldberg," he says. We admire the diagram together for a couple of minutes.

"So, can I see yours?" I ask.

"Yes, can I see yours?" He grins; I blush.

"You know what I mean."

"Yes, I do," he says, laughing. "But as I've mentioned, I like making you blush." He pulls a long, rectangular, plastic storage box out from underneath his bed. He sits down on the blue carpeted floor, and I sit down facing him, on the other side of the box. He lifts the lid off the box to reveal a handful of notebooks interspersed with loose sheets of sketching paper– pages and pages of intricate hand-drawn diagrams.

"May I?" I ask, my hands poised to pick up one of the pages.

"You may...." I study sheet after sheet. Some look like crazy mazes, others like architectural plans for zany inventions. The detail in all of them is incredible.

"These are amazing," I say. "When did you draw all of these?"

"I used to build them with my dad," he says. "The Rube Goldberg machines. It was our thing. We'd assemble them all around the basement, and sometimes around the family room, and up and down the stairs—*that* drove Mom crazy. These were the plans—I always drew out the plans before we started construction."

I examine the drawing in my hands: There's a marble poised on the brink of a sort of chute that goes downhill and then ends mid-air; what I assume is supposed to be the same marble is then represented in lighter pencil sailing off the end of the chute. Arrows point downward toward a funnel, which I see would presumably drop the marble onto a see-saw kind of a thing, which leads to a long snaking trail of dominoes that winds its way to the edge of the page.

"Wow," I say again. I thumb through the other drawings. I've never really thought about it before, but it occurs to me that Zach is smart.

"My dad was a mechanical engineer," he adds. "He kind of wanted me to be one too. I always thought maybe I'd end up being a sound engineer. Math and science are kind of easy for me, and it would be a way to combine the music with something that actually provides a salary."

I'm surprised. Not that Zach has aspirations—though I'd always assumed that his goal was to be a singer/songwriter—or that I thought he didn't have brains. Despite his lack of interest in starting his college search, and his tendency toward cutting school and getting high, Rob gets good grades—exceptionally good for someone who doesn't try all that hard. I imagine he surrounds himself with similar friends. I just never thought about Zach excelling in some academic realm. Or even as someone who would care about making money. To me, he's artsy—an artist, really.

Zach looks at the drawings with a kind of wistful expression.

"Do you miss him?" I ask

"Yup." He says it quietly and doesn't look up.

"When do you get to see him?"

"I used to go to Denver for a week every summer, but I didn't go this past summer." He shrugs. "It didn't work out." He doesn't say why and I don't ask. I'm about to change the subject when my phone dings in my back pocket. And then dings again.

I pull it out, glance at the screen. "Ugh."

"What?" he asks.

"It's my mom. I've got to go home and walk and feed Felix. My mom thought she'd be home earlier today and didn't call the dog walker." I don't want to leave Zach, but at the same time, feel slightly relieved that I have a reason to.

"But thanks for showing me these."

"Thanks for asking," he says, carefully gathering the sheets that we've scattered on the carpet around us, and placing them back in the box. I hold the pile in my hands out to him.

"They're really cool," I say.

He leans over the box and we kiss. Intensely. It's the kind of kiss that could have easily led to something more. And I'm both regretful and relieved that I have a reason to pull away and go home.

# Chapter Twenty

Alex has just talked me into playing wingwoman at boys' soccer practice while she stalks Jake. We plan that I will run out to grab snacks for the game while she picks up her portfolio from the art room. The blue uniforms catch my eye as I pass by Mr. Finnely's office on my way out of the building. I do a double take—what are the police doing here? Are they questioning students? Which students?

I slow down to get a closer look, and see the backs of the two cops as they're led into the principal's inner sanctum by Mrs. Parks, the woman who sits behind the desk. I don't see any students in there. Still, I shudder. Do they already have suspects? Are Rob and Zach on their list?

I wonder if Alex has seen the cops. I'll find out soon enough.

I hate going to boys' sports practices—I don't want to be seen as a fangirl—but I understand that Alex can't go by herself.

"Please," Alex begged as she watched me gather my things from my locker that afternoon. "Come with me." I hesitated, but knew I owed Alex this.

I can tell Alex is feeling hurt that I'm not around as much. I don't want to be one of those girls who abandons her friends the minute she starts going out with a guy, but I can't help but jump at any chance I have to be with Zach. Anyway, now that I have Zach, I want Alex to have someone too.

"Pretty please?" Alex gave me one of her irresistible smiles.

"Okay, okay," I agreed. Alex's lips curved into an even wider smile, and I knew I had made the right choice.

But as I head to the corner store, I worry that Alex has probably seen the cops at school, too, which will spark yet another conversation about the accident. Which means I will have to continue to lie, to keep up the pretense that I don't know any more about it than she does. Well, in a way I don't, really.

At the corner store, I grab a big bag of cheddar popcorn and some pretzel M&Ms. Alex's favorite. Alex rushes over when I get back to school.

"Did you see?!" Alex asks breathlessly. "The cops? At school?"

"Yeah, I saw."

"Do you think they have suspects?" I feel all the muscles in my body tensing.

"I only saw them going into Dr. Finnely's office—I didn't see any students." I pause. "Did you?"

"No," Alex says. "But they must suspect some Woodfield High student or why would they be here?" I swallow. And then she voices the question that I have been trying not to think about. "Do you think they are here to question kids who were at the party?"

"Maybe they're here to question that guy Jeremy from the football team—you know, the one who used to go out with Tara?"

"Nah—he's no longer a person of interest."

"What? Why not?" I need there to be a person of interest who isn't Zach. Who isn't Rob. "I thought you said he was at the party?"

"He left the party way too early—apparently wasn't feeling too good after downing like six beers in his first couple of hours." I don't ask Alex how she knows that. "But Sam Fields is in my English class, and she told me her older sister was there, which means the other field hockey girls were probably there..." Even though Kevin Russo is a senior, Sam's older sister is in Zach and Rob's class. That means juniors were there too. I swallow the lump that forms in my throat. And search for some reason to change the subject.

Fortunately, the soccer field comes into view, and I notice that the players are already out running back and forth, passing the black and white ball between them with their feet. I squeeze Alex's arm and nod my head toward the field. Alex looks up ahead.

"There he is," she squeals, grabbing my arm and pulling me toward the field. Attention successfully diverted.

The soccer field is inside the track, and the track is surrounded by a chain-link fence, which separates it from the soccer bleachers. I walk with Alex over to the fence, and we lean on it to watch Jake and his teammates practice. Jake looks over as he runs by and catches Alex's eye. I see him wink—Alex taps my leg to make sure I'd witnessed the moment—and I'm glad I came.

Still, I want to get home before my mother, because I suspect Zach might be there with Rob and I don't want to miss him. I glance over at the stands—and Alex follows my gaze. A couple of her friends from the school paper sit, heads together, chatting, watching the field—and the guys—out of the corners of their eyes. Alex waves, and they wave back.

"Alex, I have to get home," I say after we've been watching for a while.

"Really," Alex answers in a knowing tone. I suppress a smile.

"Okay, okay, run off to Zach," Alex teases. "You've fulfilled your wingwoman duties." She nods her head toward the stands. "I'll go watch with them."

We push away from the fence, and walk the few feet from the field to the stands together. Alex peels away from me and heads toward her newspaper friends.

"See ya Lex," I say to her back.

"See ya Banana," Alex answers, glancing over her shoulder and blowing me a kiss.

As I head home, I start worrying again about the police at school. I feel like they are closing in. *Other juniors were at the party*. It's time for me to confront Zach.

# Chapter Twenty-One

I hear the boys' raised voices the minute I open the door. They're in the basement, but they must have inadvertently left the door open, and their words carry up the stairs and into the foyer.

"You really think that *this* is a good time to choose to hook up with my sister?" Rob is saying.

"What happens between me and your sister has nothing to do with anything."

"You're just complicating things."

"It doesn't complicate anything."

"Well maybe I don't want her mixed up in this—"

"How am I mixing her up in this? She doesn't even know—"

"It doesn't matter," Rob insists. "She's a distraction and you can't be distracted right now. What if she starts talking about the accident and you slip up and tell her something?"

A chill runs through my entire body. I'm torn between remaining still, so I won't miss a single word of this conversation—and slamming the door really hard, so that I don't hear another thing. But when I hear Mom's car rolling into the driveway, my hand is forced.

I shut the door loudly, and the boys' conversation stops abruptly. Then I hear low mumbling, and harsh whispers, and before I have time to consider what I'm doing, I run toward the basement door and down the stairs, shutting the door behind me.

They look at me, shocked, as I burst in on them, invade their sacred space. Rob and Zach stand in front of the mustard-colored chenille sofa that once lived in the family room. The video game controllers lie, untouched, on the coffee table, the video game console on the floor in front of the TV, neither of them powered on.

"Stop. Talking. About. Me." I say it quietly, but firmly, looking back at the boys. I'm done keeping a low profile, done worrying about what I can and can't say to my brother and Zach. I'm tired of other people deciding what's best for me. "Whatever you have to say, you can say to my face. I'm right here."

Zach stares down at his feet, tongue-tied, hands in his jean pockets, looking like a kid who's been caught doing something bad.

Rob, on the other hand, meets my gaze. "How about you stop eavesdropping!" he answers, his voice growing louder with each word.

"Please, be quiet," I plead in a loud whisper. "Mom's home—she'll hear!" That shuts him up—at least for a few seconds—as he glances beyond me, toward the top of the stairway.

I remain frozen, at the bottom of the stairs, looking from Zach, who won't catch my eye, to Rob, who looks back at me with such venom that it makes my stomach clench. This is it, I think. The moment of reckoning.

"Like Mom's anyone to judge," Rob finally says bitterly. "You think she's so perfect? She's not." Zach shoots Rob a wary look.

I look at Rob, confused.

"Rob, don't," Zach says.

"This has nothing to do with you," Rob warns. He turns back to me. My stomach tightens again.

"What are you talking about?"

Zach shakes his head at Rob. But Rob ignores him, stays focused on me.

"Mom's cheating on Dad," he says. Zach looks at him in disbelief. As my brother's words sink in, I put my hand against the wall, to steady myself.

"What?"

"I left school early the other day and saw her getting out of Officer Scarelli's car," Rob mutters.

"So? That doesn't mean anything," I shoot back, but even as I say it, I flash back to my mother and Officer Scarelli looking at each other at the football game, to Mom's hand on his arm when she thanked him for "rescuing" me; to him emerging from our house when I came home early from school. My heart sinks.

"They were kissing," Rob adds, to drive the point home.

"Rob, you're such an asshole," Zach says finally. He moves toward me and touches my arm. "Hannah," he says, but I'm too shocked to respond.

"What?" says Rob. "She should know that Mrs. Judge-y doesn't really have the right to judge anybody."

"Rob, stop," Zach hisses.

I feel my world tilting. I look past Rob's angry face and focus on the words that are scribbled on the chalkboard wall behind the TV, but they all swirl together in a giant blur. All this time I've been worrying about Tyler Miller's family. How ironic.

"I've got to go," I choke out, turning back toward the steps. I have to get out of here before I start to cry.

"Hannah, wait," says Zach, reaching out to me. But as I push past, he drops his hand and lets me go. Before I turn toward the steps, I see him give Rob a murderous look.

"What," I hear Rob say as I run up the stairs.

I lie on my bed. Felix, who followed me upstairs, curls up beside me, as if sensing my distress. I stare up at the clouds painted on the ceiling. Though my walls are gray, with a slight hint of lavender, the ceiling is sky blue, with puffs of grayish white clouds scattered across it. The rest of my room is color-coordinated and what Alex calls teenage chic (Alex is the only friend who knows that my mother actually hired an interior decorator to design it), but the ceiling is Mom's concession to me. I'd wanted a ceiling that looked like the sky.

When I was little, my favorite thing was lying on the grass, next to Dad, and staring up at the sky.

"I see a fish," he would say, starting the cloud game.

"I see a dog," I would answer.

"My fish is swimming toward an umbrella."

"My dog is sitting next to a giant mushroom."

And so it would go, often until Mom called us in for dinner.

My favorite part of the game was that when you were busy looking for shapes in the clouds, your mind didn't have time to worry about anything that was happening down on the ground. I look up at my ceiling now, and try really hard to find shapes in the painted clouds, to find some story up there—any story—that will have a happy ending. Because whatever happens with the police investigation, with Rob, with Zach, with Mom—*Mom!*—I have a feeling that the story here, on the ground, is not going to end well.

# Chapter Twenty-Two

Alex and I sit on the worn leather sling swings that hang from the playset in my backyard, a relic from my and Rob's childhood. We move our swings in lazy circles by digging the toes of our sneakers into the grass below. One of the things I love about being with Alex is that we don't have to talk all the time. Mostly, Alex gabs nonstop, but it also feels normal to just sit together once in a while and not talk. To just go off into our own heads and still have one another as company.

Alex, whose math tutor lives in my neighborhood, stopped by on her way home, forcing me to pull myself off my bed and out of my misery. Zach and Rob were long gone, thank God— I heard their voices in the foyer and then on the front porch soon after I escaped up the stairs and shut myself in my room. I let out a long exhale once I heard the front door slam—didn't even realize I'd been holding my breath. Mom, thankfully, had been on the phone in the kitchen at the time, so didn't intercept me on my way up to my room.

"Do you ever wish that you didn't know things you knew?" I ask Alex suddenly.

"What do you mean?" Alex gives me a perplexed look.

"Like, maybe you were always wondering about something, but then when you find out the answer, you wish you could go back to not knowing."

"Actually, yes!" says Alex, enthusiastically. "Once, when I was like 10, I asked my mom how old she was. I had always assumed she was 27 for some reason, and when she said she was 34, I was so freaked out by how old she was that I wished I hadn't asked her." Then Alex narrows her eyes. "What are you talking about, anyway? What do you wish you didn't know?"

I shrug, then looked down at the ground. I trace figure eights in the grass with my sneakers, studying the temporary depression that my sneakers make in the grass.

"Is it something about Zach? Because if he told you about an old girlfriend, I don't think you have anything to worry about. He is so into you that it is beyond obvious."

I perk up and glance over at Alex.

"What do you mean," I ask, sort of knowing what she means, but wanting to hear the specifics. "How is it obvious?"

"When he looks at you," she says, "it's not like he just glances at you. His eyes are glued to you. He watches you like everything you do is utterly fascinating and interesting and—"

"And what?"

"And like he can't wait to tap that." Alex cracks up.

"Alex!" I push Alex's shoulder so that her swing swings sideways and then bumps back into me.

"Really, you're so lucky. If Jake looked at me the way that Zach looks at you, my life would be pretty much perfect."

"Believe me, my life is not perfect."

"You know what I mean." We sit there, swinging softly on the old backyard swings, gently ricocheting off one another, not saying anything.

I think about how my dad used to sit on the swings with me. Not just push me, like other dads did, but sit beside me like Alex is doing, and actually *play* with me. We would pretend we were other people, or aliens, or royalty. The backyard would become another country, or another planet, or our kingdom. We invented countless worlds and made up endless stories together.

We grew out of this game, of course, just like we'd grown out of the cloud game. I missed the one-on-one time with Dad. I knew it was normal for moms to pair off with daughters and dads to pair off with sons—I'd noticed similar dynamics in friends' families. But I envy the connection Rob has with Dad that I no longer get to have, especially now, when I no longer trust Mom and don't necessarily have any desire to pair off with her. Which leaves me with no one in my family to really talk to.

I wouldn't feel the need to talk to anyone in my family if I could only confide in Alex, but I can't, not about this. That leaves Zach, who I don't know *that* well, and who might even be a killer.

There was a time when I told Mom everything. *Everything*. Almost like a thing didn't really happen until I'd recounted it to Mom, and she'd commented on it. Was it that she validated whatever feelings I had about the stories I told her or the friends I told her about? Was it my convoluted way of gaining her approval over how I handled—or responded to—different situations? Lately it has felt like there are way more things I don't tell her about. Because maybe I think she won't approve of how I'm handling things. Or maybe I have my own doubts about how I'm handling things. Of course now her approval means nothing.

"I've gotta go home for dinner," Alex says reluctantly, jumping up from her swing and interrupting my troubling reverie. I stand too, disappointed to see her go. I don't want to be left alone with my thoughts.

"OK, see ya tomorrow."

"See ya, Hannah-ban."

I pull open the screen door to the kitchen and realize I'm thirsty. I walk over to the cabinet to get a cup, and pull out the one closest to the edge of the bottom shelf. It's the white mug with the bright, sunny smiley face, the one that my mother always brings me filled with hot lemon water and honey when I'm sick. Ever since I was a little girl.

Even now, every time my throat gets scratchy, I crave that syrupy honey and the lemony-sweet smell of the steam rising from that hot lemonade and gently enveloping my face. I yearn for the feel of my hands wrapped around the warm mug and that happy face smiling up at me. I long for the warmth of having my fuzzy throw blanket wrapped around my shoulders. Or maybe it's that version of my mother that I long for—the one who brings me the soothing beverage, who hands me the cozy blanket from the bottom of the bed, who sits by my side and says, "Maybe, when you feel better we could curl up on my bed and watch a chick flick."

From now on, it will be different. Every time I see this new version of my mother, I will think of her with Officer Scarelli, of how she betrayed Dad. I will think about how she acts one way, when she's really another. And I will think about how if you can't trust your own mother, who can you trust?

# Chapter Twenty-Three

The four of us sit around the table, quietly eating our salad. Felix lies in wait in his usual position beneath my chair. Stir fry sizzles in the wok on the kitchen island behind me, infusing the air with the aroma of soy sauce and peanut oil. Usually, my mouth would be watering in anticipation of my favorite dinner, but instead, my stomach is roiling.

If I thought family dinner had become an awkward affair since the hit and run—with my constant worry that Rob will say something suspicious, my mother relentlessly bringing up the police investigation, and my attempts to steer the conversation in other directions—now I find it almost unendurable.

"I spoke to your mother today," Mom tells Dad between forkfuls of salad. "She was all excited about the trip she and the sisters are planning to Europe." Usually, I get a kick out of hearing about my grandmother's escapades with her three sisters—the four of them spend months every year planning annual trips to far-flung destinations, as if they're still in their twenties. Now, I silently fume at my mother.

*Good strategy. Showing him what a good wife and daughter-in-law you are by talking about how you called Grandma.* I glance at Dad to gauge his reaction, but he just nods with a neutral expression and acts as if he's engrossed in devouring his dinner roll. At least Mom's not talking about the accident.

I've started analyzing my parents' every word, as well as the looks that pass between them. I scrutinize their expressions, their body language. I assess my mother's outfits and hair and makeup. Does she seem to be wearing more of it lately? Is that a new shirt? Is she wearing more form-fitting shirts, or has she always worn form-fitting shirts?

I note that Mom has recently taken to taming her typically curly brown hair with a straightening iron, which makes her look younger and more like me. (Unfortunately, I lost the genetic lottery and have only the slightest wave in my otherwise limp brown hair.) There was a time when I wanted to look like my mother—polished and self-assured, with her perfectly-imperfect curls, carefully-coordinated outfits and expertly-applied make-up. But now I don't want to be anything like her.

Mom chats on, oblivious to the reality that nobody's really listening. "They're going to start in Stockholm, and then make their way through Finland, Copenhagen, and Estonia. They're going to visit Vilnius—the town your great, great grandparents are from." She turns her attention to me and Rob.

"Cool," I say, which is all the encouragement Mom needs to continue. Though Rob sits across from me, I avoid looking at him. Even thinking about not looking at him fills me with anger. No—resentment. I resent him for telling Zach not to be with me. For not telling me what I want to know about what happened that night. And for the fact that I know anything at all.

Most of all, I resent him for knocking my mother off the pedestal on which I'd once placed her. She was annoying, yes, but she was still a good mom. I know I've distanced myself from her since everything that's happened. It's too hard for me to keep things from her—and the way she constantly brings up the accident makes me crazy. But back when I used to tell her things, she used to give really good advice. I trusted that in a lot of ways, she really did know what was best for me. But thanks to Rob, I've lost faith in her judgement—about everything. I'd never have imagined that my mom could be so devious, so unfaithful, such a liar.

As she describes Grandma's upcoming trip, Mom stands, makes her way to the wok, loads her signature mixture of spicy vegetables, chicken and sesame seeds onto the dinner plates, and then delivers them two by two to the table. She sits down, still talking. "They're hoping the tour guide will be able to find the street where their parents grew up—can you imagine?"

As soon as Mom takes a breath, I grab the opportunity to try to engage my father in conversation.

"So what's new at work, Dad?" I say, ignoring Mom's miffed look at being interrupted. I want Dad to know that someone in the family still cares about him.

"Thrilling as ever," he says, winking at me. Dad is a civil engineer who has a hand in designing bridges and tunnels and roads all around the state. He used to sketch things constantly—on the edges of the newspaper, on napkins, on his desk blotter in his office—and would regale us with detailed explanations of his projects-in-progress.

When we were little, he even used to drive me and Rob to the sites where the bridges or roads he designed were being constructed. But he doesn't sketch much anymore. And Rob and I are too old—and busy with our friends—for those kinds of field trips.

"Not too many exciting new projects at the moment," he adds. "More an effort to rescue the state's aging infrastructure and do preventive damage control. Any interesting projects on the Hannah front?"

"Not really," I answer with a smile and a shrug. "Just boring high school stuff. But I'll keep you posted." This family could have used some *preventive damage control*, I think. Is it too late for us? Can we be fixed?

The dinner conversation seems more stilted than usual. It appears to me that Mom is trying unsuccessfully to catch Dad's eye. I don't blame him for not looking—if I was him, I wouldn't look at Mom either. Does that mean he knows?

The scent of my dinner wafts up from my plate, and I half-heartedly stab at a piece of broccoli with my fork, forcing myself to take a bite. I'm not hungry. I sneak a piece of chicken off the edge of my dish, and casually slide my hand under the table, where Felix waits patiently for a bite. He snatches my offering.

"How about you Rob—anything new on the college front?" Mom asks, always grabbing any opportunity to steer the conversation to the Where-Will-Rob-Go-To-College topic. Though I guess that from Rob's perspective, if there was anything good to come out of this whole disaster, it's that Mom has something to focus on *other* than his impending college search.

"For God's sake, Julie, it's the fall of his junior year," Dad intercedes. "He doesn't need to know where he's applying to college yet."

"John," Mom says calmly, almost as if talking to a child, "he can't know where he's applying until he starts researching the possibilities. Everyone knows that junior year is the time to do that research. Why, just a couple of weeks ago, the guidance department sent out the junior questionnaires," and then taking a breath to turn to Rob—"Did you fill yours out yet, Honey?"

Rob rolls his eyes. "No, Mom. I didn't fill it out yet. Nobody has. We have actual schoolwork to do, believe it or not. And most people in our school have been focused on *other* things lately." I shoot a punishing glance at Rob. Really? He's going to get Mom started on the *other thing* again?

"Julie, lay off him already," Dad says with exasperation. "You have plenty of time to start stressing him out about college—now's not the time."

"Oh, please, I'm not stressing him out—"

Rob suddenly slams down his fork and pushes his chair away from the table. "I'm done." His exit is so swift that neither parent has a chance to react.

"Happy?" Dad says under his breath to Mom. She doesn't answer. Stranded alone with my parents, I look down at my plate. An awkward silence ensues, the clinking of silverware on our china plates the only accompaniment to our swirling thoughts.

*Please shoot me so I don't have to sit through another family dinner.* I press send and stare at the phone, waiting impatiently for Alex to text back. It occurs to me that I can assuage some of my guilt for spending less time with Alex *in person* by spending more virtual time with her. So I text her even more than usual. If only I could confide in Alex about the real reasons that being with my family has become intolerable.

I sit on my shaggy rug, my back against the beanbag chair, absent-mindedly pulling at the thick white strands in the rug as I watch the screen. Being with my family was once a reprieve, an escape from the pressures of figuring out how to navigate high school social life. Now, home life is becoming even more difficult to navigate.

Ah, finally. The dots on the screen that tell me Alex is typing....

*Tell me about it*

*Whatcha doin'*

*Procrastinating, you?*

*Yah.* I pause. There's so much I want to tell Alex, and so much I can't tell her. While I'm waffling, she texts again.

*Did you see the news?* What now, I wonder.

*No...*

*They have a person of interest – the police*

I sit up, my body suddenly on full alert.

*Who? How?*

*Someone turned in a Ring video. It showed a car that was in the right place, right time*

I think I might throw up.

*What kind of car?*

*Something black–I forget*

My stomach does a crazy dance. Rob's car is black.

*Suspect?*

*Not suspect – person of interest. Anyway, they think they got the model and maybe the guy...*

*OMG Alex who is it*

*They didn't say.* My mind is spinning. A black car. But lots of people have black cars, right? So how do they have a person of interest? And – not a suspect? What does that even mean? My brain can't handle all this.

*Alex, gotta go. Will text later*

I place my phone face down on the bed so that I can freak out without distractions.

An hour later, I'm on my floor, staring blankly at the notebook opened in front of me. My history textbook lies on one side of my notebook, a pile of mostly empty index cards on the other. How am I supposed to study? There are too many thoughts pinging around in my brain. My phone buzzes again. I reluctantly turn it over. It's Alex.

*I forgot! I need you tomorrow.*

*For what?*

*To study with me at the library after school.* Alex, study? At the library?

*LMAO*

*Very funny. Kei told me that her chemistry study group is meeting there tomorrow...*

Of course. I finish Alex's sentence:

*...And Jake is in her chemistry study group*

*exactly,* types Alex.

*OK, it's a date*

*What a pathetic life we lead...*

*Tell me about it.* I'm about to add to my text when my phone beeps, and a message from Zach flashes on the screen. Every muscle in my body tenses at once. I click on the notification.

*Hey,* he writes. I wait for him to say something about yesterday. Nothing.

*Hey,* I type back.

*Arboretum after school tomorrow?*

So that's how he's going to play it? Act like it never happened?

*Sure,* I answer, wondering if I should say more.

*Can't wait.*

*Me neither*. But after I type, I regard the phone screen with mixed feelings. I'm still excited to see him—and relieved that he still wants to see me. But now what? We can't *not* talk about what happened. Will he bring it up? Should I? I wish I could discuss my quandary with Alex. And then I realize what I've just done. *Shit.* Another text from Alex interrupts my thoughts.

*I'll see you tomorrow – gotta go to dinner. My turn to be tortured...*

I chew on the ends of my hair. Now what? I hesitate, then start typing.

*Wait!*

*Wait what*

*I forgot – I can't go to the library tomorrow, I have a dentist appointment...* Even as I type the lie, I feel terrible. I never lie to Alex.

*Nooooooooooo*

I bite my bottom lip, trying to figure out what to say next. I just *have* to resolve things with Zach.

*maybe Ami can come?*

*oh, maybe... I'll try her*

*k bye – sorry!*

*No worries, wouldn't want to interfere with your dental hygiene...bye Hannah-Ban*

I sigh, and plop my phone down on the rug. I'll make it up to Alex. She would totally understand if I could only explain it to her. Anyway, it isn't a big deal—Ami will go.

As soon as I convince myself that I don't need to feel guilty, I turn my attention back to my upcoming meeting with Zach. We have to talk about what happened. Not just yesterday, but also on the night of the accident. Especially now that the police are zeroing in. If he doesn't bring it up, I will. But how?

I lie there, my head resting on the beanbag, experimenting with different openings in my head.

*Zach, we have to talk.* No, that sounds like I'm about to break up with him. And I don't even know that we're officially boyfriend and girlfriend, which makes that approach doubly awkward.

*Zach, about yesterday*... That could work, but then what if he just says, "Yeah?" or "What about it?" Then I'll have to have figure out what to say next.

Or, I could just jump right to the hit and run. It's not like I really want to revisit the situation with my mom. But how do I even broach the accident question? Wouldn't it seem like it's sort of coming out of the blue now that I've waited so long? It's already been a whole month since Tyler's death. Even contemplating the conversation gives me butterflies and fills me with angst. But Rob might be in imminent trouble. Zach too. The police, the black car, the person of interest...I've got to move past the fear and come up with a plan.

# Chapter Twenty-Four

The heels of my black booties make tapping sounds on the concrete. I walk quickly, wondering what I will say when I see him. And what he will say to me. What-should, I-say, what-should, I-say; the words in my head synch to the rhythm of my steps.

I told Zach to pick me up at the corner store. That I have a free last period and am going to grab a birthday card for a friend. I don't want to chance Alex—or any of our friends, for that matter—seeing me getting into Zach's car. I rush out of school after my last class, feeling sneaky and deceitful, but also anxious to be with Zach again. In both a good and a bad way.

He's waiting in front of the card shop when I arrive. I spot his blue Honda from a couple of blocks away, see his elbow resting on the opened window, his hand on the top of the car—his signature parking pose. I wave at him through the passenger window and hold up my finger in a one-minute sign, barely registering the dimpled smile that greets me, then run into the card shop. I grab a lame birthday card for I don't know who. My stomach tightens as I exit the card shop and get into Zach's car.

"Hi," he says, showing that dimple again. He touches my leg quickly before putting his hand back on the steering wheel and pulling out of the space. My leg tingles where he touched.

"Hi," I say back. There's an awkward silence. His car smells like a mixture of coffee and mint and Axe deodorant. It smells like he cares what I think of him. I marvel at that for a moment. But then the silence stretches on a bit too long. Clearly, it's going to be up to me to start this conversation.

When I finally get up my nerve, and start to speak, he starts to talk at the same time. We both laugh nervously. "Go ahead," I say.

"I'm really sorry about what happened the other day," he begins. He speaks while looking straight ahead, rather than at me, though I suppose that's a good thing since he's driving. "It sucks about your mom, and Rob shouldn't have told you like that."

I sigh. "I don't really know what a good way to tell me would have been." More silence. I shift uncomfortably in my seat. It's strange to be talking to Zach about my mother's indiscretions. As much as I can't bear to think about her with Officer Scarelli, it's even worse to imagine other people thinking about her with Officer Scarelli. Zach surprises me by continuing.

"When my parents split up, I was much younger, so it was different, but I remember what a shock it was. Our family had seemed so normal—it's not like there were any signs. Although maybe there were and I just didn't pick up on them because I was a kid." He glances at me, and I give him what I think is an encouraging nod, before turning my gaze back down at my lap. I don't want him to stop talking.

"But then I found out that we weren't the regular family we appeared to be," he continues, "That when my parents got a babysitter and went out, maybe they weren't even going out together. That when my dad went on his business trips, maybe he wasn't even on business trips. Maybe he was with the other woman that he eventually moved in with. And that was the thing that I remember most—that feeling that everything was fake."

I look at him, surprised. Surprised that he is again sharing something so personal, but also that what he has chosen to tell me makes me feel so understood. I know that Rob and I don't have a perfect sibling relationship—far from it—but I've always thought we had a pretty normal family. And dependable parents. *Parents,* plural, who came together, as a pair. Who are on the same team. Had our family dinners always been a charade? Have my parents purposely cultivated the *appearance* of a healthy family unit to cover up something that is really broken?

"That's how I feel," I hear myself saying. "Like everything is fake. Especially my mom." Like Zach, I look straight ahead as I talk, even though I'm not the one driving. I'm quiet for a moment, weighing how it feels to put this personal information out there. I peek over at Zach, but he's just looking at the road, and there's no sign of judgment in his expression. So I go on.

"I also feel so guilty that everyone in our family except my father knows about it." I can't believe I'm talking so openly about my family to someone who isn't a part of it. But Zach is probably the only person who can understand what I'm going through. Even though it's scary to put these thoughts into words, it's almost a relief to get them out in the open and out of my head. When I stop talking, I feel the need to take a deep breath in, a deep breath out.

"I'm sorry," he says.

"Yeah." He puts his hand on my leg again. I look at him then and smile sadly. I like having his hand there. I like that we can talk to each other about such personal things. I put my hand on top of his and stare out the window. We don't talk for the rest of the drive. Still, what is left unsaid nags at me.

"There's something else," I say finally, as we pull into the arboretum.

He looks over at me and then presses his lips together anxiously before looking back in front of him. "Yeah," he answers. "I know."

He parks the car. Neither of us make a move to get out. He keeps his eyes fixed on the steering wheel, and I notice that his hands, now in his lap, are fidgeting.

"I need to know what happened that night," I say.

He sighs and shakes his head regretfully. "We didn't want to get you involved—"

"Unfortunately, I got involved the minute I heard you two talking in Rob's room." Zach's eyes widen in surprise.

"What? All this time? Why didn't you say anything?"

"Why didn't you?"

Zach looks down, as if ashamed.

"I just—I–I didn't want you to think I was a horrible person—I'm not a horrible person, I didn't know." His voice is shaking. He runs his hand through his hair. I don't dare move. Just watch him, remaining still.

"It was so dark, we couldn't see, they said it was just a deer—"

"Wait," I interrupt. "Who's they?"

He looks up at me then. Runs his hand through his hair again.

"Just tell me. Were you driving the car? Was Rob?"

He doesn't answer right away, just creases his forehead as if he's in pain. He puts his hand to his mouth, as if trying to hold back what's about to come out.

"Hannah, no—it wasn't like that. *We* weren't driving. I swear. We were just in the back seat. Believe me, I wish so badly that we hadn't gotten into that car, but we did..." His voice breaks and he pauses for a second. My body is flooded with such relief that I could hug him. *It wasn't Rob's car. They weren't driving.* But I need to know what happened, so I just let him speak.

"We felt the bump," he says. "We hit something really hard, he was high, he was going too fast, but it was dark, and he kept driving and we said what the fuck was that and he said a deer, and I said how do you know and he said I just know..." His words tumble out—he barely takes a breath—and his eyes start to get teary. "...and I said well shouldn't we stop and check and he said no, what are you high, and then he said oh, yeah, you are and started laughing. But I could tell he was kind of freaked out, because the laugh faded really quickly and he got this look on his face and—"

"Who's *he*? Who was driving?" How could someone laugh when they had just hit something—or some*one*—with their car?

"My cousin, and I was freaked out, obviously, because he was my cousin, and he had just hit something, and I wanted to just believe it was a deer but what if it wasn't a de-er..." His voice hitches again. "And I said we should go back and check, make sure it wasn't a person." Zach is breathing really quickly now. I want to comfort him, but something nags at me. Something Zach isn't saying.

"But what about Rob? Didn't he try to talk sense into your cousin?"

Zach is silent for a minute, as if deciding whether or not to tell me something. His silence lasts for only a second, but it terrifies me.

"I said we should go back and check, but Rob said no, it was a deer, we are *not* going back." Zach's hands grip the wheel so hard that his knuckles are stark white—it's like he is clutching onto that wheel for dear life. He drops his head down on his hands, but I can see that he's crying, because his back is trembling. How could my brother possibly be so cold? So heartless?

"What? Rob didn't want to go back?" My eyes fill with tears, and my stomach twists in knots. That can't be right. "Are you sure?" But it's as if Zach can't hear me, he just keeps talking. He's raised his head off the steering wheel and his eyes are wide, as if he's seeing the whole thing happen all over again in his head.

"He told Bryan to keep driving, said, of course it was a deer, and Bryan started saying fuck, fuck, fuck, but he kept driving—" His voice is wobbly, and he's breathing quickly and tears are running down his face.

"We were all a little high—and Rob said there's nothing we can do, that it's too late, and that it was probably just a deer, but I knew that he wasn't sure either, because he seemed really nervous and Bryan just kept saying fuck, fuck..."

Zach is full out crying now, he can only get a few words out at a time. He sobs and then sucks in his breath sharply between sentences. He rocks in his seat as he speaks, and I instinctively put my hand on his leg, almost as if to steady him.

I want to understand, I do, but I don't get it. "But why couldn't you just make them turn back?"

"I wanted to, Hannah, I really wanted to. But it wasn't just up to me." He puts his head in his hands and keeps shaking it back and forth. He sniffs and looks at me sideways without lifting his head. "We were *high*, Hannah. Maybe Rob was right. We *had* to believe it was a deer."

"But why can't you just tell the truth now?" I offer what seems to me to be the obvious solution. "I mean, not about the weed—but how it was dark, how you didn't know...." but I trail off as Zach vigorously shakes his head.

"No, no, I'm not ratting on my cousin—I'm not ruining his life—he would get in trouble for getting us the weed in the first place, and I couldn't do that to my aunt, and my mom—he could go to jail. We could all go to jail. Don't you get that, Hannah? You heard that police chief. We. Could. Go. To. Prison. JAIL. Oh my God, I can't even believe this is happening." He puts his head back down on the steering wheel and I put my hand on his back, not knowing what to say.

Suddenly Zach lifts his head and turns to me, putting his hands on my shoulders. "Hannah, you don't want me to go to jail, do you? You don't want Rob to go to jail. Right? You won't tell anyone, will you?" Tears are still running down Zach's face. I feel my own eyes filling up again. I shake my head, as the tears spill over and fall down my cheeks. And we hug and cry together.

# Chapter Twenty-Five

When we walk in the arboretum, after, we barely talk. We both have a lot to think about. We travel along a dusty path that winds its way through the trees and I notice that the branches have fewer leaves. A bright yellow or red leaf clings stubbornly to a limb here and there, but most of the foliage now litters the grass and the walkways like giant pieces of confetti.

I find myself wondering where Tyler landed when the car hit him. Had his fall been cushioned by the smattering of leaves that would have covered the street in late September? Or did it make a loud thump when his body hit the pavement? Maybe he was thrown to the grass, which would have softened his landing?

They felt a bump, he said. How could they not have gone back? I try to imagine myself in a similar scenario, but even if I thought I had hit a deer, I'd feel guilty, and would stop to see if there was any way to help the animal. I shudder and glance over at Zach. He's looking down at the ground, but his face is pinched and I can tell he's trying hard not to cry. I immediately feel sorry for him. I might wonder how it could have happened, but he must be reliving that moment over and over.

Why did Rob insist they drive on? How could my brother take that kind of a chance? Even the remote possibility that it was a person should have made them turn back and check. Did I not really know my brother at all?

I've always suffered over Rob's indifference toward me—but maybe there's a flaw in his very being, maybe he doesn't have compassion for anyone. I know we're different in this way, because it physically hurts me to see Zach like this. Hell, it hurts me to see Tyler's brother—someone I don't even know—suffering.

But if I don't say anything about what I know, doesn't that make me just as bad as my brother? Does it make me an accomplice? Could I too, go to jail? I squeeze Zach's hand, which is entwined with mine. He looks down at me and smiles weakly, keeps walking.

At least Zach wanted to do the right thing—there were extenuating circumstances that made it impossible for him to confess. He has compassion for his mother, his aunt, his cousin. For my brother. He has compassion for me.

When we kiss, finally, under a large maple, it feels completely different from our kisses before. There's an urgency to the way Zach kisses me and we press against each other in a way I find exhilarating. We kiss, and we kiss, passion, sadness, desperation and desire fusing together—our bodies fusing together. For just those few moments, I try to put aside the accident, the guilt, the fear. I focus every ounce of my being on kissing Zach.

As we drive back from the arboretum, Zach rests his hand on my leg, and I loosely hold his arm. Now that Zach has opened up to me, I feel like we have a newfound intimacy, and I can't help thinking about how something good could come from something so horrible. I quickly censor the thought. How could I even think something like that? There was nothing good about Tyler dying.

I look out the window and see that we're already back on Main Street, near school. Kids with backpacks thrown carelessly over one shoulder walk in packs and pairs away from the school, others gather in groups in front of Frank's Pizza or Carvel. I notice, in particular, the couples—kissing in the alleyway between the stationery store and DiMeo's Restaurant, others walking with their heads leaning in toward one another and their arms intertwined. We're like that now, I think. A couple. I guess I got what I wished for.

That's when I spot Alex, emerging from the corner store, probably replenishing her supply of bubblemint-flavored gum and pretzel M&Ms. What's worse is that at the same moment, she spots me. The look in her eyes changes in a split second from one of surprise, to one of confusion, and then to one of immense betrayal. I know, at that moment, that our friendship will never be the same.

# Chapter Twenty-Six

I text Alex when I get home.

*Can we talk?*

I wait a few minutes, watching the screen.

*Hello?*

No response.

*I'm sorry*

Still no response.

*Really sorry*

When Alex doesn't answer my texts, I try her number. I'm not quite sure what I will say if she answers. But I know I have to say *something*, because *not* saying something will be saying the wrong thing. The number goes right to voicemail, and I hang up without leaving a message. I hold my finger on the end call button, wondering if Alex has turned off her phone to avoid my calls. Not that I would blame her.

My eyes follow a shaft of window-light to the lavender bulletin board on the wall over my desk, and my gaze immediately zeroes in on the black and white photo strip pinned haphazardly to its surface. In the first picture, Alex and I are facing front, sticking out our tongues at the camera; in the second, we're looking at each other and the camera has caught us just as we're about to crack up. In the third, Alex is folded forward—she always falls forward when she laughs—and I'm pressing my lips together, trying to look serious. In the fourth, we're both looking back at the camera, pursing our lips and making our eyes sultry, like models. How could I have risked this amazing friendship? How could I have lied to my best friend? Maybe lying is in my genes. I plop back into my beanbag chair and look up at the clouds painted on my ceiling. Fake, fake, fake. The clouds, my "happy" family, myself. A real friend wouldn't lie to be with a boy.

# Chapter Twenty-Seven

From the moment Zach confides in me about what happened that night, I develop a newfound fascination in all things Rob. I study his expressions, his body language, his behavior. I look for clues that he might be worried, anxious, regretful. It's as if I'm a scientist, and Rob, my subject. My hypothesis: Rob was not in his right mind when he urged Zach's cousin to drive on after hitting something—or someone—and now he's paying the emotional price. I can't think the worst of him. He's my brother. And he's a human being—how could he not feel profoundly remorseful about what they did?

"How was your day, Hannah?" Mom asks at dinner. Rob is mysteriously absent from the table, yet neither of my parents mention a word about it. The number of things that my family doesn't talk about seems to increase by the day.

"Fine. Where's Rob?" Despite my two disturbing encounters with Rob, I find it difficult to be around my parents without him. I want him to bear witness to every encounter between our parents, in case there's anything important to interpret at some later time.

"He has a group project due tomorrow," Mom answers. "He's having dinner at Nick's house so that they can finish it." I'm instantly suspicious: Since when does Rob ever work into the night on a project? But it's the quick glance my mother shoots at my father after she says it that makes my stomach clench. *What now?*

Dad eats, silently, abnormally focused on the slab of steak that he carefully cuts into pieces and forks into his mouth. Then again, maybe he's thinking about his wife, his marriage, Officer Scarelli. Technically, he has as much to worry about as I do, though I'm not sure exactly how much he knows about either situation. Technically, his world is on the brink of falling apart, just as mine is.

"I got an A on my *Of Mice and Men* paper," I throw out in an effort to get Dad to say something. He typically takes extreme pride in my accomplishments—why not give him something positive to think about.

"That's awesome, Han," he says, giving me a weak smile. I find his lack of enthusiasm unexpectedly stinging. I haven't appreciated, up until this moment, how much of the satisfaction I take in my academic achievements is tied up in my father's reaction to them.

"That's great, Hannah," Mom adds, sounding equally unenthusiastic. She concentrates for a little too much time on her salad bowl, and securing a piece of lettuce onto her fork. Then asks: "How's Alex?"

The question feels like a kick in the gut, and it must show on my face, because Mom says, "Hannah, what's wrong?"

Everything, I feel like saying. "Oh, nothing major. We just had a misunderstanding." Understatement of the year.

"What happened?" Mom looks at me expectantly. Even Dad is paying attention now—Alex and I never fight. In the old days, I would have told my mother about how Alex was mad at me, but first of all, my parents don't know anything about Zach, and secondly,

I no longer feel my mother deserves to be privy to anything that I think or do. She certainly doesn't share what she thinks and does with anyone else in the family, does she?

"I don't really want to talk about it—it's dumb anyway," I say.

"I'm sure whatever it is, you two will resolve it," Dad says.

"Yeah." I turn my attention to my meal, in the hopes that my parents will turn their attention away from me, and try to convince myself that maybe it really *isn't* that big of a deal.

Maybe Alex just needs some time to cool down. We're best friends—even best friends have arguments. I will call her again. And again. Until Alex lets me apologize.

School the next day is a nightmare. Not only does Alex purposely avoid me, but as I pass through the hall between classes, I can't shake the feeling that the entire student body is looking at me—and talking about me.

I corner Kei at her locker. "What's going on with everyone? Is there something I'm missing?"

Kei hesitates before answering. "You must know that your brother and your um, *boyfriend*, are suspects...." She speaks slowly, waiting for my reaction.

"What?" Even as I say it, I know that this is what I've been expecting, no, waiting for—and dreading—all along. Did the police figure out that the car in that video belongs to Zach's cousin? Does he also have a black car? My stress level shoots so high that I feel actual pressure building inside my body, as if the anxiety is about to burst out of me. Still, I struggle to contain it, to maintain an outer calm.

How could I have thought that I could keep the boys' secret forever? That the rumors percolating around town wouldn't eventually target those who were truly to blame?

"I'm sure you know that a bunch of students who had been at Kevin's party were questioned by the police in Dr. Finnely's office yesterday..." Kei's voice rises at the end of the sentence, suggesting she suspects that maybe I don't. My stomach twists in knots. I can't even respond—I just shake my head slowly.

"I mean it's not like *nobody* saw them getting high outside of Kevin's party that night," Kei says knowingly, though she'd been nowhere near that party. She had, in fact, been holed up in Ami's basement several neighborhoods away along with me, Alex and Ami, watching *27 Dresses* for the millionth time while eating bagsful of Skinny Pop, Twizzlers, and pretzel M&Ms.

"I'm sure a lot of people were getting high *and* drunk outside—and inside—Kevin's party. What does that have to do with the hit and run?"

"Well, according to Alex—she's doing a story about it—*Rob* and *Zach* were there almost till the bitter end, but left with some other kid who doesn't go to Woodfield High....I'm just saying, the timing was kind of suspect...." *According to Alex? She's doing a story?* I suddenly feel the floor dropping beneath me, and have to put my hand on the locker to steady myself. How could Alex betray me like this? If this is revenge, it is *way* out of proportion to my tiny lie.

I feel a desperate need to defend Rob and Zach, to come up with alibis, for reasons it couldn't have been them. But I can't think of what to say.

"That does not mean *anything*," I say, not even convincing myself.

"Wait," says Kei, before I can respond. She puts her hand on her hip. "I know you are majorly crushing on Zach, but you aren't actually defending him, are you? After what he did?"

"What is there to defend? That they were at a party with half the school? That they stayed late? Other people obviously stayed late too, or there wouldn't be anyone to make up these rumors." I notice that passers-by are definitely looking in our direction and whispering to one another. Why do I suddenly feel like the accused?

"You are speaking about my brother too, Kei," I say quietly. "So please make sure you have your facts straight before you spread any more rumors." Kei seems momentarily dumbstruck. I take the opportunity to rush away to my next class, focusing straight ahead and trying not to notice who's looking at me and how.

I'm relieved to arrive at physics—which is ironic in itself—and I slide behind my desk, open my book and stare at the words without reading. The typeface blurs, but I furiously fight to keep my eyes from crying. Not only would it be humiliating, but I feel like it would be an admission of guilt. I sink down in my chair. I will definitely be calling in sick tomorrow.

# Chapter Twenty-Eight

I play nauseous in the morning. Not that home is any better than school. I have a feeling that Mom somehow *mysteriously* knows that the police suspect Rob. Dad too. Would the school have called them about the questioning? Or is it that Mom has an inside source...

They try to act normal in front of me, but Dad's unusually quiet during breakfast and Mom's quick movements and tensed facial muscles give her away.

I pull the smiley-faced mug out of the cabinet and shuffle through the tea bags with my empty hand to find the Morning Breakfast.

"Here, let me help," Mom says, hurrying over.

"I got it," I say, ignoring her wounded look, and continuing my search. Mom, meanwhile, gets the kettle off the stovetop and pours steaming water into my cup, her lips pressed together.

"So, have you heard anything at school about the investigation into the accident?" she asks.

"No, have you?" I don't look up, but stand, still, waiting for my mother's response.

"No." Her reticence on the subject, itself, is suspect. Typically she loves to regale me with all the latest accident gossip. I look over at Dad, but he doesn't even lift his eyes from the newspaper.

As I climb the stairs, heading back to bed, I hear them whispering furiously together. At first I think they're fighting. But then I hear the word "lawyer." That's how I know they know.

I return to school the next day. I stare up at the building from across the street, bracing myself for the day to come. Maybe I'm being paranoid, but again, it seems like all eyes are on me as I enter the building. Could Alex's article have come out? I glance over at the table in the corner of the entryway that typically holds stacks of the school paper when it's published each quarter, but thankfully the table's empty.

I don't even bother looking for my friends—Alex is clearly no longer my friend, and after my conversation with Kei, I'm wary about approaching my other friends too. I can't bear it if they all turn against me. So I walk down the hallway with my head down, eyes lowered, trying to avoid the other kids' accusing eyes. Then I bump into Caitlin Steele.

"Excuuuuuse me?" Caitlin says loudly and dramatically, stopping in her tracks, and thus forcing me to do the same. I've never liked Caitlin—she's so fake and judge-y. And I have no patience for mean girls. Caitlin, on the other hand, has never acknowledged my existence enough to even form an opinion of me.

"Sorry," I mumble, attempting to walk around her.

Caitlin steps to the side, blocking my way. "Why don't you look where you're going?" Caitlin speaks as if she's acting in a play, aware that she has a growing audience. "Are you trying to *run me over* or something?" She looks to her friends for a reaction. They laugh, stare me down.

I decide in the moment that escape is the best possible response. I try, again, to circumvent Caitlin.

"Runs in the family, huh?" Caitlin says under her breath, more for her friends' benefit— and mine—than for any of the other onlookers that have gathered in the hallway. Even she must realize she's taking things a bit too far.

Something snaps. I'm suddenly seething.

"Are you kidding me, Caitlin? Are you actually making a joke about a student's *death?* Does *this* make you feel superior? My brother is as upset over Tyler as anyone. And whoever is responsible—and to my knowledge no one has yet been charged—that's what it was, an *accident.* Unlike you, my brother would never, ever *joke* about it."

Caitlin stands there with her mouth open. But I'm pissed. I glance around at the other kids in the hall, daring anyone to pipe in, but I seem to have shocked everyone into silence. I turn around and storm back to the front lobby of the school, out the door, and through the parking lot. When I'm far enough away from the building, I break into a run, heading across the athletic fields and into the woods.

# Chapter Twenty-Nine

At the edge of the woods, I bend forward, hands on my knees, to catch my breath. I wipe my nose on the edge of my sleeve, but let the tears flow freely down my face. I don't know where I'm going. I only know I want to go where everyone else isn't.

I start walking again, just to do something. It's quiet, aside from the crunching of the leaves beneath my feet and the occasional bird cry. The air is cold, and I hug my arms around my chest for warmth. The morning sun shoots narrow rays down through the branches, lighting up small patches of fallen leaves. A cluster of abandoned beer bottles and discarded cigarette butts reminds me that the woods are not as remote as they feel to me at this moment—I know it's early, probably still homeroom period, so the kids who usually hang out in the woods haven't made their way out here yet. They have to be marked in attendance before cutting out of their classes. I don't want to be accounted for: I just want to disappear.

I breathe in the pine-scented air deeply, trying to calm myself. *Breathe in 2,3,4. Breathe out 2,3,4.* That's what Alex's mom used to tell Alex when she got panic attacks as a kid. Now Alex and I say it jokingly to each other whenever one of us is freaking out about a boy, or a test. *Breathe in 2,3,4...* Then we laugh, of course, diffusing whatever anxiety has sparked the freak out in the first place. Well, that's what we used to do, anyway. We probably won't be doing it anymore.

Glancing around, I realize I'm on the same path I'd taken with Zach just a few weeks earlier. What a turn my life has taken since that day. The Robert Frost poem we studied in English last year pops into my head: *Two roads diverged in a yellow wood...* Perhaps I chose the wrong path. Maybe I should have stayed away from Zach. If I wasn't with Zach, I wouldn't have screwed up my friendship with Alex. And I wouldn't know what I now know about Rob.

I just can't see my way out of this situation. It's bound to end badly—the case, Zach and Rob, my parents. I don't even have a best friend anymore. How could I ever walk back into that school building? I'm sobbing now, big, ugly sobs that practically choke me—and probably make me look like a freak—but I don't even care. There's no one to judge me out here.

I walk fast, keeping my eyes on the path, dodging larger branches as I tearfully wind my way through the trees. I only want to put more distance between me and Woodfield High. The unexpected crack of a branch and rustling of leaves alerts me to another's presence. I look up quickly, just as I'm about to bump into a hoodie-clad figure emerging from between the trees. My heart almost jumps out of my chest. I freeze.

"What are *you* doing here?" says a familiar voice.

Rob? I wipe my sleeve across my face.

"Rob." I'm about to ask him what *he* is doing here, but then realize he probably needs to escape even more than I do. Not to mention the fact that he probably spends more time in these woods than he does in his classes. I instinctively glance at his hand and see that it holds a joint. Normally, I'd think it's kind of early for that—but nothing is normal these days.

He lifts the joint, sucks in some smoke, holds it in his mouth and then blows it out. He looks at me, as if daring me to say something. He seems peeved that I've disturbed his solitude. I don't react. Instead, I attempt to compose myself. But a sob escapes.

The change in Rob's expression then, from irritation to disbelief to—is it possible?— concern, catches me completely off guard. He actually puts his hand on my shoulder in a...*brotherly* way. I can't remember him ever having done that. My eyes well up.

"Hannah, what's wrong?"

"Everything." I start to cry again. Rob takes a step back and runs his hand through his hair, nervously, then holds it there for a moment, as if debating what to do. He looks around.

"Um, come sit over here," he suggests, leading me to a fallen log. I let him. I sit down and feel the protrusions of the bark poke into my jeans. He sits too, leaving a bit of space between us, and looks at me expectantly, waiting for me to say something.

I take a deep breath.

"Everyone hates me," I say, finally, slumping down in defeat.

"I'm sure Alex doesn't hate you," Rob says diplomatically. I look down at my hands, in my lap, playing with the edges of my jacket with my fingers.

"Actually, she does....." I admit. "I lied to her to be with Zach."

"Hmm. OK, that was shitty. But Zach *clearly* doesn't hate you...." He says it begrudgingly, I know, and even sort of rolls his eyes as he says it. But I'll take it. My brother is actually being nice to me.

"Everyone's talking about how you and Zach are suspects and how you were both at that party," I blurt out. "And even though nobody knows *anything* they just assume things and now everyone's looking at me like *I* did something wrong."

"What are you talking about?" He tries to make the question sound dismissive—aggressive, even—but he's not convincing. He suddenly looks nervous, on edge.

"I actually had to defend you to Caitlin Steele—who normally never even stoops low enough to talk to me, but had the nerve—"

"You defended me?" He looks at me like he's seeing me for the first time.

"Of course, I did—you're my brother." He nods, but doesn't say anything, just looks straight ahead.

What I really want to say was, "What did you tell the police? Why didn't you turn back? Why did you make them keep driving?" But I'm seeing a different side of Rob, and I know my questions will ruin it. Right now, I need an ally. I never would have expected to find one in Rob, but the surprising turn gives me a glimmer of hope.

"What do you think is going to happen with Mom and Dad?" I ask instead, looking down at my fingers as I run them along the rough edges of the log's bark.

"I don't know." Rob draws circles in the dirt with the toe of his sneaker. I watch.

"What *do* you know?" I ask him. "I mean, you said you saw her kissing Officer Scarelli—where were they? And, like, *really* kissing? Like, definitely romantically?"

Rob gives me a look. "Hannah, come on, give me a little credit here—they were kissing. And it's not an image I want to keep revisiting, if you know what I mean." He fake-shudders to drive his point home.

"Okay, okay, but just tell me where you saw them."

Rob sighs loudly, as if to let me know that I'm being an annoying sister but that he's going to indulge me anyway. "I was dropping off a friend who lives on other side of town. By that strip center. On Route 6 with the Dunkin Donuts. And then I saw them. They were making out in the parking lot." His words make my skin crawl.

"In a car?"

" No—right out in the open. Like fucking teenagers." He grimaces as he says it. I feel sick.

"I wasn't sure it was her," he continues, "but then I saw that her car was right there—they were fucking leaning on it. I was so shocked that I didn't see the light turn until the car behind me started honking at me...." He trails off. He brings his joint to his lips and inhales deeply. He turns away from me and blows out the smoke. "As I said, not an image I want to revisit."

At any other time, I'd be surprised that Rob would smoke in front of me. I might have even seen it as a positive sign—that he sees me as a peer, someone he can be himself in front of. But all I can think of now is my mother kissing this man that isn't my father and my face crinkles up in disgust.

"Why him?" I mutter, only halfway talking to Rob.

"What?"

"I mean, what can she possibly see in Mr. Scarelli?"

Rob shrugs. "It's messed up." He drops his joint in the dirt, and grinds it into the leaves with his heel.

I have so many questions: I want to ask Rob if he thinks Mom is unhappy with Dad, if he thinks our parents will get a divorce. Who he thinks we would end up living with. But how would he know, really? I think about how this is what siblings are supposed to do: talk about family stuff that they couldn't, or wouldn't, bring up with people who aren't part of the family. That people outside of the family could never understand. But why did my family have to start falling apart in order for me to finally be granted this kind of moment with my brother?

Still, I grope for a way to make the conversation continue. I want some kind of reassurance from Rob, but don't quite know how to ask for it. He, meanwhile, is hyper-focused on a giant ant navigating its way around one of his sneakers—he's pushing at the dirt with his other shoe to bury the insect under a mound of fallen leaves. I wonder what he's thinking. I always wonder what my brother is thinking.

Aside from the chirping of birds, and insects, and the periodic rustle of leaves in response to the autumn breeze, the quiet is so noticeable that it almost feels awkward. It doesn't exactly come naturally, talking to one another. We haven't yet found a comfortable rhythm for our conversation.

"I think Dad knows about Mom," I say, watching Rob's shoes and the patterns they make in the dirt.

"Yeah, me too," he answers. "But I sure as hell wouldn't be as calm as he's being about it." That's strange, coming from him. Someone who's been involved in a hit and run, yet is carrying on as if it's just life as usual.

I picture Zach at the arboretum, his body wracked with sobs, his head on the steering wheel. I imagine the regret, the worry, the guilt that he must have been hiding behind his flirty bravado up until that moment. Maybe Rob's nonchalance is also a facade. Maybe, though he tries to come off as cool and collected, he's really scared shitless.

"I have to ask you something." I try to ignore the fluttering in my stomach.

"What?" There's a slight change to his tone. But we're actually sitting together, talking; he's being nice. This is my chance, right?

"Why didn't you go back?" I blurt out.

There, I'd asked it. I looked Rob in the eye. "Why didn't you go back and check on him? How could you keep driving?"

I regret the words the minute they leave my mouth, the minute I see the bewilderment, and then disbelief in Rob's eyes. I watch his face getting red.

He doesn't answer at first. He clenches and unclenches his fists. Why did I have to ruin the moment? He was finally talking to me heart to heart, I should have just kept talking about Mom and Dad—in some screwed up way, that was a safer topic.

"Hannah, don't ask questions that you don't want answers to."

"What's that supposed to mean?"

He seems to weigh his words carefully. "It means that sometimes ignorance is bliss. Zach shouldn't be involving you in this—I've been telling him that all along, he shouldn't have said *anything* to you about that night..."

He isn't exactly yelling, but his voice is getting louder. He's clearly mad, though the fact that he's mad about Zach telling me makes me angry too.

"He *trusts* me, at least," I say, rising from the log and looking down at my brother. "*He* knows I would never tell anyone anything."

"If he trusts you so much, then you shouldn't need me to answer that question, because you would already know the answer."

"WILL YOU STOP ALREADY!" I stamp my foot in frustration. "He can't tell me what was in *your* head! He can't tell me why *you* insisted that they keep driving, why *you* wouldn't let them turn back."

Rob jumps up from the log, takes a couple of steps away, and then turns back toward me. "*That's* what he told you? Are you *shitting* me? That fucking liar..." I freeze at the word liar. Is Rob really so distrustful of me that he's going to deny the truth?

He paces back and forth quickly, taking a couple of steps in one direction, and then back in the other, like some kind of trapped animal.

I remain still, though I feel my hands shaking. My stomach is in knots. Rob locks eyes with me.

"And of course you believed him."

He turns, then, and walks away from me.

"Rob, wait. I'm sorry, come back," I yell as he disappears into the trees.

# Chapter Thirty

I stay in the woods after Rob leaves, rewinding our conversation in my head, wondering if it could have gone differently, trying to figure out exactly what made Rob so angry. But all my thoughts keep circling back to Rob's final words: *And of course you believed him.*

It never even occurred to me to not believe Zach. Why wouldn't I? We've gotten so close in recent weeks—he opened up to me so much about his father, his family, the accident. Why would I have any reason to doubt anything he told me?

Zach isn't a liar. I'm sure of it. He's a good person. So kind to his mother, staying home with her sometimes on weekend nights so that she won't be by herself. Someone like that doesn't lie, not about big, important things. And not to me. Would he?

I can't stand to be alone with my thoughts. I stand, brush the dirt off my bottom, and head back toward school. Imagining that Zach could have lied to me makes me feel sick. If he lied to me about that, then can I believe anything he says? Can I believe the way he looks at me, the way he kisses me—is it all a lie? The mere thought makes my heart break.

I emerge from the woods after a few minutes, and look across the soccer field at the school building. The thought of going back fills me with dread, but what choice do I have? There's a lot I don't know at this moment, but one thing I'm sure of: My classmates—and so-called friends—have no right to condemn Zach and Rob based on gossip. *I* don't even know what really happened that night. And they certainly have no right to make me feel *less than* because Rob's my brother or because I'm with Zach. I will stand up for myself. I don't care what girls like Caitlin think of me. The stakes are higher now. I have to focus on what really matters.

Still, climbing the stairs up to the front door of the building is torture. If only I at least had Alex in my corner. One friend, that's all I really need. Someone to talk to who isn't part of my family, who isn't Zach. I know Alex: I can't believe she would write anything bad about my brother—or Zach—in the school paper, even if she was mad at me. Still, she shouldn't have said anything to Kei about them staying late at the party. Maybe I should just confront her, in person. Walk right up to her and tell her I'm sorry. That I'll never ever lie to her again. Beg her not to write that story. Tell her how betrayed I feel. If she can forgive me for lying to her, I can forgive her for spilling to Kei about Zach and Rob.

I glance at the black and white clock hanging on the wall across from the school's entry. 9:10. I've already missed most of first period. The old me—the good girl me—would have gone to class anyway. But the new me thinks *It doesn't matter.* I hide out from the hall monitor in the bathroom and wait to intercept Alex at her locker. She always stops at her locker between first and second periods, because she has Art first period and hates lugging her oversized sketchbook with her to her other classes.

I make my way to Alex's locker just as the end-of-period bell rings, keeping my head bent toward the ground in front of me while at the same time sneaking furtive sideway glances to see if I spot her. I try *not* to notice people peering my way and whispering to one another—though it's hard not to notice—and scan the faces filling the hallway hopefully.

Finally, I notice Alex's springy hair, and the black-rimmed glasses she has recently taken to wearing (Alex thinks they exude a Brooklyn/intellectual-chic vibe). I will Alex to look my way, try to catch her eye. It works! Alex locks eyes with me. I'm flooded with relief. Then she turns and walks the other way.

I get through the rest of the morning by making myself invisible. I don't look out for friends as I usually do between classes, or take longer routes to pass by their lockers. I'm not quite sure who is still my friend. If anyone. I walk through the hallways with my gaze directed at the floor in front of me. I slip into seats in the back corners of classrooms, keeping my eyes down—on my books, my notebooks, my desk. This strategy works until English, when Mr. Broza calls on me.

"Miss Greene," he bellows in his deep, booming baritone. "Tell us about how Shakespeare symbolically makes use of light and dark in the scenes we read about in *Hamlet* this week."

Mr. Broza is my favorite teacher, and English my favorite class, so I'm not about to disappoint him—or myself—by not answering. I know the answer of course. I always know the answer in English. But when I respond, I look only at my notebook. I don't want to see if other students give one another looks or whisper about me.

I'm especially wary about attracting the attention of Marissa, one of Caitlin's crew who happens to be in the class—and who was also there this morning when Caitlin decided to make me the object of her withering attention.

"Well, darkness represents evil, and light represents good," I say quietly. I let my hair hang down like a veil over the side of my face so that it blocks my view of my classmates. "Hamlet's father is murdered at night while he sleeps, and the ghost appears at night, in the dark. Ophelia, who is pure and virtuous wears white, and the king, who was innocent when he was killed, is draped in white."

"Yes, that's right, Miss Greene," Mr. Broza says. Someone had written C.K + T.P. in a heart on the surface of my desk—I stare at the initials as I speak. But I assume Mr. Broza has walked around his desk, as he typically does, and is approaching the class, since his voice grows louder as he continues questioning me.

"And can you give us an example of this in the text?" he asks. I flip through the pages nervously until I find what I'm looking for.

"Yes, when Ophelia sings about the dead king she says, "white his shroud as the mountain snow."

Apparently satisfied, Dr. Broza calls on Mike. But before I can even release a silent sigh of relief, I hear someone whisper something with the words "she" and "ironic" and "someone innocent being killed." They're relentless. I sink deeper into my seat.

What would I do at lunch? I feel sudden empathy for all those weirdos who sit by themselves in the cafeteria, or eat alone on the wall outside. I'm so relieved when my phone vibrates as I leave English. I swing down my backpack, which I'd slung over my right shoulder, and reach in as if grasping for a life preserver. It's Zach.

*Franks?* I assume it's unlikely that Rob will be with Zach, considering how pissed off he is at him—hell, he probably didn't even go back to school.

*OK, see you soon.*

We don't make it to Frank's. He leans against the building at the corner of Main waiting for me. He lifts one hand in a pseudo-wave, but I break down crying the minute I see him. His expression immediately turns to one of concern, and he puts his arm around me in a protective way.

"Let's walk," he says.

I nod, leaning my head onto his chest and letting my tears drip onto his rugby shirt.

"What's wrong? Did something happen?" he whispers.

I nod again, but say, "Let's just walk." I don't have it in me to revisit my disastrous morning.

We walk down Main Street, past Frank's, past the shops, and the bakery, past Baskin-Robbins and the library and the movie theater. We walk all the way to the town pond, find a wooden bench to sit on, and stare out at the water. I think about what a mess everything is. Still, it feels nice to be with someone who isn't judging me.

Finally, I tell Zach about what had happened in school. I forget that what I'm telling him has even greater repercussions for him than it does for me, until I feel his body tensing, see his eyes widening.

"Oh my God, Zach, I'm sorry, I didn't mean to freak you out too—"

"No, Hannah, it's not your fault, you didn't do anything wrong," he says, trying to keep his voice steady, though I notice that one of his legs is suddenly bouncing up and down really quickly. I put my hand on his leg to still it.

"I feel terrible," he says, shaking his head slowly. "I should never have told you—Rob was right—I should have kept you out of this."

"At least you're willing to confide in me. My own brother lied to my face—I ran into Rob in the woods behind the soccer field—I had to get away from people and well, you know, my body just automatically walked in that direction..." I let my voice fade as I notice that Zach goes pale when I mention Rob. My heart sinks.

"What's wrong? Was he not lying?"

"No, no, I don't even know what he said to you," Zach says. "It's just that he must be really pissed that I told you anything about the accident at all."

I want to ask him about what Rob said, but I've already ruined things with my brother—I don't want to do the same with Zach.

"You wouldn't lie to me, would you Zach?" I ask quietly.

He has one arm around me, but takes the other hand and gently brushes a piece of hair away from my eye and behind my ear. It's such a tender gesture.

"Of course I wouldn't." I bite my lower lip and study his face. His expression is so sincere, attentive, caring. I turn my gaze to the water and lean my head on his shoulder. He pulls me closer. We sit together like that for a few minutes without talking. I savor the moment of calm. Bask in his nearness.

"You're the only person I can really talk to right now," I say, finally. I feel so grateful for his presence—and I think the feeling is mutual.

"I'm always here," he whispers into my hair. I feel a little better going back to school after that.

I lay low for rest of the afternoon, not speaking to anyone. I don't sit next to Megan Albert, like I usually do in social studies, because I can't face her once I remember that she lives next door to the Millers. I walk home by myself, avoiding the bus. Avoiding will be my new norm.

# Chapter Thirty-One

Nobody is there when I get home, so I go straight to my room, close the door, and flop down on my bed. At least I have Zach, or I would've gone through the entire day without talking to a single other person. But "having" Zach has become so complicated. I turn my head and gaze over at the bulletin board above my desk, and the photo strip of me and Alex. Even though I'm mad at her, I want my best friend back.

How can I get her to talk to me? Or at least to listen to me? She won't answer my texts or phone calls. I could send an email, but what if she doesn't open it? Maybe I'll send her a real letter. Even hand deliver it to her mailbox. Alex won't be able to resist an actual letter—she loves that kind of vintage-y thing.

I grab a pen from my nightstand, then pull a notebook from my backpack.

*Dear Alex,* I write, then pause for a few minutes, biting on the tip of my pen and trying to decide what to write. The truth?

*I messed up. Big time. I should never have lied to you to be with Zach. No boy is worth losing your friendship. I miss you so much. I keep wanting to talk to you, to text you, to tell you things. And it kills me that I can't. You're my best friend, still, and I'll be your wingwoman anytime. Please forgive me, Hannah-Ban*

I read the note a few times, think about embellishing it, and then decide to leave it alone. I get up, open my door, and go into my parents' office for an envelope.

My parents' office is really my mother's office, as evidenced by the feminine décor—floral balloon shades, a slipcover in a coordinating red and beige stripe on the desk chair, a toile-upholstered chaise in the corner. And then there are the motivational speech therapy posters that say things like "Mistakes are just proof that you are trying" and "Not being able to speak is not the same as not having anything to say." I'm not exactly sure why Mom even needs an office, since she works in an office every Monday through Friday in Southbury, but at least it provides a home for the desktop and office supplies.

I reach onto a shelf in the supply closet and grab an envelope, and am turning to leave the room when I notice the blankets folded neatly at the foot of the chaise. And underneath them, a pillow. Is one of my parents sleeping in here? I feel the now-familiar knot in my stomach. Are things so bad between Mom and Dad that they can't even bear to sleep in the same room together? The thought of it just compounds my sorrow.

I try to intercept Rob when he comes home, a while later, to report what I've found, but he barrels past me with an angry look on his face and goes straight down into the basement. I don't dare follow him.

I attempt to catch his eye at dinner, a couple of hours later, but he avoids looking at me. My parents don't speak to each other either. I listen to the silverware clinking against the plates, the dog obsessively licking his back leg, the kitchen clock ticking loudly. I glance at each of my parents, and again at Rob.

"Can I have the sour cream?" I ask, just to break the silence.

"Sure," Dad says, passing the red and white container. His smile seems forced. I spoon an extra dollop of it onto my chili. I don't even like sour cream.

The unexpected ring of the phone cuts into the quiet, making me start. Mom pops out of her seat, as if glad to have a reason to leave the tension at the table.

"Hello?" We all watch her as we eat.

"Oh, hi," she says, turning away from the table. And then more quietly: "Is everything okay?" She starts to pace.

"I see," she says, as she walks the length of the kitchen island. Back and forth, back and forth, nodding. "Yes, okay," she says quietly. I feel a knot in the pit of my stomach again. Has someone else died?

Mom hangs up. We all look at her expectantly.

"Who was that?" Dad asks.

"It was Paul," she answers solemnly, causing Rob to push his chair away from the table and bang his hand on the arm of his chair.

"How could you take a phone call from *him* in front of all of us?" he demands angrily.

Mom, stunned, tears up. But she only looks at Rob for a moment—then she turns to Dad. "The police want to question Rob about the hit and run."

Rob freezes. I gulp, but it suddenly feels like there's a big lump in my throat.

"Oh, no," says Dad, dropping his head into his hand. But, really, he looks more resigned than surprised, like he's been expecting this. He glances at Rob, whose face has gone completely pale, and then at me.

"But I thought he was already questioned at school," I blurt out.

"Well, Principal Finnely did advise parents that the police might meet with groups of students in his office to ask informal questions about anything they might have seen that night as part of their information-gathering," he tells me, "but they can't officially question teenage suspects without their parents present." I look down at my plate. Instead of worrying that I've just revealed I know more than I've let on, I think about how he said teenage *suspects*.

"When do they want to question him?" he asks my mother. Rob remains deathly quiet, his eyes moving back and forth, from one parent to the other, as they discuss his fate.

"Tomorrow." *Tomorrow?!* I remain still on the outside and become frantic on the inside. Are they also going to question Zach? I have to warn him.

"We are going to sit here right now," Dad says firmly, eyes back on Rob.

"And you are going to tell us what happened."

# Chapter Thirty-Two

Everyone watches Rob, waiting for him to speak.

"Rob, I'm serious. I want answers." But Rob's eyes are focused on his fork, which he grips so hard that his knuckles turn white. His eyes dart around the table nervously, landing on me.

"Maybe you should ask your daughter," he says, his angry words like arrows. "*She* seems to be an expert on what 'really' happened that night." Rob makes quotes with his fingers as he says the word *really*. I can't believe he's throwing me under the bus. After all I've gone through trying to keep his secret. So much for sibling solidarity.

"Wow, Rob," I say.

"Hannah, *you* know what happened?" Mom regards me with disbelief. But Dad doesn't let Rob off the hook so easily.

"Rob, my guess is that Hannah wasn't in the car that night," he says. "Were *you*?"

Rob runs his hands through his hair, losing his composure. "Yeah, I was," he says, nodding his head a little too quickly, like he's about to lose it. He puts his head in his hands, like it's just too much effort to hold it up anymore. Are his shoulders actually shaking? Is Rob *crying*? I can't remember ever seeing my brother cry.

Dad puts his hand on Rob's arm. Mom, too, leans in toward her son and rubs his shoulder. "Rob, listen, we'll figure out what to do here—we're on your side no matter what," Dad says. "But you have to tell us what happened."

Rob takes a deep breath, and swallows loudly. He sits up and nods slowly.

"We were driving home from a party—"

"The party at the Russo's?" Mom interjects, as if she already knows the answer.

Rob gives her a not-very-friendly look, and says "Yeah, Mom, at the Russo's." He knows where she got that information.

Mom purses her lips and sits back primly in her seat, the way she often does when she's wounded by something I've said—or the manner in which I've said it. Her brow furrows and I know she's afraid. She wraps her arms around her body as if trying to protect herself from the secrets her son is about to divulge.

"Who's we?" Dad says. "Who was in the car with you?" His gaze is fixed on Rob's face with such intensity that Rob has no choice but to respond.

"It was me, Zach, and Zach's cousin Bryan." My stomach clenches at the mention of Zach's name. "It was still dark—it was like five in the morning—and we were on that curvy road over by Birch where you can't really see what's coming around the corner—especially in the dark—unless it's lit up by your headlights..." Rob speaks really fast, his words tumbling out as he grips the edge of the table. He focuses on the salt and pepper shakers.

"But it was really late, it was foggy, and we weren't totally—we were a little—" I can tell he's trying to figure out a way to say they were drunk or high without really saying they were drunk or high. "We were really tired and we were talking about something on the radio and not really paying attention and we felt a bump—" A bump? I feel as if I've been gut-punched.

"A bump?!" Mom's hand flies to her chest. "A bump?!" She sounds like she's about to hyperventilate.

"Julie—let him finish," Dad says. But his face has gone almost white. I realize I'm holding my breath.

"We didn't see anything—I mean Bryan and I weren't even looking at the road, we were slumped down in our seats, he in the front, me in the back, and he was playing with the radio dial and we were talking about a song—" Why is he only talking about him and Bryan? I feel a growing sense of dread.

"Rob, how could Bryan not see anything if he was the one driving?" I demand. Our parents glance over at me as if they've forgotten I'm here.

"Because *he* wasn't the one driving," Rob says as if I'm a moron. "Zach was driving." My jaw drops.

I hold onto the edges of my seat, to keep myself from falling out of it. I think I might throw up. "Or maybe he left out that little detail when he *confessed* everything to you, because he *trusted* you so much," Rob spits in my direction.

Mom stares at me as if something is just dawning on her. I feel her looking, but don't say anything, and don't turn my head. I just keep my eyes riveted on my brother. I try to keep my face still, even though I want to scream or cry or just disappear.

"Hannah?" Mom says.

But Dad won't be deterred from hearing the rest of Rob's story. "Go on, Rob," he says. "So what happened after you felt the bump?"

"I said 'What the fuck was that?' and Zach said 'I don't fucking know…And Bryan said 'Holy shit' and then Zach said 'It was probably a deer' and Bryan said 'Maybe it was a dog' and I said 'Maybe we should go back and see' and Zach said 'No way are we going back there. There's no reason to. It was a deer, I'm sure of it.' But I knew he wasn't sure of it. How could he be sure of it?"

I couldn't listen to another word. "You're lying," I scream, cutting him off. "Zach didn't say that! He's the one that wanted to go back and you wouldn't let him!"

"Is *that* what he told you?"

I am still.

"That asshole. That fucking liar. It figures you'd believe him over me. I don't know why I…." Rob pushes his chair out and stands up. "This is useless. If my own family doesn't believe me, who will?" He storms out of the kitchen and up the stairs. His angry footsteps make Mom's china teacup collection jingle in their saucers.

Mom looks at me again. "Hannah?" But I look down at the table. I can't bear to talk about Zach at this moment. All I can think about is the possibility that he has been lying to me all along. About everything.

# Chapter Thirty-Three

When I come downstairs in the morning, the rest of the family is already huddled in the family room, Mom and Dad in their usual chairs by the fireplace, Rob slouched forward in one corner of the couch. I'm surprised to see him awake so early. Though, really, how could he sleep at all?

Our parents, both with their hands wrapped around their coffee mugs, look like they've hardly slept either. Dad's hair stands up in different directions, and Mom has dark shadows beneath her eyes. They're focused on Rob, who's apparently retelling the story of what happened. I hesitate in the doorway, and Rob stops talking. Mom and Dad look up at me.

I start to turn around, to retreat upstairs to my room, but Mom says "Hannah, you stay. I'm sure you know something about this too. I know Zach has been hanging around here quite a bit." Dad raises his eyebrows in surprise, then quickly rearranges his expression.

I'm shocked that Mom knows anything about me spending time with Zach. Hoping that nobody notices my face getting hot, I sit on the carpet, facing them, and hug my legs to my chest.

Our parents direct their attention back at Rob, and so I do too. "So tell us again," Dad says, nodding his head in Rob's direction. "What happened after you felt the car hit—something."

"I told you—I said we should go back," Rob says. He looks at me pointedly. I look down at the carpet. "*Zach. Said. No.*" My head jolts up. "He said 'Absolutely not. It was a deer. I know it was a deer.'" Was it *Zach* who really said no? Who am I supposed to believe? Rob's eyes start to get teary, but this time he doesn't cry. Still, he pauses, as if to collect himself. "It wasn't a deer."

As Rob speaks, I feel like he's tightening the knot in my stomach. I won't cry, not in front of my family, and besides, I'm all cried out, having spent most of the night crying into my pillow. What kind of person would blame his best friend? Would lie to his girlfriend about something like this? Would try to pit her against her own brother? I just don't think Zach has it in him. But would Rob lie to Mom and Dad? To me about Zach?

Rob's hair is disheveled and he's still wearing the ratty t-shirt he'd had on at dinner. He looks like a boy who's been dragged out of bed too early. He does not look like a convict. Will he end up having to go to jail? Will Zach? I shudder.

I'd struggled last night over whether to confront Zach. But instead, I ignored his usual goodnight texts. Let him think my phone ran out of battery, I'd thought. I think I was afraid that Rob was telling the truth. In which case, I would hear it in Zach's voice. In which case, I didn't even know who Zach was anymore.

"What are we going to do?" Mom looks at Dad with a kind of desperate appeal. Her face is slightly twisted, as if she's trying not to cry.

"Well," Dad says, looking at Rob. "For one thing, you are going to tell the lawyer everything. The truth. And no one in this family—" and now he looks at me—"is going to talk about this with *anyone* else." He speaks sternly, but I can tell he's shaken. His voice sounds gruff.

"It was an accident," he says, almost as if to convince himself. "I mean, you should have come forward right away, but what it all comes down to is that it was an accident." And then, as if something has just occurred to him, Dad looks at Rob and asks, "Had you boys been drinking?"

Rob lifts his head from his hands, but doesn't answer right away. Would he tell our parents they were high?

"A little," he answers. He wasn't lying, just omitting. It's Dad's turn to put his head in his hand. Mom, meanwhile, just makes a sound that's a cross between a gasp and a squeal, and covers her mouth with her hand.

"I didn't come forward because I didn't want to be a snitch," Rob said. "Zach was my best friend." I notice he says *was*.

"Well it's time to be honest," Mom says. "You don't want to ruin your life, go to jail instead of college..." She tapers off with a sob.

"Oh my God, you're still on my back about college at a time like this?"

But Dad unexpectedly backs up Mom. "Your mother's right, Rob. Your whole future rides on how we handle this," he says. Mom looks surprised.

"So this lawyer—Todd's friend—handles criminal cases," Dad falters for a moment, as if realizing the weight of what he's just said—the fact that his son needs a *criminal* lawyer—but then quickly regains his composure. "She's coming by early this afternoon." Todd is Dad's best friend, yet I'm surprised my father has talked about this with him. But of course, if the kids at school know Rob is a suspect, so, probably, do some of their parents.

"This way there will be plenty of time for her to get what she needs," Dad says. "And to prepare us before the police get here." He says this part more quietly, even though there's nobody here but us. No one says anything for a minute—it's a lot for all of us to take in.

Mom breaks the silence. "I'll pick you up after 4th period," she tells us. I'd hoped that maybe we'd both get a stay-home-from-school pass, considering, but no, I'm going to have to go back to the wolves. I sigh. I'm not sure which is worse right now—being at home or being at school.

Rob gets up immediately, disappearing up the stairs before I can even lift myself off the ground.

"Hannah," Mom says as I slowly raise myself into standing position.

"Yeah?" I answer, feeling suddenly defiant. I haven't done anything wrong. I meet my parents' stares.

"Is there something you want to tell us about Zach?"

No, not really. But I know I have to say something. "Um, we've been going out," I say, dropping my eyes back to the ground. My voice cracks as I say it.

And then, before either of them could respond, I add, "But I'd rather not talk about it right now."

Mom starts to speak, but Dad puts his hand out to stop her. He nods at me. "Okay," he says. "But we're not done here." I nod, not really sure what I'm agreeing to, and head out of the room. I climb the stairs, then pause outside Rob's door. I think about how quick I'd been to believe what Zach said about my brother. Now, I don't know who to believe.

# Chapter Thirty-Four

I slip into school right as the homeroom bell rings. Maybe, if I keep my head down in the hallways, and just go straight from class to class, I can avoid catching anyone's attention. Just as I finish reassuring myself, my sneaker bumps up against a Doc Marten. I freeze when I look up and recognize who I've walked into. Kevin Miller.

I haven't seen him since the accident, probably because he's missed a lot of school since his brother's death. Plus, he and I don't have any classes together, since he's a year younger. But here he is. *Zach* may have killed his brother. And my brother said nothing. I feel ashamed and scared and sick that he might know who I am.

To make things worse, Kevin is trailed closely by Caitlin's crew. Not only is Caitlin's sister in his grade, I remember, but Caitlin typically befriends anyone who achieves any kind of temporary rise in social status—and being Tyler's brother has definitely earned Kevin Miller his five minutes of high school fame.

Flustered, I mutter an apology and try to walk around him. But as I start to pass, I see out of the corner of my eye that Caitlin grabs Kevin's shoulder and whispers something in his ear. He abruptly turns to me, as Caitlin and her posse strategically block my way.

"You tell your murderer brother—" he hisses, pointing his finger in my face, "AND your murderer boyfriend, that I am going to kick their fucking, cowardly asses."

Caitlin nods her approval. And gives me a withering look. How am I supposed to respond to that? I can actually feel myself trembling, but my feet are frozen in place.

"Where *was* your brother the night my brother was killed?" Kevin demands, bringing his face up to my face. "Where was your *boyfriend*?" I instinctively take a step back, but hear whispers among the students who have gathered behind me. I feel trapped and begin to panic. I can't breathe. Then, suddenly, Alex swoops in and comes to my rescue.

"What is this, an inquisition?" Alex says, whisking me away and steering me through the crowd of students now standing around me and the others. Too shocked to speak, I allow myself to be led through the hallway and out the nearest emergency exit by Alex, who I wasn't even sure was still my friend.

Once outside, we lean against the outside of the building. I start hyperventilating, try to catch my breath. Feeling the cool brick through the seat of my jeans, I wrap my open jacket more tightly around my body and slide down the wall until I'm sitting on the ground. Alex slides down beside me.

"Thank you—for, in there—I didn't know what to do—I don't—"

"Just don't ever lie to me again," she says quietly.

"Alex," I start, my eyes filling with tears. "I'm so sorry—"

Alex doesn't answer, but she nods her head slightly, as if she knows.

"I'm really sorry," I say again, my voice breaking. We sit quietly together, staring ahead at cars in the parking lot. I'm happy to be beside Alex again, I am. But it occurs to me, as we sit there, that there must be a reason why everyone suddenly seems to think that Rob and Zach are responsible for the hit and run. Is it because of Alex?

I turn back to Alex. "Alex, how could you tell Kei that Rob and Zach stayed late at the party? And if the police questioned lots of students who were at the party, why is everyone suddenly just blaming Rob and Zach? Is Kei not the only one you told? Or is it because of the story you are writing for the paper?"

"Really, Hannah? You think I'd tell everyone in school that kind of thing about your brother? About Zach?" She looks hurt. And kind of pissed. But I don't know what to think. Alex sighs loudly, lowers her eyes. "Look, I'm sorry, I shouldn't have said anything to Kei. I just didn't have you to talk to anymore, and she was at my house, and we were talking about the hit and run, and I was feeling guilty that I finally had this information about your brother and your boyfriend and couldn't tell you about it and—and it just came out." She looks up at me. "I regretted it the minute I said it—but no one else was there, I swear, and I swore her to secrecy. And I didn't tell *anyone* else. Not even Ami."

"So how—"

"Kevin's been telling people—maybe he knows from his lawyer?" Ah, that makes sense. "And, you know, Evan Riley and Mia Scarelli both have parents who are cops." I cringe. Even the mention of that slime's last name sends my heart racing. And if Alex is writing a story about the investigation, who knows what else everyone will know.

"But you're writing an *article*? About the hit and run?"

"I *was* writing an article. Or thinking about writing an article. I thought a story about the accident could be my big break—that I could maybe get the inside scoop and even get an article picked up by a real paper. But when I found out that Zach and Rob were being questioned—when I realized it was the scoop or our friendship—I picked our friendship." I breathe out slowly, feeling a rush of gratitude. I have Alex back.

"So you're done investigating?"

"I'm done investigating," she says, holding her hand to her heart.

"Your friendship is so important to me," I say. "I just, I can't get through this year without you." My voice breaks again, so I stop talking.

"I've missed you too," Alex says, looking back at me. "I read your letter like ten times." I smile weakly at Alex and then look down at the ground. I pick up a pebble from the crevice where the pavement meets the wall, and turn it around in my hand, trying hard not to cry.

"I will never ever lie to you again, I promise. I just want to be with Zach all the time—but that doesn't mean I don't want to be there for you too. To be honest, I don't even know about Zach anymore."

Alex lifts an eyebrow.

"I really, really liked him, I mean, I do, but I don't know if I can trust him anymore." I lower my voice to a whisper. "I'm so scared that he and Rob are going to go to jail."

"Do you even know what happened?" Alex asks quietly.

"No," I say, shaking my head. I know what Zach says happened. And I know what Rob says happened. But it's not like I know what *actually* happened.

"But you have to believe me," I add, "They just can't be responsible for Tyler's death. We know them—they wouldn't do that." I will it to be true, but feel guilty as I say it. According to Zach, neither he nor Rob were driving the car. Yes, they should have gone back, but they weren't driving the car. I don't believe Rob—I can't believe him. He's just mad at Zach for twisting the story and making him out to be the bad guy. He's probably just trying to get him back by turning me against him. "Don't you think there has to be a different explanation?"

I want so much for Alex to agree with me, for her to convince me that I might be right. I hope—more than I'd ever hoped for anything—that what I'm saying is true.

Alex nods solemnly. We sit quietly together some more. It's almost like old times.

"Did you go to the soccer game?" I ask Alex after a while.

"Yes," she says, one side of her mouth curving up in the beginning a smile.

"Yes, and?"

"Yes and—something happened."

"Really?!" I'm genuinely excited for her. "Like, what?"

"Well, we ended up talking after the game, and then he asked if I wanted to grab some pizza with him and the guys, and then Jake walked me home and along the way, well....you know...." Alex gives me a wide smile as she shrugs. I nudge her with my shoulder.

"You go, girl."

We both laugh. But I quickly sober, remembering why we're out here together. Then I think about the lawyer, and what will come after. I slump against the wall.

"Alex, I really don't know what to do."

"What do you mean?"

"It's torture to be in school. It's torture to be home." I turn to Alex and look her in the eye. "I have to tell you something that you have to *swear* you won't tell anyone else."

"What?"

"Do you swear?"

Alex puts her hand on her hip and gives me a look. "Hannah."

"I know, I know." One thing about Alex, she isn't a gossip. What just happened—that was an aberration. Usually, telling her secrets is like depositing them into a vault.

I take a deep breath.

"I think my mom is having an affair," I whisper. Alex's eyes widen.

"My family is falling apart. Everything is falling apart. I just don't know what to do." My eyes fill again and I start crying.

But Alex is here, so things are a little bit better.

# Chapter Thirty-Five

Rob doesn't even look up when I climb in the car after fourth period. Mom doesn't ask how my day was, like she usually does. I lean back and close my eyes for just a minute, breathing in the smell of gum and coffee. Then I start wondering why Rob didn't drive himself to school. And start obsessing over the fact that Rob isn't driving his car.

"Why didn't you drive your car to school today, Rob?" I finally blurt out.

He just gives me a look that implies I'm stupid, and then turns back to his phone. Of course. There's no way Dad would let him drive after hearing he'd been drinking and driving. But as Mom pulls away from the school, without saying anything, I think back over the past few weeks and realize that I can't even remember the last time I saw Rob driving. I comb my memory. I can't recall hearing Rob's car pull into the driveway on *any* recent day.

Has his car been sitting idle in the garage all this time without me realizing it? Has Rob not driven *anywhere* since that night? And if not, why? I don't even want to think about the answer.

We pull into the driveway, and as Mom turns off the car, she turns her body to face us. "Now, the lawyer is going to be here at about three," she says. "She's going to want to talk to you, Rob first, obviously, but she's also going to want to talk to all of us together. Then she'll come back at around 5:30, to be here when the police officer comes to question Rob."

My stomach tightens when Mom mentions the police officer, and I instinctively glance over at Rob. The police are coming to *our* house! To question *my* brother! Rob's eyes are lowered but he's no longer looking at his phone. I notice, in fact, that he grips his phone really tightly, so tightly, that I worry it might break. I feel bad for him. He must be freaking out. I feel guilty for having doubted him.

I decide, right then, that I'm going to confront Zach, make him tell me the truth. Or maybe the real truth will come out in just a little while, when Rob is forced to tell the lawyer what *really* happened.

"Okay," Rob says quietly, then gets out of the car, punches the garage code into the keypad on the side of the door, and goes inside.

Mom looks at me. "I don't know what Zachary has told you," she says, "but the lawyer is probably going to want to know that as well." She catches me off guard.

"What?"

"Hannah," Mom says quietly, "we're trying to prevent your brother from going to jail." Her voice is firm and she looks right into my eyes. "Any information you have could help Frankie defend him."

"So now *I* have to be a snitch?"

"If Zachary is not going to tell the truth—if you know his version of the events, I think the lawyer is going to need to know that to properly prepare for what's coming. This is your brother we're talking about, Hannah..." Mom falters for a minute, and then regains her composure. "...and I'm sorry that you are being put in this position. I don't know exactly what's going on between you and Zach because you haven't shared that with me—but family comes first. Don't forget that." Family comes first. My mother is such a hypocrite.

I ignore the dig about how I haven't told Mom about Zach—as far as I'm concerned, my mother is in no position to be expecting such confidences—we all know she's been keeping her own secrets. But now I'm supposed to break Zach's confidence? Betray him?

"Hannah?" Mom waits for a response. I nod my head without saying anything. That seems to satisfy her—she gathers her keys and bag, gets out of the car and goes into the house.

I stay where I am, consider all I'm about to lose. And then, suddenly, I look up, and notice Rob's car sitting in the garage. I get out of Mom's car, and slowly walk toward the front of Rob's. Wouldn't there be a mark on his car if he hit someone? I bend down and examine the front of the car. Nothing. The black finish is pristine. I run my hand along the front fender. Smooth as can be. I let out a breath, stand up and walk into the house.

# Chapter Thirty-Six

The lawyer wears a stylish black blazer and a slim gray skirt, with dark tights and pointy tweed pumps. Her hair is cut in a bob that is angled toward the front, so that when she turns her head, it hangs on a diagonal. She's very chic.

I watch from the stairway as the lawyer introduces herself to my parents. "I'm Frankie Holloway," she says as she extends her hand. She stands very straight, employing what Mom used to refer to as "ballerina posture" when I was younger and she was trying to make a dancer out of me.

Mom and Dad take turns shaking the lawyer's hand. "I can't thank you enough for taking this case on with such short notice," Dad says.

"Of course," the lawyer says warmly. "I can imagine how difficult this has all been for you. I'm happy to be able to help."

Mom turns toward the stairs. "Rob? Rob, come down." My mom's eyes register my presence at the top of the stairs. "We'll deal with you later," her eyes seem to say. But then she cranes her neck to look beyond me to see if Rob is coming. I hear his door open, and turn toward him as he passes, head down, hands in his pockets. He lifts his head for a moment to scowl at me. Whatever progress I'd made with my brother—it's like it never even happened. I flash back to the two of us sitting on that log in the woods, actually talking to each other about something real. And sigh.

Mom introduces Rob to the lawyer. He looks miserable. The lawyer seems sympathetic, but professional.

"All I ask is that you are completely honest with me," she tells Rob as Dad ushers them all into the living room, a room we rarely ever use. The lawyer places her hand on Rob's arm as she speaks to him. "I will do my best to get the best outcome here. You're a minor, so you've got that in your favor..." Before Mom closes the door to the living room, she looks up at me.

"I'll call you down when the lawyer is done talking to Rob," she says quietly.

I watch as the door closes, then tiptoe down the stairs. There's no way I'm missing this. I sit on the bottom step, rest my elbows on my lap and my chin in my hands, and listen.

"...went to the party at Kevin Russo's house," Rob is saying. He speaks quietly, so I have to strain to hear.

"And who were you with?"

"My friend—" He falters for a second. "Zachary. Zachary Kirkland. And his cousin, Bryan. I don't know his last name. He doesn't go to our school." I've never heard Rob call Zach by his full name.

"Around what time did you arrive at the party?" the lawyer asks. Drawing from the TV shows I've watched, I imagine the lawyer taking notes as my brother speaks.

"I don't remember—"

"An approximation?"

There's a pause.

"Rob, just a guess," Dad prompts, "Whatever you can recall about that night—"

"12 maybe?"

The lawyer's voice is muffled, but I hear part of her next question. "....do at the party? Drink? Drugs?"

"He doesn't do drugs—" Mom pipes in.

"Let him talk, Julie," Dad says.

"...a beer or two," Rob answers.

"And that was all?" the lawyer asks. There's another pause. I wish I could see what's going on in there. I scooch to the edge of the step and lean forward.

"And we smoked a little pot." He says this even more quietly, but I hear him pretty clearly.

"Oh God—"

Oh my God, I think, echoing my mother's response. I can't believe he's admitting to that in front of our parents. Should he be admitting that to anyone? Even the lawyer? I don't know. I hope this lawyer can be trusted.

"Julie," Dad says again. Sternly, like a warning.

"How much pot did you smoke?" the lawyer asks.

"I don't know."

"Were you all smoking?"

"Yeah."

"Where?"

"Outside, in the backyard."

"Were you with other people?"

"No, just Zach and Bryan."

"Were there others outside?"

"Yeah, but everyone was doing their own thing. We were kind of off behind the bushes."

"Can you give me an idea of how much you were smoking? Were you smoking joints? Were you vaping?"

"Joints," he mutters. I'm sitting up straight now, my head turned slightly so that my ear is closer to the family room. I feel my nails digging into my palms. I wish I could see my parents' expressions.

"We just shared one joint at the party. We were there for a few hours..." I imagine Mom making that disapproving "tsk" sound she makes with her tongue on the top of her mouth.

"What about before the party?" Boy this lawyer is thorough.

"Yeah, we might have had another joint in the car."

"In the car?!" Mom can't contain herself. I hear Dad sigh loudly. Wow, Rob isn't holding anything back. I'm actually shocked at how honest he's being. And kind of impressed.

"Jesus," Dad mutters. Rob's car will be sitting idle in the garage for a long time after this conversation.

"....interact with anyone at the party?" The lawyer is questioning Rob again.

"I don't know....I mean I guess. I said hi to a couple of people.... Beer...some girls from school in the kitchen...." What girls, I wonder. Was Zach flirting with any of those girls? That was technically before we hooked up. I know I shouldn't care, but I do. I purposely push Zach out of my mind and focus on listening to what's going on in the family room.

I can't hear everything Rob says. He speaks quietly and it sounds like someone is walking around. Pacing, maybe. Probably Dad—he tends to do that when he's stressed. He often paces when he lectures me or Rob. It always drives us crazy.

"John, sit down for God's sake," I hear Mom say.

I quietly rise from the steps, and silently make my way closer to the door. I press my back against the wall next to the door and hold my ear near the crack at its edge.

"....did you leave the party?" The lawyer's getting to the important part. I brace myself. I can feel my heart beating against the inside of my chest.

"I don't know. 4:30? 5:00? But we didn't leave right away. We chilled in the car for a while before we left...."

"What does chilling mean, Rob? Does it mean smoking more pot?" Dad sounds angry.

The lawyer says something quietly, and everyone is silent again.

"Rob?" she says.

"We were just hanging out...."

"Who was sitting where in the car?" I tense.

"I was in the back, Bryan was in front of me, in the passenger seat, and Zach was in the driver's seat." I gasp, and slide down the wall. Try to process what I'm hearing. Zach in the driver's seat. Not Bryan. Rob wasn't lying to our parents, to me.

So if Rob is telling the truth—and of course he isn't dumb enough to lie to his own lawyer—it means that not only did Zach lie about who had been behind the wheel, but he was probably also lying about Rob being the one to insist they keep driving. He's not the person I thought he was. He's a liar. I swallow hard. He's a murderer. My boyfriend is a murderer.

My heart starts racing. I don't realize I'm crying until I feel the tears dripping off my chin and dropping onto the back of my hands, my hands that are clenching the material at the bottom of my sweatshirt.

Has he been using me this entire time? A sob explodes from me. And then I'm full out crying, hard, so hard I can't catch my breath.

The door to the family room opens and my parents burst out. "Hannah?" Dad says. "What's going on?" But I can't talk, can't even stop crying. I can't breathe. I take big gulping breaths – letting out loud sobs.

"Oh, Hannah," Dad says, sitting down next to me and hugging me to him. I wish we could stay like this forever, but I know that this moment—like many other things in my life—is about to come to an end.

# Chapter Thirty-Seven

I lie back in my beanbag, staring up at the clouds on my ceiling. I was given a pass on the lawyer meeting due to my little "panic attack." That's what my parents called it, anyway, when they told Frankie that I'd talk to her later. Needless to say, I'm embarrassed about the meltdown. And worried it will happen again. I've never felt so physically out of control. I literally couldn't breathe. Just thinking about it compels me to take a really deep breath.

Still, my mind keeps going back to the thing that set off my anxiety in the first place. Has the whole thing between me and Zach been a lie? Did he just hook up with me to keep me quiet? To keep Rob quiet? But when would he have decided that?

I think back to when we first bumped into each other at The Music Shoppe. Before the accident even happened. There was something there, even in the very beginning, wasn't there?

I remember how he flirted, how he said "Hi Rob's sister," even though he knew my name perfectly well. How he smiled at me and showed me his dimple when I said hi back. How that innocent moment led to a series of increasingly less-innocent moments between us.

I pull my phone out of my back pocket, and hold it up above my face.

*How could you?* I type.

Dots appear immediately beneath my text. That was quick.

*What are you talking about?*

*I know the truth, Zach.*

*The truth?*

*About that night..* There's a pause. Zach doesn't answer so quickly this time.

Then...*Hannah, let's talk about this in person.*

*You lied to me.*

*What did Rob tell you?*

I ignore the question. Can't believe he even has the nerve to ask it.

*And if you lied to me about that, what else have you lied to me about?*

*Hannah, please. Let's talk in person.*

My eyes start tearing up again.

*I've gotta go.*

Before I have a chance to turn off my phone, it starts ringing. Zach's ring. The song "Hey Love." I resist the urge to answer and hold down the power off button. I'm not going to talk to Zach in person. I'm not going to talk to Zach. Period.

# Chapter Thirty-Eight

I hear footsteps on the stairs. Then in the hallway outside my room. Rob's door bangs shut. He'll probably stay holed up in his room until the police arrive. The police, God. Is this really my life?

A knock.

"Hannah?" It's Mom.

"What," I say, not really wanting her to come in.

Mom walks in anyway, closing the door behind her. I hate when she just comes in without waiting for me to answer. What's the point of knocking?

"Did you and Dad agree that *you* should come speak to me? What – Is this *mother-daughter* territory?" I feel a rush of anger.

She sits on the edge of my bed. My muscles tense.

"Hannah," she begins.

"What, Mom!" It comes out harsher than I intend. She gives me her "wounded" look, but I'm not letting her guilt me this time.

"Hannah, do you want to talk about Zach? "

"No, Mom. Do you want to talk about Officer Scarelli?" I practically spit his name.

"Hannah!"

I don't dare look my mother in the eye. Even though part of me feels that she deserves my rage, I sense I'm crossing a line. Then I feel my mother's hand on mine. I look at her hand, surprised, and then at her. There are tears in her eyes.

"Mom, I'm sorry, I didn't mean to say that, it's just—"

"No Hannah, I owe you an explanation." She says it quietly, but I hear her loud and clear. I brace myself for more information I don't want. "I made a big mistake. A really big mistake. I don't expect you to understand why. Your father is a good man, but—" She stops and looks at the ceiling, and the window, anywhere but at me. "Well, as you can imagine this not an easy thing to talk to you about."

"Mom, you don't have to tell me," I put up my hand as I say it, as if to signal that she can stop. *Please stop.* But she doesn't.

"Hannah, let me just assure you that I'm going to put an end to this. Our family has to stick together for Rob's sake."

I can't believe what I'm hearing. Is my mother actually admitting to me that she is having an *affair*? Or, rather, ending one? "Only for Rob's sake? Not for Dad's sake? How could you even have *started* this?" I'm trying not to scream.

Mom doesn't answer right away. My feelings are all jumbled together in my head. Disbelief that my mom and I are actually having this conversation. Revulsion—is she *actually* attracted to Officer Scarelli? Anger—how could she do this to our family?

On top of everything, I feel guilty. This is *Dad* we're talking about. Is he going to be able to tell that I know? Is this just another thing I'm going to have to pretend not to know at the dinner table?

"But Mom, why?" That's what I really want to know. Or do I? I'm not sure. Still, Mom has given me an opening. How can I not take it?

"Why did you do it?" It comes out in a small, pleading voice. *Please don't say anything I don't want to hear*. What *do* I want to hear?

"I don't know, Hannah" she says thoughtfully, staring down at her hand on mine. "I guess I liked the attention...it was a stupid thing to...I didn't think of the repercussions...it was impulsive."

"Are you and Dad going to get a divorce?" I say this so quietly that I'm not even sure Mom hears it. I say it so quietly that it's almost as if I haven't said it at all.

"No, Hannah, no." She strokes my hand and speaks in her reassuring Mom voice. "This family is staying together. Dad and I are going to work everything out. Please, don't worry. I'm ending this." I feel a tiny bit relieved, but then have a horrifying thought.

"Wait, he won't take it out on Rob, will he?"

"No," she answers. "No, no. Paul isn't like that." I flinch when she says his name. "He'll just be sad." Mom looks kind of sad too.

"Mom, I'm going to end things with Zach too," I say. I don't even know I'm going to do it until I say it out loud.

"I mean, I really, really like—liked—him. *Really* liked. We've been spending a lot of time together. He's been teaching me a lot of guitar—he's so talented. And, I don't know, it's just so easy to be with him." It feels good to be able to tell my mother these things.

Mom nods. "I always did like Zach," she says with a sad smile. She, too, had been taken in by Zach's charms. She, too, has been disappointed by him, has to reframe the way she looks at him. After all, Zach is now, in a way, the enemy.

"But he lied to me," I say quietly. "Figures, I finally get a boyfriend and..."

"Hannah, you are going to have plenty of boyfriends." She's putting on that reassuring Mom voice again. "I know that doesn't make this any easier, and I know—"

"It doesn't matter," I say. "Zach is the person I wanted to be with. And now I can't be with him anymore. Boys suck." I stare up at the clouds on my ceiling, in part to keep my eyes from tearing up again. It feels kind of nice to have my mom on the bed next to me.

"Yes, sometimes they do," Mom says unexpectedly. I would laugh if I wasn't so miserable. Instead I give Mom a weak, half-hearted smile.

"The thing is," I say, "it's not like he's a bad person. It's not like he ever wanted this to happen." I can't believe I'm still trying to protect him, even after everything he's done. He betrayed my brother—his best friend! And he betrayed me. I hate him. And maybe I also love him.

# Chapter Thirty-Nine

As it turns out, the police never end up coming to our house. Instead, Frankie Holloway calls someone she knows at the department and makes arrangements to bring Rob and our parents down to the station the next morning. I beg my parents to let me come, but they are adamant. Rob, surprisingly, agrees with them.

"You need to stay out of this," he says. His eyes are bloodshot, as if he's been crying. He doesn't say it in an angry way, the way he usually talks to me. He says it almost in a protective way. I stop protesting.

"You'll stay home, and go to your make-up guitar lesson," Mom says. Eric had a rare Saturday opening, and I grabbed it—but that was before everything started unraveling, and my brother became an official police suspect. Do they really think I can just go about my life as if nothing has changed?

I remember when my grandfather died. I was 11—he was the first person I knew who'd ever died. At the funeral, I stared at the coffin, which looked too small to fit my grandfather's oversized body. Holding Mom's hand, I cried.

Lots of people came to our house after, aunts and uncles and other adults who hugged me tightly on their way in and out. The next day, my parents woke me up for school, and sent me off as if it was just a regular day. How could life just go on like normal, I wondered then. I wonder it again now.

"There's no reason for you to come to the station," Dad adds. "No need to give them the idea that *you* might be worth questioning too."

"Okay," I agree. I definitely do *not* want them to ask *me* questions.

But from the moment my parents and Rob leave the house—he, looking miserable, my parents looking nervous, though I can tell they are trying to put up a brave front—I find even the one-hour wait until my lesson to be excruciating. I pace around downstairs, foyer to kitchen, kitchen to foyer, as my mind races.

What are they asking him? Does he have to go into one of those interrogation rooms like on TV? Is there a bad cop and a good cop, the one trying to intimidate him into a confession, the other being understanding and trying to win his trust (and thus, ultimately, his confession)? When I envision Rob in one of those interrogation rooms, my eyes get teary and my stomach, tight. I feel really bad for Rob at this moment. And sorry that I ever doubted his story.

Still, it doesn't take my mind long to jump to another scenario, one that I expect will be taking place very soon. Zach has to be next on their list. Especially after Rob tells them Zach was driving. I imagine his mom, alone, no dad, driving her son to the police station. He could go to jail! How can I not warn him? That the police are probably going to want to question him too? So he can be prepared?

On the other hand, how can I do anything to help him? If helping him might be hurting Rob? It all makes my head hurt.

I pull my phone out of my back pocket and stare at it for a moment. Instead of typing in Zach's number, I type in Alex's.

*Hey,* she types back.

*Can you talk?*

*Ya*

I plop down on the bottom step and dial Alex.

"Hi, you. What's going on?" We rarely call each other—usually we just text or go over to each other's houses. But this is an emergency.

"Alex, I don't know what to do," I say. "You can't tell anyone anything I'm about to tell you."

"Hannah, you KNOW I don't tell people stuff you tell me."

"I know, I know. This is just—my brother is being questioned by the police."

"Oh. Wow."

"Yeah. And I'm sure they're going to also want to question Zach, because—and you can't tell anyone this...."

"Hannah."

"Okay, okay. They were both in the car."

"WHAT? Hannah, what are you telling me."

"I'll tell you more when I see you, but –"

"Hannah, who was driving?" she whispers.

"I don't know," I whisper back.

Alex is quiet on the other end of the phone.

"Alex?"

"Why are you just telling me this now? We've been talking about this nonstop for weeks....how could you not say anything? I'd never keep such a huge secret from you."

"Alex, please, don't be mad. I shouldn't even be telling you now—my father would kill me if he knew."

"You told me you would never lie to me again," she says. "And then you lied. Again. You told me you didn't know what happened."

"I didn't," I say. "I maybe suspected some things, but I didn't really know for sure until now."

"I thought we told each other everything," Alex says quietly. She isn't just angry. She's hurt.

I don't know what to say.

"I have a guitar lesson this morning, but we can get together after and I can tell you everything I know," I finally offer. I can't risk losing Alex's friendship again.

"I'm going to the soccer game this afternoon," she says coldly. She isn't cutting me a break.

"Alex, I'm sorry. Really. I should have told you. I've been wanting to, believe me. This is too much for me to handle by myself." My voice hitches. "It's just my dad—"

"You *could* come to the soccer game too..." Alex interrupts, her tone warming a bit.

"OK, but Alex—"

"Yeah?"

"I don't know if Zach's mom can afford a lawyer. I'm really mad at him right now—he hasn't been honest with me—but I don't want him to go to jail..."

Alex lets out a loud breath. "This is some heavy stuff...."

"I think I need to warn him...."

"Yeah, maybe you should.

"I'm going to text him now," I say, making up my mind. "I'll meet you at the soccer game after."

"Okay, but don't forget—you have to tell me everything."

I click end call and stare at the phone for a moment. I feel a wave of guilt. I've directly disobeyed my parents. And am about to again. I take a deep breath. Then start typing.

*Are you alone?*

The dots appear immediately—it's as if Zach has been sitting there waiting for me to text him.

*Yes, why?*

And then, right after:

*I'm so happy to hear from you Hannah.*

My heart flutters in my chest.

*I'm just texting you to warn you. The police are probably going to want to question you very soon. They're questioning Rob today at the station.*

There's a brief pause.

*What is he telling them?*

*I don't know, Zach. And that's not why I'm texting you.* Why am I texting him?

*I just wanted you to be prepared*

*Hannah, I don't know what to do. I miss you so much. Can you meet me? What if I come over while they're all gone? Can we talk?*

I want to say yes. But I know I shouldn't. No way can he come to our house. Plus, I don't trust myself not to tell him things and I promised Dad that I won't.

*That's not a good idea. Not today. I'm sorry, Zach. I've got to go. I've got a makeup guitar lesson in a little while.*

I turn off my phone before he can text back. I know I shouldn't see him. But if he happens to show up at The Music Shoppe? That's out of my control.

# Chapter Forty

I brace myself as I open the door to The Music Shoppe. I've been too preoccupied to practice, so I'll have to face Eric's disappointment. And that's the least of it. I might see Zach. I shouldn't have told him about my music lesson. And yet.

As I slowly make my way to the back of the shop, my mind flashes back to Tyler's brother sitting in the waiting area, swinging his little feet, looking too sad, too solemn for his age. What if he has a makeup lesson today too? Does he know who I am? No, how would he.

I breathe a sigh of relief when I see that the waiting area is empty. Out of habit, I strain to hear the sounds of Zach's guitar, but all I hear is someone sampling the keyboards out front, playing the introduction to the Green Day song I love over and over. What's it called? I rack my brain. *Wake Me Up When September Ends*. Maybe I'll ask Eric to teach it to me. The intro is really meant for guitar anyway.

I glance at the clock above the door to Eric's lesson room. Two minutes until my lesson. On a typical Thursday, I'd get butterflies waiting for the door to open, for Zach to emerge. I'm thankful that today, someone else will be coming through that door.

"I gather you haven't spent much time with your guitar these last couple of weeks?" Eric says after I struggle through a lackluster rendition of "I'm Yours."

"You gather correctly." I sigh.

"You know you're not going to progress if you don't practice."

"I know, I know," I say. "Maybe I need a new song to motivate me." *Maybe I need to not have my brother being questioned by the police. Maybe I need for my boyfriend not to be a liar. Maybe I need for my mother not to—*

"Okay," he says, bringing me back to the moment. "Do you have something in mind?"

I try to focus. I nod. "Wake Me Up When September Ends?"

"Ah, Green Day. One of my favorites," he says, plucking the first few notes of the intro on his strings. "Great intro. We can do that. Let me go get the music." I nod again, and he leaves the room.

I let out a breath that I didn't even realize I'd been holding. I wonder what Zach is doing at this moment. Is he looking through the music outside? Will Eric see him there? Will he know that Zach is waiting for me? Does Eric even know that we're a thing?

We're not a thing anymore. I'm going to put Zach out of my mind. At least for the rest of the hour. I'm going to focus on my guitar. Maybe he's not even going to show up—that'd probably be best. I pick up my instrument and try to figure out the first few notes of the intro while I wait for Eric to return.

I pack up my guitar and music slowly at the end of the lesson. Glance uneasily around the music store as I make my way to the front. I'm kind of relieved when there's no sign of him. But then I peek through the glass door, and there he is, of course, sitting on the sidewalk, his back against the storefront's brick wall. He hasn't seen me yet, so I have a chance to look at him, unobserved.

Seeing him softens me, dissolves my anger. A brown wave hangs down over his left eye, so I can't really see his expression. Still, something about his demeanor is so—sad. Maybe it's his posture: His head hangs down, so that he seems to be looking at his hands, which are fidgeting nervously in his lap. His jean jacket rides up a little in the back, so that I can see a piece of his flannel shirt, and even a bit of his bare back that peeks out above his worn jeans. I get a physical reaction, seeing his skin, a stirring that I try to ignore.

His guitar case is propped against the wall next to him, but had it been laying opened in front of him, I swear people would be tempted to put money into it. He just looks so—dejected. And vulnerable. I feel a wave of empathy for him. He doesn't deserve it.

I take a deep breath before pushing open the door to the icy air outside. Zach looks up eagerly when the door opens. He seems so grateful to see me that it almost breaks my heart.

He scrambles to his feet. "Hannah."

My heart starts racing, and something flutters in my stomach. Why is he so damn cute?

"Hey," he says softly, grabbing my free hand. I don't pull it away.

"Hey." I look down at my guitar, which hangs in its case from my other hand.

"I've missed you," he says. My heart flips in my chest, but I don't say anything right away. I don't know what to say. I've missed him too, but it really pisses me off that I miss him. That he still has that effect on me.

As I open my mouth to respond, Eric opens the door and exits the music shop. We quickly disengage.

"Oh, look who's here," Eric says lightly, though he must sense the tension between me and Zach, because he gives us a casual goodbye salute and discreetly continues toward the parking lot without stopping to chat.

"See ya," Zach says awkwardly.

"Yeah, bye," I add.

We watch Eric get in his car and drive away, then turn back toward each other.

"I've *really* missed you," he says.

"Let's walk," I say, barely slowing down to wait for Zach. I don't trust my body when it's near his body. It's hard to stand so close to him without touching. But I also don't trust *him* anymore. I quicken my pace.

He picks up his guitar and jogs a few steps to catch up to me.

"Hannah, wait." I stop, but don't look at him. Just look at my feet, trying to sort out my conflicting feelings, trying to figure out what I want to say.

"Hannah," he says, lifting my chin so that I'm facing him. "I can't take this. You not talking to me. Not answering my calls, my texts." His eyes bore into mine—I look away. "Please, Hannah. Talk to me."

Part of me wants to gaze back into Zach's eyes, to reach out and touch his face, or his arm. How did we get here? But I know how we got here. He's a liar. And I can't let myself be taken in by his charm.

"How could you lie to me, Zach? " I say to the ground.

"I didn't mean to lie to you," he says quietly. It doesn't matter whether he *meant* to lie. It just mattered that he did. I lock eyes with him. "How could you make me think badly about my own brother? How *could* you?"

"I didn't want you to think badly of me," he says, even more quietly.

"But you wanted me to think badly about Rob? Your supposed best friend?" As I speak, I become more incensed. "What kind of friend are you?"

He looks down at his feet.

"I've got to go," I say. I turn away from Zach and walk toward school and the soccer field. But as I walk away from Zach, I don't feel any satisfaction. Just shame. I think of Alex.

"What kind of friend are *you*, Hannah?" I ask myself.

# Chapter Forty-One

*Where are you?* I silently will Alex to answer. I don't want to be alone with my thoughts about Zach. And don't want to think about what's happening at the police station. I'm relieved to see the dots indicating that Alex is responding.

*Just leaving my house. You?*

*On my way back from guitar. Just saw Zach*

*He was at guitar?*

*Well, yeah, I kind of told him I was going there*

*Of course you did*

*Yeah...ugh...I don't know what to do about him*

*What did he say?*

*I'll tell you when I see you*

*Hannah!*

*Meet you by the West lot*

*Ugh, OK*

Then I text Mom.

*I'm not going to be home when you get back – going to a home soccer game*

*Really?! Aren't you even going to ask what happened? Do you know what your brother just went through?*

I bite my lip. How could I be so selfish? And yet....

*Of course I want to know what happened. Rob wasn't arrested, was he?*

*No, of course not. These things don't happen* that *quickly...But I would think you would want to be with the family at a time like this... And we have things to discuss...* I hate how my mom puts a million ellipses in her texts. It's so passive aggressive.

*I just need some time to process all of this Mom.* I pause, then type some more. *I'm going to the soccer game to make up with Alex. I probably won't make it home for dinner.* I definitely won't make it home for dinner. *I know we have to talk, and I promise, we can talk when I get home.*

I haven't told her that I've made up with Alex—if I promise to talk later, Mom will probably take pity on me and give me a pass. Especially if she thinks I'm resolving my problems with Alex. She's all about resolving problems.

*Fine.* Well, not exactly an enthusiastic response. In fact, Mom usually says "Fine" when things aren't. But I'll take it. Dots appeared on my screen—Mom's not done.

*I'm glad you girls are patching things up.* She's so predictable. More dots.

*But be careful what you say to Alex...* I don't respond. Instead, I stick the phone in my back pocket and go to meet my friend.

# Chapter Forty-Two

"What exactly did you hear?" Alex whispers. We sit in our usual spot on the stone wall by the school's entrance, our legs dangling in front of us. The soccer field is on the other side of the building, so we'll have privacy here. I feel the cold stone on my butt through my jeans, but the sun on my back warms me. We speak in low voices, even though nobody's around. "Start at the beginning," Alex said when we first sat down, and so I had.

"I could only hear like every few words, but Zach was upset about something and kept saying 'Shit, shit...'" Alex's eyes widen as she listens. My heart races as I recall how the boys' panicked voices traveled through the shared wall between our bedrooms. I have the same sick feeling in my stomach now as I'd had then. As I return to that moment. As I reveal the secret I've guarded for so long. I don't say the part about them being too high to drive. Not even my parents or Frankie knew the boys were "too high to drive."

"Rob was trying to calm him down, but he didn't sound calm either."

"Oh my God," Alex says.

"They didn't know—they thought it was a deer," I add, instinctively wanting to protect them, still. "Zach told me, eventually, but he said that his cousin was driving, and that he wanted to go back but Rob wouldn't let him." I pause. Am I betraying Zach? Am I betraying my brother? "But Rob said Zach was driving. That *he* was the one that wouldn't go back."

Alex lets out a low whistle. "Wow."

"Zach was waiting for me after my lesson." My eyes tear up. *Do not to cry*. "I asked him why he lied and he said that he didn't want me to think badly about him."

"So he admitted it?" Alex whispers in disbelief.

I think about it for a moment. "Well, not exactly."

"What? You mean you didn't ask him what he meant? Or what really happened?"

"Well, I assumed that he was saying that he lied about all of it," I say. It dawns on me that I really don't know exactly which lie Zach was confessing to. That he was driving? Or that he was the one who didn't want to go back? "I mean, I assume Rob was telling the lawyer the truth—"

"But can you really assume that?" asks Alex. She has her reporter voice on now. "You can never really assume anything."

No matter how I look at it, every possibility is equally terrible. Zach lied to me, and tried to throw my brother under the bus. He may or may not have killed someone. And Rob? Even if he is telling the truth—my brother was still in the car that killed Tyler. And here I am, opening my stupid mouth about it. I grab Alex's arms. Look her in the eye.

"Alex. You. Can. Not. Tell Jake. Any of this."

"Hannah," she says, looking hurt. "How could you say that to me? You know you can trust me."

I let go, and slump forward. How pissed Rob had been when I revealed what Zach told me. Was it possible that Rob said Zach was driving just to get back at him for what he'd told me? "I just don't know what to do." I give Alex a sideward glance. "And I still like him," I say in a whisper.

"Oh, Han," Alex says, putting her arm around me. Voices drift over to us from the direction of the soccer field, and we hear cars pulling into the parking lot on the side of the school.

"Listen," she says. "I'll help you figure out what to do. But you need a break from all this. Try to get your mind off of things. Come watch the game, we'll have some beers with Jake and his friends after, and you can forget your troubles for a little while..."

Forget my troubles? As if. I do *not* feel like going to the soccer game. I do not feel like drinking beers with Jake and his friends. I don't even like beer. The only thing I feel like doing is curling up into a ball and crying my eyes out.

Plus, who knows what I'll be walking into when I finally get home. I'd hung up on Mom, and surely Dad will be disappointed in me for not being there for the family today. And Rob. He'd been questioned by the police, for God's sake.

But I can see that Alex, who has already jumped off the wall and reached into her pocket to pull out a tube of lip gloss, is excited to see Jake. And I owe Alex. Big time. So I nod my head, jump down from the wall, and brush the dirt off the butt of my jeans. I'll be Alex's wingwoman today. And deal with the consequences later.

I try to focus on the game, to listen to Alex's running commentary on Jake's every move. I make myself clap whenever the students around us cheer—and jump up with Alex and join in the cheering when Jake makes a goal. But my mind keeps returning to Zach. *I didn't mean to lie to you. I didn't want you to think badly of me. I've missed you.* I can't get our conversation out of my head.

The soccer game goes into overtime, providing me with an excuse to stay away from home for even longer. Not going home allows me to be in denial for at least an extra hour. Denial that my family is about to fall apart. That everything will be different at home now that my brother is officially a *criminal suspect.*

I don't rush home when the game ends, either. Instead, I stick around beneath the bleachers with Alex, Jake and his friends. I don't say much—I'm not in the mood—I simply smile when appropriate, pretend to sip from a red plastic cup filled with warm beer, listen to the banter between Jake and his teammates. They won, and spirits are high. Everyone's but mine anyway.

I watch Alex and Jake, he with his arm draped casually around her shoulder, she flirty, laughing at all his jokes. I feel envious, wish that things between me and Zach could be as easy. Alex, maybe sensing my distress, pulls me closer, and hooks her free arm with mine.

"Cheer up, Han," she whispers. I nod. Alex, to her credit, has not brought up the accident again. I know I've got to be strong. For myself, and for my family. I take a deep breath, rearrange my expression to read "happy," hold up my cup in a toast to Alex, and make myself down the rest of my beer. Cheers to the new me, I think, though I'm feeling anything but cheerful. I'm surprised by how quickly the fuzzy feeling from the beer spreads through my body, all the way up to my head.

I linger longer than I should, ignoring my vibrating phone. It's Zach or Mom, and I don't feel like talking to either one of them. Instead, I let Jake refill my cup, embrace the buzz from the beer. I join Alex in laughing at the boys' jokes, which seem to be getting funnier and funnier. When I realize that dusk has at some point turned to dark, I text Mom.

*The game went overtime. Waiting for Alex and our friend from the team to walk me home.*

I don't look at her response. I want to remain in my slightly drunken haze for a bit longer. Reality can wait.

# Chapter Forty-Three

I climb the stairs quietly, but with a growing sense of dread. Why isn't anyone listening for me? Demanding to know where I've been? What happened while I was gone?

Jake and Alex walked me home, elbows linked, Jake on one side of Alex, me on the other. We tried to match one another's strides, cracking up whenever one of us tripped in the process. I knew that once I got home, the laughing would be over.

But nobody's downstairs when I finally get my key to fit into the lock. When I let myself in, only the light in the hallway is on. It *is* 9 pm already, but still kind of early for everyone to have gone to bed. And very unlike Mom to not be waiting up for me.

When I reach the top of the stairs, no doors open, no one shouts out for me. Am I actually going to get a pass? I'm about to slip into my room when I hear raised voices coming from my parents' room.

"It's not like you're a paragon of honesty, here," Dad is saying. I freeze.

"I've told you a million times how sorry I am." Then, as if realizing that she's speaking a bit too loudly, Mom lowers the volume. I can still hear. My stomach clenches.

"Are you going to punish me forever?" she whispers loudly.

Something makes me turn my head. I notice that Rob's bedroom door has opened slightly, and that he too, stands there, still and quiet, listening to our parents fight. We exchange a look. He doesn't look at me with anger, exactly. More like we're co-conspirators, listening to something important that is going to affect us both.

"Do you expect me to just say okay, honey, I forgive you, and we go resume life like nothing happened? I can't exactly trust you anymore—"

The phone rings, startling us both and interrupting our parents' conversation.

Dad's angry voice erupts loud and clear. "You have some nerve calling here." But then he quiets.

"Oh," he says. "Yeah. I understand." Pause. "No, I get it, thanks." Another pause. "Yeah, we'll bring him. No need for anyone to come here." We hear the phone receiver click in its receiver.

I look over at Rob, who suddenly seems a few shades paler. He glances nervously at me, and then we both look back toward our parents' room.

"They are going to arrest Rob," we hear Dad say, his voice shaky. Mom lets out a sob. Rob grips his doorframe, almost as if to keep himself steady. "Paul said that if Rob agrees to come willingly and turn himself in, it's okay if we bring him in tomorrow morning."

I can't help it. I gasp, then clap my hand to my mouth. Our parents' door opens and they see me standing there. I glance over at Rob, but he has already disappeared and shut the door behind him.

# Chapter Forty-Four

I stand next to Mom, clutching her hand, as Dad disappears into Rob's room and whispers with Rob behind the closed door for what seems like an eternity. It doesn't matter anymore that I ignored Mom's calls, stayed away when my parents wanted me home. The worst thing that could happen is about to happen. I'd been worried that Mom would smell the beer on my breath, but she doesn't notice. She's on the verge of falling apart. Her son is about to be arrested. Now, instead, I worry that my mother will have a nervous breakdown. I clasp her hand more tightly.

"What's going to happen?" I ask Mom quietly, as we wait for him to emerge. My stomach is churning. I'm not sure if it's from the beer or just nerves. My brother is about to be arrested.

"I don't know, Han," she says, shaking her head. "I don't know."

I'm not sure how much time goes by before Dad finally emerges, his eyes red, his expression grim—life has become surreal and even the way that time passes has changed. Every minute is excruciating.

"I'm going to call Frankie," he says, heading back into their room and to his nightstand. He dials. We wait in the doorway, listening fearfully to one side of their conversation.

"Yes, he said they are going to arrest Rob." Mom inhales sharply, but I don't hear her exhale. I know that if I turn my head, I'll see her eyes brimming with tears, but my eyes are laser-focused on Dad. I watch his every expression for clues to what he's hearing. Wait anxiously for every word that comes out of his mouth.

"Not sure, but he said that they could avoid showing up at the house and making a scene if Rob was willing to turn himself in." Dad runs his hand through his hair, in a way that reminds me of Rob. I picture police officers knocking our door down, leading Rob away in handcuffs. I force my mind back onto my father's conversation, but the fear in his expression only makes me feel worse. It scares me to see my father so unmoored.

"Yeah, in the morning."

"I didn't even think of that. You think they know?" Think of what? Who was "they?" What was he talking about? My heart thumps in my chest.

"Cameras? Jesus. How can we avoid it?" Cameras? Was my family going to be on the news? I think of the news stories where the perpetrators shield their faces from the cameras as they pass throngs of reporters. Is that going to be us? Are they going to be shoving cameras and microphones in my face again? I clutch my mother's hand even more tightly. Mom squeezes back.

"As early as you want."

"A deal? But is it safe for him to..." Dad falters. "I don't want them to take it as a confession of guilt. I mean...yeah, but...Whatever you think is best, but Frankie, it's my son..." He seems to choke on his words.

"Frankie, just keep my son out of jail."

No one says a word when Dad hangs up. I wait for him to make some pronouncement that will make us all feel better. Mom looks at him with her eyebrows raised, as if she's having the same thought.

"So, Frankie is going to pick us up in the morning, early," he finally says. "Before the press gets wind of this."

Mom lets go of my hand, and brings her hand to her mouth, pressing it there, her eyes wide. I can tell she's trying not to cry. It occurs to me that if my parents hadn't been fighting, if Mom had not been cheating on Dad, he would probably be stepping forward right about now to try to comfort her. Hug her or something. But he doesn't move any closer. He just leaves her there. Eventually, Mom wraps her arms around herself.

"The press," Mom says to no one in particular, as if trying to comprehend this new reality. I move in and put my own arm around her. Mom, teary-eyed, draws me closer to her side.

"We'll do what Frankie says, and everything will be okay," Mom says, as if trying to convince herself.

"Exactly," says Dad. He doesn't look directly at either one of us as he says it.

"But what if reporters are there?" I ask, remembering how claustrophobic and trapped I felt when journalists were closing in on me at the memorial service.

"Frankie will keep us away from the reporters," Dad says. "She's going to take us in a back entrance." When had our life turned into an episode of *American Crime*?

"They're not really going to put a 17-year-old boy in jail, are they?" Mom asks quietly, desperately almost, her eyes boring into Dad with such intensity that I have to look away.

"Frankie says she thinks they will release him into our custody," he says. "But we'll have to post bail...."

"Bail?!" I blurt out. "Will that be a lot of money?"

"Whatever it is," Dad says, putting his hand on my arm "we'll handle it. Rob is a minor—he is not going to go to jail." He doesn't say it with his typical certainty. I don't feel reassured.

The three of us stand together, silently. So many questions swirl in my head. Is Zach going to be arrested too? Does he have a lawyer who can bring him to the secret door at the police station—or will he be besieged by press as he walks into the precinct? Or worse, will they come to his house and put him in handcuffs, press his head down as they force him into a police car? While all his neighbors stand around and watch? Will people film it on their phones and share it on social media, and in the hallways at school?

"Hannah, I think you should stay here again when we bring him in." Dad's words interrupt my spiraling thoughts.

"But I don't want to stay here myself." I imagine reporters gathering outside our house, ringing the doorbell. My stomach churns again and my skin suddenly feels clammy. I instantly regret drinking that beer.

"No one has to know you're here," Mom says. "You'll stay in your room, we'll keep the lights out in the house, and hopefully we'll be back relatively quickly." I have a fleeting moment of gratitude that I no longer have to handle all of this on my own, that at least I have my parents here to tell me what to do. I think of Zach, who only has his mom. But my mother's words are tinged with uncertainty. And I realize in this moment that I've always taken for granted the fact that my parents would take care of everything. That they have it all under control, that no matter what, everything would be okay.

This might not be okay. This could ruin Rob's future. This could change our life—hell, hasn't it already? My parents are entering this new territory right along with me, and having them on the same shaky footing is terrifying.

# Chapter Forty-Five

When I notice sunlight appearing at the edges of my blinds the next morning, I feel strangely relieved. I've barely slept, and the official arrival of morning means I can finally get out of bed.

Up until now, I've restrained myself from peeking at my phone. When I could no longer stand to listen to it vibrate, I'd shut it off, knowing that Zach had probably both called and texted multiple times. But all through the night I fretted about him getting arrested, and eight hours of sleepless worry has worn away at my resolve.

I reach for the phone, press the on button, and turn on the sound. I'm barraged by a long series of beeps, as the phone registers the last ten hours-worth of activity. There are a series of missed calls—and texts—from my mother from when I was at the soccer game, and then a long string of texts and calls from Zach. I'm about to click on one of Zach's texts when I notice a message from a number that

I don't recognize. I click on it. The first few words—*This is Zach's cousin Bryan*—sends chills up my spine.

How did he get my number? I feel the hairs on my arms standing up, like when Alex and I watch scary movies together. I sit up in bed, and read on.

*I know you don't know me, so it probably doesn't matter to you if I go to jail. But do you want Zach to go to jail? Because his mom can't afford to get him a good lawyer. My cousin is so in love with you. Don't you care what happens to him? Just because Rob's your brother, it doesn't mean he's telling the truth. If you care about Zach at all, you'll keep quiet when they ask you questions.*

My heart is racing. I throw the phone down on my bed. Cover it with my blanket. I pull on jeans and a sweatshirt, and leave my room in a hurry.

I peer through my parents' open door. The bed's already made, and the room is empty. I run down the stairs, two at a time, and head toward the sounds of spoons clinking against coffee cups. I stop in the doorway, relieved to find my parents at the kitchen table. They both look up.

"Hi Han," Dad says. He sips his coffee.

"Hi Hannah," Mom echoes. She stirs her coffee far longer than she has to, and never even bothers to take a sip. Her eyes have big bags under them. Dad's do too.

"This is early for you to be up," he says. "Did you have trouble sleeping?"

"Yeah," I say, wanting to tell them about the text, but knowing I really can't. They would probably want to show it to the lawyer, make me even more of a traitor than I already am. *He is so in love with you.* Zach has never said the "L" word. But can he feel as strongly about me as I do about him? Am I really going to betray him when the lawyer asks me what he'd told me? Can I really tell the lawyer—or anyone—how Zach cried in the car that day as he confessed everything?

Or maybe they're both just playing me. Maybe Zach never loved me at all. Maybe Bryan's text—and everything that ever happened with Zach—are all lies. Ways for them to protect themselves, to keep themselves out of jail. Maybe they both want to throw Rob under the bus. I sink against the doorframe. I'm so tired.

Dad comes over and puts an arm around me. I lean against him. Mom gets up too, puts her hand on my arm, and says, "I'm going to help Rob get ready."

Dad glances at his watch. "Frankie's going to be here in like ten minutes," he says, as if I'd asked.

Dad pulls me in closer. It's like he's offering me the comfort he had withheld from Mom. It makes me sad, but I nod into the soft flannel of his shirt.

I look down at my feet, and realize I'm wearing my fuzzy purple slippers—I don't even remember putting them on. Alex used to say that they made my feet look like they belonged to Barney—the talking dinosaur from the kid's TV show we'd watched on repeat when we were toddlers—on a bad hair day. She would tell me to put on grown-up shoes. I always found the whole exchange hysterically funny—but I never changed out of the slippers. They were like a favorite blankie or stuffed animal that I'd never quite outgrown. Today, seeing those slippers makes my heart heavy.

I don't know how long Dad and I stand in the kitchen doorway, but finally, the creak of the stairs—and the soft padding of Rob and Mom's footsteps on the stairway carpet—make us both look up. Rob comes first. He wears a button-down shirt and khakis—clearly Mom has picked out his clothes. He seems scared, and younger somehow—like a little boy in grown-up clothing. I pull away from Dad and throw my hands around Rob's waist, hug him. A move that surprises me as much as it does Rob.

I pull away quickly, a little embarrassed, and then am amazed when my brother sort of tousles the top of my hair before turning toward the front door. The moment is so fleeting, that I don't even have a chance to savor it—or examine it—but I could swear Rob's eyes look a little teary as he passes by.

The doorbell rings just then, making Rob shrink back, but startling Mom and Dad into nervous action.

"Oh, she's here," Mom says, looking at Dad and then back at the door. I can make out Frankie's blurry form behind the frosted glass panel next to the front door. Mom touches my shoulder as she passes, gives me an apologetic smile, but is out the door before I have a chance to say anything.

"We'll see you later Han-Han," Dad says, as he leads Rob to the door. He hasn't called me that in a while. It makes me sad. "Don't worry." And just like that, my parents and my brother are off. To jail.

# Chapter Forty-Six

I sit down on the bottom stair, stunned, as the reality of what is happening sinks in. *You'll keep quiet. Zach is so in love with you. You'll keep quiet. Zach is so in love with you.* The two phrases bounce around my head, crashing into each other. My heart pounds.

As angry as I am at Zach, as suspicious as I am about his motives, I still care about what happens to him. Will he go to jail? Will his mom be left alone? I feel sorry for everyone. Then I think about Tyler and his family. Even if Zach or Rob go to jail, they will not be gone forever. Am I a bad person for worrying about the wrong people? The people who killed Tyler? I swallow. Feel ashamed. But I can't help it.

I pull myself up and slowly climb the steps. I open my door, head toward the bed, pull away the blanket and retrieve my phone. I start typing.

*Zach, we need to talk.*

Dots appear immediately. Is he just sitting there, waiting for me to call? Maybe he really does love me?

*What are you doing now?*

*Nothing, let's meet.* I hesitate for a moment before pressing send, but push the doubt away. If I can see his face, if I look into his eyes, I'll be able to tell whether what he's saying is real. Won't I? I press send.

More dots. But before even waiting to see his response—because of course I know what his response will be—I send another text. *Can you pick me up?*

My heart beats almost as quickly as my fingers type. I know I'm being reckless. But this could be the last time I see Zach for a really long time. I want one last chance to find out the truth about the accident, about what this is between us. If it is—or has ever been—real. One last time to be with him before he's arrested, before he and Rob are pitted against each other in court. One last time to be with him in case he ends up in jail. I shiver, even though I'm not cold.

*Yes, I'll be there in 10.* Ten minutes! I try to ignore the hollow feeling in my stomach. I drop the phone on my bed, and scoot over to the mirror. Run my hands through my hair, pull it around one side of my shoulder. Examine my face in the glass. I look tired, but tired will have to do.

I take the steps two at a time, then suddenly, freeze at the bottom of the staircase. What if Zach's cousin is with him? What if the two of them were waiting together for me to call?

I text Alex. Again, reckless, but I'm driven by fear.

*Alex, I'm going to share my location with you.* It's too early for Alex to be up on a Sunday, but I'm desperate. Maybe she'll hear her phone buzz.

Apparently she does.

*Where are you going????*

*I'm going to see Zach. But I'm afraid his cousin will be there and I'm kind of scared of him.*

*What are you talking about? The cousin who was in the car with them? Have you even met him? Why are you scared of him?*

*I think he maybe threatened me? But I might be blowing this out of proportion. I just want you to know where I am.*

*Hannah, you're worrying me. What happened? When did you even talk to him?*

*I don't have time to explain. He might not even be there. I'm being crazy. Just keep track of me. I'll call you later.*

*Omg Hannah, you better.*

I'm about to open the door and go onto the front porch to wait for Zach, when suddenly I remember about the reporters. I freeze, again, and actually feel myself shaking. *Get a hold of yourself, Hannah.* I walk slowly toward the door, and put my eye up against the tiny little peephole in its center. I let out my breath, in relief. No one is there. Still, I don't want to take any chances. I pull out my phone again.

*Pick me up at the corner of McAllister and Pine, OK?* To be safe, I'll go out the back door and cut through the neighbor's woods.

*OK, almost there*

Swallowing to get rid of the lump in my throat, I grab my keys from a tray on the table in the foyer, exit out the back door, and cut through the woods. Zach's blue Honda pulls up just as I get to the road. I open the door and slide into the passenger seat. I've barely turned to Zach when he throws his arms around me and kisses me—I mean *really* kisses me—on the lips. I melt into the kiss and my fear falls away. How could I have been scared of Zach? It's just Zach.

I don't know how long the kiss lasts. Seconds? Minutes? But when he pulls away and softly says "Hi," it is the old Zach I recognize.

Maybe it's always been the old Zach. It's the circumstances that have changed, not him.

"Hi." I love his face. I study his profile as he looks through the windshield and puts the car into gear. I try to imprint on my memory the way his hooded eyelids and long lashes make his eyes look sleepy-sexy, the way his nose slopes up slightly at the tip. A dip and a rise that I would sometimes trace with my finger when we were lying next to one another. The feel of those soft lips pressed on mine. The way he wrapped his arms around me the minute I got into the car.

"I'll drive to the arboretum?"

"Yeah." I close my eyes for a second, memorizing the look and feel of him. Then open them. I can't let myself lose sight of why I'm here, why we're in this situation.

"Zach, did they question you?" A shadow seems to pass over his face.

"Yeah." I wait for him to continue, but he doesn't. Just stares straight ahead at the road.

"What did you say?" Zach is quiet for a minute. He looks at his rearview mirror, puts on his turn signal, is suddenly very focused on his driving. My heart starts speeding up again.

"Zach?"

"Hannah—" The way he says my name, I just know. It's because of whatever Zach said that Rob is being arrested at this very moment. But what did I think? I try to harden myself to him. I have to remember that he's the enemy. Not what he was to me before.

"Zach, what did you say? Are you the reason they are arresting Rob right now?"

"Oh, my God," he says. "They're arresting him? Right now?" I've blindsided him. He had no idea. I see how his hands tighten on the wheel, I watch the beads of sweat form on his forehead. His breaths, in and out, become quicker and more pronounced. He turns into the arboretum.

What am I doing? How could I kiss the person who is sending my brother to jail? I'm a terrible person.

Zach drives down the long, windy entryway, and then makes a right. He pulls the car over on the side of a road that's almost completely shaded by a canopy of trees. There isn't another car—or person—in sight. There's no reason to be scared—this is Zach. I wish there was something—anything—he could say to make this better.

"Hannah," he says, looking into my eyes. I notice the little bits of green that fleck the dark brown of his irises. "Look, my mom can't afford a fancy lawyer like your parents can. Rob will be fine." He looks down at his lap. "I had to answer all their questions," he adds. "I had no choice."

Of course he can't look me in the eye as he basically admits that he's caused Rob to be arrested. How could he? Doesn't he care about me at all? And isn't Rob supposed to be his best friend?

"So you told them it was Rob's decision not to turn back..." Zach's doesn't answer right away. His silence scares me. "Zach?"

"Hannah..." He hesitates, and his hesitation makes my stomach all twisty. *Please.* I think. *Don't make this any worse.* And then he does. "Rob was the one driving."

I am stunned into silence. Stunned that Zach would take his lies this far. Heartbroken, again, over his disregard for Rob, for me.

"And let me guess," I say, my heartbreak morphing into anger. "Bryan also told the police that Rob was driving." Zach doesn't answer. Just keeps his eyes down.

"Zach, you told me your cousin was driving. How could you lie to the police?"

He looks at me, then. "I told them the truth." But his words are hollow.

"I didn't want to tell you about Rob, and I didn't think I needed to," he says. "I never thought things would get this far." I don't believe him. I just can't. In fact, I realize at this moment that it doesn't matter what he says, about that night, about what he told the police—and even about the two of us. I can't believe him anymore.

"Hannah, I can't go to jail." There's something desperate in his eyes, his tone. He tries to put his hand on mine, but I pull it away. A flash of hurt crosses his face. He puts his hand back in his lap, grips it with his other one. Then stares directly into my eyes.

"Hannah, I can't. Do this. To my mom. To my cousin," he speaks slowly, emphatically. His brow is dented with two lines. "Rob will be fine, but we won't. You can't tell the police anything. If they question you, you have to act like you don't know anything—just say I never talked to you about any of it." Again, I'm dumbstruck. *What is happening here?* I think of Bryan's text.

"Zach, was any of this—you and me—real?" I ask quietly, my voice breaking. "Or did you just go out with me to keep me quiet?" I try hard not to cry, but tears well up in my eyes. I swipe at them angrily with the back of my hand.

"Hannah, no," he tries to embrace me, but again, I pulled away. He looks stricken. "Hannah, please, don't be like that. This was real. Is real."

He lets out a breath and starts over. "Okay," he says. "I'm going to be completely honest with you."

"It's about time." I cross my arms, shielding myself from what's coming.

"I was obviously attracted to you from that first day at the Music Shoppe," he says.

"Obviously? Nothing is obvious to me anymore..."

"Hannah, you know I was. That was before the accident had even happened." I don't say anything, so he continues.

"I might have—uh—accelerated things, afterward, because I wanted you to be on my side." His words are like arrows. Sure, I'd had my suspicions, but I didn't *really* believe that he could have made that stuff up.

"Wow." I feel winded, like I've been punched. I wrap my arms tighter around my body, focus my gaze on the windshield. *Accelerated things?*

"Wait, let me finish," he says quickly. "I wanted to show you that I was a good person, so that you wouldn't tell anyone what you had heard."

"A good person?" I say, turning back toward him. "What kind of good person does that?"

Zach swallows.

"Hannah, listen. I didn't expect to like you so much. I mean, Hannah, I don't just like you. And I know this is bad timing, and I don't want to say this for the first time in the middle of all this—" he waves his hands around, as if that could aptly capture the mess we find ourselves in. I hold my breath, wanting him to say it, but not wanting him to say it. Because what a waste. We can never be together. Not now.

"But I actually think I love you." He shrugs his shoulders as he says it, looking me right in the eyes. Naked, vulnerable, at my mercy. His words flood me with both relief and sadness. When I don't answer, he continues.

"Do you really think I could have faked the way I felt when we were together?" No, deep down, I don't. Which is why I've been so confused. "I've told you things—showed you things—that I've never shared with anyone."

"But Zach," I say, holding his gaze. "If you really feel that way about me, how could you do this to my brother, my family? My brother could end up in jail because of you."

It's Zach's turn to be dumbstruck—he has no response. He just looks down and fiddles with the edges of his shirt, shaking his head slowly. His eyes fill with tears.

"I think we should go back," I whisper.

"Hannah—"

"I need to go home. Now." I bite my lip so that I won't cry.

"Okay," he says. He turns the key, still dangling from the ignition, and re-starts the car. I look out the window, away from Zach. I'm done talking to him.

But as he drives me home, it occurs to me that there's a tiny possibility that he is actually telling the truth. What if Rob *was* driving the car? What if Zach had initially lied to me to protect him? Or to protect me? I turn to ask him, again, but stop myself. He won't tell me the truth anyway.

# Chapter Forty-Seven

I slink through my neighbor's backyard after Zach drops me off, staying close to the shrubs along the edges of the property. My feet make squishing sounds in the grass, still wet from the sprinklers. I slip into my house through the back door. The house is silent, thankfully—my parents haven't beat me home. I remain in the kitchen, in case there are reporters out front. I don't want anyone to know I'm in the house.

Leaning against the kitchen counter, I dial Alex's number. I start to cry the minute she picks up.

"Oh, Hannah," is all Alex says.

"He said the L word," I say, sniffling. "Can you believe that?" I have fantasized about hearing these words from a boy someday, from this boy. But this isn't how I imagined feeling after hearing them.

"Wow," Alex scoffs. "Gotta love his timing."

Neither of us says anything for a while.

"Alex, they arrested my brother," I whisper into the phone. Alex gasps.

"Whoa, Hannah. You buried the lede!" Alex loves to pepper her speech with journalistic catch-phrases. "But then why didn't they arrest—Ohhh. That asshole...he didn't."

"Yeah. He did." I swallow. "I thought they were *all* going to be arrested, but I guess Zach and his cousin both blamed Rob..."

"But wait," Alex says. "Didn't you say he told you that his cousin was driving?"

"Apparently he didn't want to 'burden' me with the 'truth,'" I say bitterly. "Who the hell knows if he's ever told me the truth. About anything."

"But Hannah, don't you see?"

"See what?"

"You have to tell the police what Zach told you! You can get your brother out...."

"Wait, wait, wait—you don't get it. I lied to my parents! I told them I didn't know anything. Isn't that like withholding evidence? Can't *I* get arrested for that?" I shiver at the thought.

"Hmm," says Alex, considering what I've said. "We'll have to do some research on that. But there's got to be some way to prove who was really driving."

"Well, as you know, that Ring camera video was too blurry to see the people inside the car."

"Yeah, those houses on Willet are set too far back...But maybe there are traffic cameras—don't they have traffic cameras?"

"In Woodfield? I doubt it. And anyway, don't you think they would have checked those already if they existed? "

"Maybe they got gas?" Alex asks.

"At five in the morning?"

"Yeah, probably not."

"Maybe someone at the party saw them get into the car?"

"Well we know someone told the police they were there late or the police wouldn't have suspected them—but if whoever ratted them out saw who was driving they probably would have told the police that too…" Both of us are silent for a moment.

"But, Alex," I finally whisper. "What if Zach is telling the truth?" I bite my lip as I wait for her answer.

I hear the garage door opening. "I've gotta go," I say to Alex. "My parents are back." I click the phone off before Alex has a chance to respond, and collect myself. I have to act like I've been here the whole time.

I run over to the pantry and grab a box of Cheerios, pull a bowl out of the cupboard next to the sink, and dump some cereal into it. The last thing I feel like doing is eating, but I need to look like I'm doing *something*.

Mom walks in. Her eyes are red and swollen. She's alone.

"Where's Rob? Where's Dad?" I ask, dropping my spoon.

"They're still processing the arrest. Dad's staying with Frankie and Rob. They're filling out paperwork and—uh—taking photos…." Her voice breaks, and she stops herself.

"Mug shots?" I whisper. *Is this really happening?*

Mom nods, pushing her knuckles into her closed lips, as if to stop herself from crying out. Then she collects herself and comes closer. She puts her arm on my shoulder. "Han, Frankie needs to talk to you. She needs to know if Zach told you anything, anything at all, that could help your brother."

My heart starts racing.

"Why does she think he would tell me something—did you tell him we were—"

"Of course, Hannah—Rob told her too. We have to be completely honest with Frankie so that she can help us. Hannah, why do you have that look on your face? What are you not telling me?"

I'm not ready to tell Mom about the conversation I just had with Zach. Then again, wouldn't *anyone* be upset if their brother had just been arrested?

"Any 'look' I have on my face is because my brother is having his mugshots taken and is about to be in jail! Don't you think I care about what happens to Rob?" I start crying. I'm not sure if I'm actually crying because of Rob or because of Zach, but either way, it works. Mom's suspicion turns to sympathy.

"Hannah, nobody is blaming you for anything." Mom hugs me. "I know this is hard for you too, especially because of you and Zach." She speaks in a soothing voice, and it occurs to me that my parents probably consider me to be fragile now after my recent meltdown. I'll take it, if it means they'll leave me alone and not grill me about Zach. But I know she isn't going to let me off so easy.

I don't even try to stop crying, because I don't want to create an opening for Mom to question me again. Should I tell my parents and the lawyer what Zach told me? I have no problem sacrificing Bryan, whom I don't even know, to save Rob and Zach. But what if Zach has been lying about Bryan, too? What if Rob is telling the truth and Zach was driving?

Another thought makes its way through the noise in my brain: What if Bryan finds out that I'm responsible for ratting him out? Will he text me, call me, come find me? I shudder as fear permeates my entire body. And if Zach really loves me, how could I—

"Hannah?" Her mother's concerned voice interrupts my train of thought. She's stepped back, though she keeps her hands on my shoulders. She peers into my teary eyes. "Is there something you want to tell me?"

I shake my head. "I just don't want to get Zach arrested too," I whisper.

"Hannah, nothing you say is going to get Zach arrested. If Zach is arrested, it is because of choices he made that night that Tyler Miller died—not because of anything you say to Frankie." I notice that Mom says "that night that Tyler Miller died," as if it was a passive thing that happened, not something that was caused by the car that Rob, her son, my brother, had been in. Whether or not he had been driving it. Her son, my brother, may or may not have told his friends that there was no way they could turn back—a "choice" that might have made the difference between Tyler dying, or just getting very hurt.

I nod slowly, to let her know that I've heard what she's saying.

"But what you say," Mom continues, keeping her eyes locked on mine, "and anything you might know that you aren't saying, might save your brother from going to jail and ruining his life."

I gulp, but before I can answer, Mom's cell phone buzzes. She scoops it up so quickly that I'm afraid she might knock herself out with it.

"Hello? John? Are you coming home? Are you and Rob coming home?" She looks like she's holding her breath for a minute, but she slowly releases it, and I can tell by the way her shoulders drop away from her ears, and the way the hand that grips the phone softens so that the color comes back into her knuckles, that the answer is yes.

"Thank God," she says. "How is he?" Hannah watches her mother's expression change.

"You don't have to be nasty," she says under her breath, though I can still hear. "I'm just concerned. See you when you get here." She hangs up quickly, and tries to rearrange her face. But I know that Dad probably said something sarcastic, and am reminded that even if Rob is coming home, my father could at any time decide that *he* is not.

Still, I get why Dad's being sarcastic—of course Rob's not okay. But at least he doesn't have to stay in jail. Will Zach be so lucky if they arrest him? And will either of them be able to *stay* out of jail?

"I'm going to lie down for a few minutes," I say, feeling suddenly exhausted by all the overwhelming possibilities. I need time to figure out a strategy. What I should say to Frankie. To my parents.

"Hannah," Mom says in a harsh voice, but then must rethink whatever she is about to say. "Okay, fine, go lie down for a few minutes," she says in a more compassionate tone. She's trying to be understanding—I'll give her that. Though, of course, she can't possibly understand. "Frankie is coming over this afternoon, so you can talk to her then."

I nod, though on the inside I'm screaming.

I leave the kitchen quickly, before Mom can change her mind, and run up the stairs and into my room, shutting the door behind me. If only I could just sleep all day. And not have to talk to Frankie. I head toward my bed, then pause and pivot, go back to the door and quietly lock it behind me.

I plop down on my bed and immediately pull out my phone.

*Alex!! Help!!!!*

*What?!*

*The lawyer wants to know what Zach told me! What do I do?????*

*You. Tell. Her. That his cousin was driving.*

*But what if he wasn't*

*What are you saying*

*What if Zach was driving*

*Hannah*

*What*

Suddenly the phone buzzes. It's Alex. I click on the green receiver icon.

"Alex," I whisper.

"Listen to me, Hannah. I know you really, really like Zach. But if he was driving, and he said your brother was driving, he's kind of....a dick."

"True..."

"More than a dick. A pathological liar. Hannah, he or his cousin *killed* someone. Not just someone. *Tyler.* He's basically accusing your brother—his supposed best friend—of murder. Or at least involuntary manslaughter. " I let Alex's words sink in. It's not like I haven't been thinking these thoughts. But to hear Alex say them out loud is chilling.

"Yeah, I know, but—"

"No buts. Seriously, Hannah. You tell the lawyer that he said the cousin was driving. And, I don't know. Maybe they'll get his car for evidence or something. Maybe they can tell." A new worry pops into my head: It occurs to me that though I've ridden in Zach's car, I've never really examined the front of it. But no, he wouldn't be driving it around if there was any evidence of—no. Anyway, his car is blue—didn't the news say it was a black car? It had to be Bryan's car, whoever was driving.

"But what if his cousin finds out?" Even voicing this fear makes my heart start pounding. He hasn't texted again, but I'm scared every time I check my phone.

"His cousin isn't going to find out."

"Okay...." I'm not convinced.

"Tell me what the lawyer says."

"Yeah, okay." I sigh.

I'm on my own.

# Chapter Forty-Eight

I wake to knocking.

"Hannah, open the door." It's Mom. Sounding impatient. I look around my room, disoriented. Did I actually fall asleep? Light streams through my open blinds, making sun stripes on the carpet. It's still daytime. More knocking. I remember that I locked the door.

"Coming, coming," I say, slowly swinging my feet over the side of the bed and making my way over to unlock it.

"Frankie's here," Mom says when I open it. My body instantly tenses.

"Come down," Mom says. Then, after thinking a moment, she adds, "Or if you want, I can send her up here."

"Up here." I hug my arms around my body, dig my fingers into my upper arms. I don't want to face Rob. And I definitely don't want to have an audience when I speak to Frankie.

"Ok, then." Mom leaves me standing by the door. I remain there, awkwardly, in my own embrace, waiting for whatever's coming next.

I hear Frankie's heels clicking on the steps before I see her head—and then her body—appear over the edge of the stairwell. What should I tell her?

"Hi Hannah," Frankie says warmly. "Let's have us a chat." She understands my predicament, I can tell. It's the way she looks at me, the way she touches my arm and keeps her hand there as we walk into my room. It's the way she bends her head toward me, looking at me expectantly, but waiting patiently for me to be ready. Trust me, she's saying without words. I will guide you through this.

So I tell her everything.

# Chapter Forty-Nine

"I can't believe that a-hole had the nerve to threaten you," Rob mutters angrily.

"Rob," my parents say at the same time. They can't help themselves. Frankie has just left, said she was going back to her office to review the case now that I have "enlightened her further." That's the only part of the conversation I catch as I join the rest of my family in the family room. I'm not sure exactly what Frankie has told them. But she promised me she'd make sure my family knows what's going on so that I won't have to repeat my story.

After Frankie leaves, Rob alternates between a zombie-like state and being steaming mad. He's especially fixated on Bryan's text. I showed the text to Frankie, but asked her not to tell my family about the "Zach loves you" part.

"What? I just never knew Bryan was such a d—"

"That text is probably going to work in your favor," Dad says, cutting Rob off before he can swear again. I sit beside Dad on the couch; he rests his hand over mine, as if to say "I'll protect you." At least that's how I take it. I do feel a slight bit of relief that my parents now know about Bryan's text.

Frankie's going to speak to "her contacts" in the police department to let them know there's some "discrepancy" in the boys' testimony. She told me it's likely that the police are going to want to question me. The thought of it makes me so anxious that I try to push it out of my mind. But the damage is done. I've betrayed Zach simply by telling Frankie what he said. What I'd heard.

It seems like ages ago that I'd sat in my room, staring at Tyler Miller's draped body on my computer screen. That I became privy to a secret that I didn't want to be privy to. But I remember the boys' voices coming through the wall—and the words they carried—as if it just happened. "Shit, shit shit." And "What are we going to do?" Zach doesn't stand a chance. *He* had been the one asking the question, now that I think about it. And wasn't it Rob who tried to reassure Zach?

"And the worst of it," Rob is saying, "is Zach giving him your number. What a fucking—"

"Rob, enough," Dad warns. But Rob is right. This is the piece of it that I can't wrap my head around. That Zach would give Bryan my number so that he could send me that threatening text. I try to think of alternate explanations. *Maybe he saw the number on Zach's phone?*

"Really, Hannah? You're still defending him?" Had I actually said that out loud? Rob's question comes out more weary-sounding than mean. He just shakes his head. Zach wouldn't conspire with his cousin to scare me. Would he?

"Zach seemed like such a great kid," Mom says, deflated, shaking her head. "You just never know people..."

"No, you don't," Dad says pointedly. That sure shuts Mom up. Mom purses her lips, and I feel the tension rising in the room. Mom busies herself straightening some magazines on the table next to her chair. I glance quickly at Rob, in time to see him shift uncomfortably in his seat.

I feel my phone buzzing in my back pocket, but ignore it. Zach is probably texting me. He got Rob arrested, I keep reminding myself. I'm just trying to save my brother. Still, I'm consumed with guilt. Zach trusted me and I betrayed him. And now he could go to jail because of me. What if he was *the one*?

I've always believed that there's a person out there for everyone, a soulmate, and that you and your soulmate will eventually find each other. Alex and I don't disagree about much, but Alex has a very different philosophy when it comes to love. Alex thinks there are many possible soulmates, and that the choices you make in life are like forking paths that will lead you to one of them. If Alex is right, then it's my own fault that I'm in this mess. I chose to let things happen with Zach, to accept, no, to invite his attention, even when I knew that he could be involved in the hit and run. But the ball had already been rolling at that point—I was smitten. How could I have turned my back on the possibility of love?

I think of Zach's Rube Goldberg drawings, and of how when you drop that one marble or push that one domino, it makes all the dominos tumble down, and then sets off a whole series of events along the dominos' path. I could have disrupted the whole chain reaction—could have stopped the whole runaway train in its tracks—but I didn't. Maybe, deep down, I thought Zach might be the one. But if he truly loved me, how could he put me in this impossible situation?

Just maybe—it will be Bryan going to jail. Maybe Zach will be just fine. I look at Rob, will him to look back at me. Somehow, he does.

"Are you sure it wasn't Bryan driving the car?" I can see immediately by his expression that I shouldn't have voiced the question.

"Haven't you listened to a word I've said?" he says between gritted teeth. "Your perfect little Zach isn't so perfect. HE was driving. HE hit Tyler Miller. HE refused to turn back. He probably just hooked up with you so that you would take his side—and look, it's working."

His words hit me like an unexpected slap. They *sting*. Sure, Zach basically admitted that he *accelerated* things. But to hear it the way my brother puts it...

"Rob, enough." Dad stands up, taking over. "This is not productive. Let's all take a little while to cool down, and we can sit together at the dinner table to discuss what happens next."

"Oh yeah, we can all sit down like a happy little family and have dinner together, what a great idea," Rob says as he gets up from the couch. He makes a quick exit before either of our parents can respond.

"Hannah, you want to talk?" my father asks gently.

"Can we talk later?" He nods.

"Sure, honey, go rest—we can talk later," Mom adds, regaining her composure. As I make my escape, I overhear yet another snippet of conversation that I wish I could unhear.

"Maybe I should call Paul and see whether this new information might get Rob off the hook?" Her mother's voice is tentative. "Well maybe not off the hook, exactly, but make him less the focal point...." Her voice trails off.

"Yeah, *sure honey*," Dad says, but when he says "honey" it doesn't sound affectionate at all. "Call Paul. Another great idea." As I slip into my room, I hear the door to the family room slam, and then hear my father's footsteps pounding up the stairs.

I lean against my closed door. I feel my breaths getting quicker and becoming more shallow. Once again, I can't seem to get enough air into my lungs. I also started to breathe a little quicker while I told Frankie about Zach, but I told myself that I just had to get it over with and get my story out and somehow managed to get my breathing back to normal.

I thought maybe Frankie hadn't noticed, but on her way out of the room she turned around and said, "You know, when I was in high school, I used to have panic attacks. I learned to stop them from coming by focusing on my breaths and counting. I'd inhale for five seconds and exhale for five seconds. It worked like a charm." She didn't put me on the spot, didn't wait for me to say anything. Just offered up the information, tapped on the doorframe and nodded goodbye.

I do that now: Inhale deeply—1, 2, 3, 4, 5—and exhale—1, 2, 3, 4, 5. I do it again. And again. And it works. My breathing slows. I think about Alex telling me to "Breathe 2, 3, 4," and how we used to crack up when she said it. But it isn't so funny now.

I make my way over to my beanbag and drop into it. My phone buzzes in my back pocket again. Against my better judgement, I reach my hand into my pocket, pull it out and look at the screen.

Three missed calls from Zach. Three texts.

*Hannah please answer*

*They're here*

*They're coming to arrest me*

# Chapter Fifty

I drop the phone. My hands are shaking. It's my fault. *I* had gotten Zach arrested. How can I text him back? How can I not?

I stare down at my trembling hands, not knowing what to do. He probably can't answer anyway. For all I know, he's already in jail. *Jail*! I stand up, not sure what to do with myself, then collapse onto my bed as tears well up in my eyes. I let them roll, unchecked, down the sides of my face.

Even if Zach is wrong—even if he's just being questioned again, not arrested—he's definitely at the police station by now. I can't risk calling him.

What would I say, anyway? Sorry, I told the police that it was you? *Oh my God. I basically accused my own boyfriend of being a murderer.* I'm a horrible person. I try to imagine Zach, scared, all alone at the police station. But instead, an image of Tyler Miller flashes into my mind.

It had been just an ordinary school day, a few years ago, when Rob and Zach and Tyler and me were all in middle school. The next period was about to start, and I realized I'd left my math notebook in my locker. I was balancing a bunch of textbooks and notebooks in one arm, while attempting to open the lock on my locker with the other, and as I yanked the lock open, I lost hold of my pile of books, and several of them thunked down onto the linoleum floor, scattering across the hallway.

As I turned around to retrieve them, I found myself looking into the dazzling blue eyes of Tyler, who had just scooped them up, and was handing them back to me. Flustered, and blushing—he was a ninth grader, after all, not to mention super popular and super hot—I mumbled a shy "Thanks" as he handed me the books. I remember noticing that his eyes held a trace of a smile as he backed up, gave me a thumbs up sign, and turned around, continuing down the hall.

Now he's dead. Not just a random person. *Him.* And it was probably Zach's fault. He or Rob maybe could have saved him. And because of their selfishness, he had to die alone. The thought of Tyler, lying on the ground by himself—after—makes my heart hurt.

Still, he's gone, I tell myself. But now I may have just ruined someone else's life too. Not just *someone*—Zach. The person I've been falling in love with. The irony of it all is that even though I did it to save Rob, my brother still sees me as a traitor. I believed Zach over Rob, and I doubt Rob will ever forget that.

I make myself get up. Stash my phone in my back pocket. I can't sit here thinking about all of this anymore—I'm making myself crazy. I need to find out what's going to happen next. I don't even know what the police told my father, told Rob. I open my bedroom door, walk quietly across the hall, and tap on my parents' door.

"Hey, honey," Dad says as he opens it.

"Hey, Dad." He studies my face for a minute, then motions for me to come inside. But he doesn't take his eyes off my face.

"What's up Han-Han?" he says gently. He sits down on the side of their bed, patting the blanket next to him. I sit down beside him.

"Dad, what's going to happen to Rob now?"

"Well," he says, taking a deep breath. "Frankie stayed behind at the police station to make sure they keep the case in juvenile court. You know, since Rob is a minor, the case should be heard by the juvenile court judge, but because someone, uh, died..." Dad gets quiet for a minute. "Because someone died—and because there's a lot of pressure on the police department to solve this—he could, technically, be tried as an adult."

My stomach drops. That means the same could happen to Zach. Dad must have noticed some change in my expression, because he quickly adds, "But that's not likely to happen. Frankie said it should stay in juvenile court." Of course he thinks I'm worried about Rob—which I am, of course. But like Zach said, we can afford to have Frankie. I don't even know if Zach has a lawyer. I don't share any of this with Dad. He won't understand that I still care about Zach. To my parents, Zach is now the enemy.

Dad sighs. I don't know what that would mean, technically, but I assume that a judge will be more lenient with a kid than with an adult.

"What we're really hoping, of course, is that Rob won't get tried at all—since he wasn't even driving..." Dad's voice trails off. I wonder if Dad is as sure of that fact as he tries to appear. Does he trust his children so implicitly that it wouldn't even cross his mind that his son could be lying?

"So, anyway," Dad continues, "then they will set a court date for the arraignment."

"The arraignment?"

"Yes, that's where they formally charge Rob and he enters his plea."

"Just Rob?"

"Well, I guess it depends if they arrest the others," Dad says.

"I think they did," I say quietly. Dad gives me a quizzical look, and then his expression changes, and his eyes narrow.

"Hannah, you're not still talking to Zach are you?" When I don't answer right away, he continues, his volume rising. "We're talking about the boy whose lies got your brother arrested! Your answer had better be no." His words are clipped. Angry. He never raises his voice at me. I can't bear to disappoint him. But I don't want to lie, either. My dad's been lied to enough. So I deflect the question.

"Well, he texted me a little while ago and said he was about to be arrested." My voice cracks when I say the word arrested. I start to cry and my father's expression softens. He hugs me to his side.

"You did the right thing, Hannah." His tone is no longer reproachful—it's reassuring. "Telling the truth is always the right thing."

Maybe, I think, as I remain safely within my father's embrace, letting my tears soak into the blue fabric of his button-down shirt. *But what if you don't actually know what the truth is?*

# Chapter Fifty-One

I search Tyler Miller's name on my phone, along with the word "arrest." Several articles come up. I click on the first.

*Woodfield, CT, October 28, 2018 – Three Woodfield teenagers have been arrested in connection with the hit-and-run accident that killed local football star Tyler Miller last month. Town police, who have been investigating the Woodfield High School junior's death since he was struck while jogging on Willet Road early on the morning of September 23rd, have declined to release the names of the suspects because they are all minors.*

The rest of the article is about Tyler. My heart hammers against my chest as I read all about what a promising athlete and upstanding human being he had been. I suddenly remember going with Ami to see her brother Darian, who has Downs Syndrome, compete in a Special Olympics Flag Football game. We were in seventh grade—so Tyler had just re-appeared on our radar—and I was surprised to see the swoon-worthy Woodfield Middle School football star running along the sidelines, cheering on one of Darian's teammates.

"Oh, he coaches one of the kids," Ami had told me, like it was no big deal. *Lucky kid*, I recall thinking at the time. The way Tyler ran onto the field and actually picked up the kid after he successfully grabbed one of the other team's flags, the way he was practically jumping up and down as he propped up the kid while the kid waved the flag wildly in the air and smiled widely—it stuck with me. The memory just makes me sad, so I push it away and continue reading. The article doesn't say anything about who was driving, or whether the boys were in jail or at home, in the custody of their parents. But it does state the date of the arraignment. October 31. Halloween. Less than a week away. *Great. The whole world knows when we will be at the court house.*

I know I'm not supposed to contact Zach. But I just have to make sure that he's home. That they've released him to his mother, just as my brother has been released to our parents. That he has a lawyer who can help him. It was an accident, after all, and no matter how angry I am at Zach for lying to me, I don't want his life to be ruined because he made a mistake.

I pull out my phone.

*Are you there?*

He doesn't answer.

Frankie stops in at the end of the day to fill us in. She says Zach's cousin was arrested around the same time as Zach. My heart thumps wildly when I think of what Bryan will do if he realizes that it's my fault he was arrested.

"Do we know what kind of charges Rob is facing?" Dad asks the lawyer.

"I'm not sure," Frankie says. "The police are being close-lipped about the investigation. They did finally find the cousin's car—" We all perk up.

"So that's good, right?" Mom interrupts.

"Well, not necessarily," Frankie says, slowly. "The car was parked in some municipal garage in Middlebury—which could be construed as tampering with evidence or at least interfering with an investigation." Dad glances at Rob, whose eyes remain glued on Frankie. "There was a dent in the fender, and..." She takes a deep breath. "They found a trace of material on the metal that matched the sweatshirt Tyler Miller had been wearing." No one makes a sound. The knot in my stomach tightens and I look at the others. Dad presses his lips together. Mom puts her fist against her mouth. Rob bows his head.

"Also, all three boys' fingerprints were on the steering wheel," she continues. My heart sinks. I'd hoped that once they found the car, there would finally be evidence in Rob's favor.

"But that's because I drove to the party," Rob says suddenly. "Because Bryan was already drinking. Not because I drove back..."

"And that will be part of our defense," Frankie reassures everyone. She explains that if they can somehow prove that Zach was behind the wheel, Rob—and Bryan—might just be charged with interfering with an officer or impeding an investigation. I'm afraid to ask Frankie what Zach would be charged with in that scenario. Murder?

I look up "charges for hit and run" on my laptop. *Evading responsibility.* That's the State's fancier way of saying leaving the scene of a crime that results in serious injury or death. When I see that Connecticut considers Evading Responsibility to be a felony, I slam my computer shut. And almost hyperventilate. I do the slow breathing thing that Frankie showed me. But it doesn't really help.

My phone buzzes in my hand, and my heart rate quickens as I switch over to the text screen, expecting to see a text from Zach. It's Alex.

*WOW. So you told the lawyer*

*Yes. But Alex, please please please YOU CAN'T TELL ANYONE*

*Hannah.*

*I know, I know. I feel so guilty. I don't want Zach to go to jail*

*I know you don't. But you don't want Rob to go to jail either*

*For all I know he will anyway. For interfering with an investigation...*

*I don't think so, Hannah. I've been doing some research on the internet. Since he's a minor, he could just get a fine. Or community service...*

For the first time in months, I feel a tiny bit of relief.

*Alex, I'm afraid to go to the court.* I haven't voiced that fear to anyone. But I dread seeing Bryan. I dread seeing Zach. I worry about reporters sticking microphones and cameras into my face.

*I wish I could come with you. But only the family of the accused and their lawyers can go in.* How does she know so much about this already? She's such a journalist.

*Do you think there will be a lot of reporters outside?*

*Wish I could say no but TBH, yeah, probably. I can come stand outside for moral support?*

*Yeah. That would be great.* It *would* be nice to see a friendly face in the crowd. Since I don't expect there to be many of those. I think about how I would feel if Rob and Zach weren't involved. Or worse, if it were Rob or Zach who had been hit instead of Tyler. I would *hate* the person who had caused that to happen. I would want them to pay for their mistake. For not turning back. And for the first time, I really let myself think about how Tyler's family must feel. How they must picture their son, their brother, struck by the car, dying, alone, by the side of the road. Because of Zach and Rob. How they would want them to pay for leaving their son there. How they might feel about someone who knew the truth about what happened to Tyler and kept quiet. The guilt sits in my stomach like lead. I feel sick.

*Gotta go Hannah-Ban. My mom's calling me for dinner. I'll text later.*

*K, bye*

*Bye*

I put my phone down, and drop my head into my hands. On top of everything, it occurs to me that my father would not be too happy that I'm texting with Alex about the case either.

"You can't talk to anybody outside the family about this," he had warned back when Rob first told them the truth. Or his version of the truth, anyway. Not only did I eventually tell Alex everything—and continue to text with Zach—I *saw* Zach. I even *kissed* him. I kissed the person who tried to put my brother in jail. The person who left someone to die in the street. *What kind of person am I? How could I want to be with someone like that? How could I betray my own family?*

But then I think about my mother. That's what real betrayal looks like. She lied to all of us. Broke her wedding vows. She could end up breaking up our whole family. I imagine our family splitting in two, my father and brother, on one team, and me and Mom, the two traitors, on another. I would deserve it.

According to Frankie, the courts rarely schedule an arraignment so soon after an arrest. But that it isn't surprising considering the media frenzy surrounding the hit and run and the investigation. It's once again become the top story on all the news stations.

Still, the next couple of days drag on. By Tuesday, I've bitten off all my nails, and have fallen completely behind on my school work. All I can think about is the arraignment. About having to walk through crowds of pushy reporters shouting questions at me and my family. About having to see Zach. And Bryan.

Alex texts me the same question every day—*Did you see the news today* —which doesn't help. And of course I have. My parents have it on 24 hours a day. On low volume, of course, so Rob won't hear. As if he isn't watching on his laptop, upstairs.

Hearing Zach and Rob mentioned on the news gives me a perpetual stomach ache. Seeing their school photos plastered up on the TV screen like mugshots makes me want to cry. Seeing Bryan's photo—with his buzz-cut hair and mean-looking eyes—makes my heart beat so uncontrollably that I think it will fly right out of my chest.

*I'm swearing off TV and social media,* I finally tell Alex the next time she asks if I've seen the news. She gets the hint. She stops asking.

# Chapter Fifty-Two

The scene outside the courthouse is worse than I expected. There are throngs of reporters speaking into microphones marked with the call letters of their TV stations and pointing toward the court building. Cameramen aiming their cameras first at these reporters, and then at me and my family as we emerge from the car that Frankie sent for us. Just our luck that the court date coincides with one of the high school faculty's "personal development" days, so students were dismissed at noon. It seems like practically the whole town is here.

As we walk toward the courthouse—the walk of shame—Rob, Mom, and I are sandwiched between Frankie and Dad, who lead us toward the courthouse steps with their inside arms and hold their outside arms up to block reporters from coming too close. I keep my head down, feel my face getting hot. I glance furtively to my sides and up ahead to see if I can spot Alex in the crowd. That's when I lock eyes with Tyler's little brother, the one I'd seen in the weeks after the accident at The Music Shoppe.

When he sees me, his eyes widen in recognition, and I feel like I've wronged him somehow. I follow the arm wrapped around his chest with my eyes and see Tyler's mother's face. And the hateful look in her eyes. Which are laser-focused on Rob.

My stomach flips—I feel like I might throw up. I quickly look back down at my feet. Concentrate on each step as we mount the seemingly endless staircase leading to the courthouse door. One step. Then another. Then another. There's so much noise, so many reporters shouting questions at my family. "Who was driving the car?" And "Rob, is there anything you'd like to say to Tyler's family?" I don't dare to look at my brother, but I feel for him in that moment, and impulsively grab his hand as we are squeezed together by the crowds. He doesn't pull it away.

# Chapter Fifty-Three

I cross and uncross my legs. I've picked out a pencil skirt, white blouse and black tights for today. It's just like TV. Almost. It's less of a formal court of law, and more of an auditorium-turned-courtroom. Still, the judge sits behind a high desk set up on a platform in the front of the room, facing the accused in her black robes and looking solemn and imposing. Will she have compassion for Rob and Zach? Or will all her compassion be reserved for Tyler's family? Everything rests in her hands. I only hope the case stays here, in juvenile court. We'll know soon.

There are four tables set up across the front row facing the judge. Rob and Frankie sit at the one directly in front of me and my parents. To the left is another table with Zach and an older man who I don't recognize. A lawyer. Thank God. I stare at Zach's back. Like Rob, he wears a navy blazer. It stretches tight across his back, as if he has almost outgrown it. His waves graze the top of his blue and white striped collar. I think of how I put my fingers in those waves when we kissed.

The thoughts I don't want to think come back: Did he really kiss me just to get me on his side? Was he that good at faking it? I watch his leg move up and down quickly beneath the table. It hurts my heart to watch it bouncing.

Bryan—it can only be Bryan—sits with his lawyer at a table to the left of Zach's. He has that buzz cut, like in his high school photo, and broad shoulders. Just seeing Bryan's back makes my heart pound. *You'll keep quiet....* I hadn't. And he knew it.

I look away and toward the right, where a woman and man sit huddled over a pile of documents at the table across the makeshift aisle. And then behind them, Tyler's family. His parents sit stiffly in their seats, the brothers between them. Kevin glares at Rob's back with such hatred that it makes my skin crawl.

I can literally feel the nervous energy emanating from my parents, who sit on either side of me. They keep glancing over at the town lawyers or prosecutors or district attorneys—whoever they are—with their documents, documents that probably spell out Rob and Zach's fates. They don't look at Tyler's family.

We wait for what feels like hours for things to start. Mom keeps rearranging her hands in her lap—wrapping one around the other then switching them around. What's it called? *Wringing your hands.* Frankie whispers something to Rob, and he nods his head slightly, slowly. Beads of sweat collect on the back of my brother's neck.

The thump of the judge's gavel startles me—my parents flinch too—as she calls for the courtroom's attention. The sound of wood on wood echoes against the walls of the large room, which—as Alex predicted—remains empty of spectators, aside from the lawyers, a couple of police officers who stand in front of the doors to the chamber, and the boys' families. I stare at the profile of the woman who is clearly Zach's mom. There's something familiar about the slope of her nose, something slightly heartbreaking about the way her eyes are trained on the back of her only son.

"We are going to begin the arraignment proceedings for the trials of State of Connecticut vs. Robert Greene, State of Connecticut vs. Zachary Kirkland, and State of Connecticut vs. Bryan Kirkland." Hearing Zach's surname attached to Bryan is disturbing. It reminds me of their familial bond and makes me again doubt whether I can trust anything Zach has said to me.

"The prosecutor will present the charges against each of these gentlemen. And then I will ask each of you to enter your plea." She turns toward the boys, lowering her head and looking at each of them over her thick black-rimmed glasses. "Understood?" They each nod, but almost imperceptibly, as if the tension-filled air makes the act of moving their heads almost too much effort to bear. Even Zach's cousin looks nervous. He keeps grabbing at the sides of his pants with his hands, like he doesn't know what to do with them. It makes me a little less afraid of him.

The woman at the table on the right stands. She reads from the typed sheet she holds before her. "The State of Connecticut charges Robert Greene, the driver of the car that struck and killed Tyler Miller, with one count of interfering with an officer, a misdemeanor, one felony count of negligent homicide, and one felony count of Evading Responsibility for leaving the scene of an accident that resulted in a death."

My mother lets out a loud sob, and then quickly presses her fist to her mouth to stifle it. I freeze. My father stiffens beside her. Rob's fingers grip the seat of his chair so tightly that it makes his knuckles white. *They believed Zach and Bryan.*

"Mr. Greene, please stand," the judge says. Frankie gently puts one hand on Rob's back, and the other on his left arm to help him stand. She leaves her hands where they are, as if she doesn't think he will be able to keep standing without her support. *Please don't let him fall.* "How do you plead? Admit or Deny?"

"Deny," Rob says. His voice wobbles as he speaks.

"Because of the serious nature of this crime, its tragic consequences, and the accused's failure to report the accident or to come forward during this investigation," the prosecutor continues, "the State of Connecticut recommends that this case be remanded to the judicial district court in Southbury, CT, and that Mr. Greene be tried as an adult."

Dad sits up stick straight and sucks in his breath. There's murmuring among the boys and their lawyers, and among the handful of family members in the seats behind them. My heart sinks like a stone. Rob turns to our parents with a panicked look, but Frankie quickly puts her arm on his, and draws his attention back toward her. She whispers what I imagine must be encouraging words. But what could she possibly say that could comfort him now?

Frankie stands. "I object," she says. "The defendant is a minor, with no previous record."

"Objection sustained," the judge says. "I will take this into consideration."

"H-h-how?" Mom whispers to Dad in horror. "How is this possible?" They lean over me, almost as if I'm not there, united—for once—in their despair. Dad puts his hand on Mom's knee, and she looks into his face. I catch the surprised expression on her face.

"I don't know," he says quietly. "I – I, let's see what they charge the others with. Frankie has a plan—" His unconvincing words of reassurance are cut off by the prosecutor, who continues reading from her script.

"The State of Connecticut charges Bryan Kirkland with interfering with an officer, a misdemeanor."

"Mr. Kirkland," the judge says. "Please stand." Hannah steals a glance at Bryan as he and his lawyer—a fat white-haired man in a shiny-looking grey suit jacket—stand. "How do you plead? Admit or Deny?"

"I deny," he says so quietly that I wonder how the judge can even hear him. He doesn't sound so tough now.

"Please speak up, Mr. Kirkland," the judge says, almost impatiently. "The court stenographer has to be able to hear your plea clearly." For the first time, I notice a woman with electric blue glasses and a matching skirt sitting off to the corner of the room, slightly in front of the judge. She sits with her fingers poised above the keys of her computer keyboard, waiting for someone to speak.

Bryan looks toward his lawyer, who gives him a nod. "I deny," he says more forcefully. The woman's fingers descend back onto the keys, and I can hear the faint click click click as they tap the keys rapidly, recording Bryan's words. Bryan glances nervously around the courtroom behind him as he lowers himself into his seat. His eyes narrow when they spot me. I look down quickly, and keep my eyes lowered, hoping my stillness will mask the quickening pace—and force—of my heartbeat.

"The State of Connecticut charges Zachary Kirkland with interfering with an officer, a misdemeanor," the prosecutor continues. What?! Interfering with an officer? That's it? I look up in surprise. In that moment, my compassion for Zach melts away and turns into anger. They are actually going to get away with teaming up against Rob. Rob faces possible adult felony charges —and prison—because Zach figured he could afford a lawyer who could get him off? How many years does "adult" and "felony" translate into? How could I have trusted Zach? How could I have loved him?

I don't even notice the tears welling up in my eyes, even when they drop over the ledge of my bottom lid and roll down my cheeks. This is my fault. I should have come forward sooner. I shouldn't have warned Zach, given him time to concoct this plan with his cousin.

I glance over at him then, and the sight of him exchanging glances with his cousin fuels my anger and fills me with regret.

It's over between us. I know that now, yet my anger is mingled with grief. Zach turns around and catches my eye. When he sees me his face turns red and he lowers his eyes. He looks ashamed. Is he ashamed? It doesn't matter anymore. But I hope so.

I listen as Bryan, and then Zach, plead not guilty. It's all such a show. Of course they're guilty. They're all guilty, even my brother. And the judge and the prosecutors and the boys and their families all know it. But it's a game, and we're all playing along. I don't blame Tyler's family for wanting Rob and his friends to pay for what they did. I feel bad that they have to witness this. Not guilty? It was an accident, yes. But it was not an accident that they left the Miller's son lying there by the road, dying, alone. And didn't even bother to call an ambulance.

I force myself to pay attention to the judge, to get out of my head. It isn't a place I want to linger—especially today. "The defendants are all 17 years old," the judge is saying. I notice that my parents' hands, each of which had been resting on one of my legs in a reassuring kind of way, are now clasped together tightly across my lap as they listen to the judge decide their child's fate. I try not to read too much into it, but it makes me hopeful.

"Therefore, I am going to keep this case in the juvenile court," the judge says. Mom, Dad and I let out a collective breath. I feel Dad squeeze Mom's hand. *Thank you, thank you.*

"Thank God," Dad says quietly. The state's lawyers mumble to one another. They do not look happy.

"This is good," I hear Frankie whisper to Rob, "this is good." Rob nods slightly, but otherwise keeps his body unnaturally still. He doesn't take his eyes off the judge. His whole future rests in this woman's hands. "We will reconvene one week from today, on November 7th, for the hearing," she continues. "Court dismissed."

And just like that, it's over. It's back to waiting. The unbearable waiting. But at least the case is staying in juvenile court. That's a good thing, I reassure myself, echoing Frankie. Not just for Rob, but for Zach too. Not that I care about what happens to Zach.

Then suddenly, everyone's standing—even me, though I can't even remember getting to my feet. My parents hug Rob—Mom with tears in her eyes—and Frankie is ushering us all toward the aisle.

There's no sneaking out the back door of the court house: There's only one way out. Through the front door. And into the masses: masses of hostile townspeople, reporters and our classmates, all hungry for drama, and a few of them, for revenge.

"This is good," Frankie repeats to them in a low voice as they move toward the aisle. "Keeping this in the juvenile court system is the right thing. Let's just get out of here, and keep our heads down, and get to the car. You don't need to answer any questions, just keep walking." She quietly imparts her instructions as she leads us toward the door.

But as we arrive at the door there's a bit of a traffic jam—everyone trying to get out at the same time. I notice Rob turning his head, and I turn mine to see where he's looking. And there's Zach. Right behind us. Wearing a pained expression, not a victorious one. His face reddens and he looks down. That's right, I think. You shouldn't be able to look either of us in the eye.

Rob scowls at him and turns back toward the door. I turn too—I don't want to see Bryan, or God forbid, catch his eye. But as Zach—and his mother and his lawyer—move around us, Zach's arm brushes against mine and a jolt of electricity passes through my skin.

"I'm sorry," he whispers, so quietly that I'm not even sure he has said it. I don't dare to look at him again, not with all these people around, not with my parents or Rob or Frankie within sight. But I hide his apology away in my brain to be examined later, in the privacy of my bedroom. A tiny gift—too late, but still precious. Later, when I have time to think about today, I will replay his "I'm sorry" over and over in my mind, will imagine it floating from his lips and landing on my ears like a gentle caress. But for now, I have to get through the crowds.

Police escorts lead the way through the double doors out of the juvenile court house, and then join other officers just outside in creating a narrow passageway for us all to walk through. Still, reporters and cameramen press in on us, seemingly disembodied cameras and microphones lining the passageway—I barely notice the faces behind them. Just the microphones and the cameras, cameras turned on Rob, poor Rob, who keeps his head down to the ground as if he is wearing blinders.

"Rob, how do you feel?"

"Rob, do you think it's fair that you are not being tried as an adult?"

"Rob, do you have anything to say to Tyler's family?"

"No comment, no comment, no comment," Frankie says to one reporter after the other, as she leads us through all the people. I try to keep my head down, but can't help scanning the crowd. Caitlin's here, of course—she and her friends whisper to one another while looking at me with contempt. I realize I'm looking for Alex, the one person who I know is on my side, my family's side. And there she is, as promised, squeezed between the reporters on the frontlines of the crowd, trying to catch my eye. As soon as she does, she puts her hands on her heart and I feel like crying. But then my eyes land on a less friendly face. The face of Tyler's brother Kevin. He has come out of the courthouse ahead of my family and waits for us to pass.

"I hope you rot in prison," he hisses at Rob. Shivers run down my spine as I realize that Rob is somehow no longer flanked by our parents and Frankie—Frankie's slightly ahead of us, and our parents slightly behind. Rob seems so...vulnerable. I move to the other side of Rob, blocking him from Kevin's view, link my arm in his, and pull him slightly back so that we're in line with our parents. We walk together as a family until we're safely tucked back inside the car.

# Chapter Fifty-Four

"Who was there? What were people saying?" I lie on my bed, my head propped up by two pillows, my phone pressed against my ear. I couldn't bring myself to watch the news reports about the case when I got home, though I was so, so tempted. I knew it would only make me more freaked out than I already was. Still, when Alex calls, I can't resist barraging her with questions.

"You really want to know?" Alex asks.

"I don't know. Yes."

"First of all, they weren't just blaming Rob," she starts, trying to ease the blow in advance, I suspect. "They thought all three of them should pay for what they did to Tyler."

I feel nauseous. I know it's like picking at an already-inflamed wound, but I need to know more. "Who was saying it?"

"Well, Caitlin, of course. And her faithful little kiss-ass friends—you know, Brynn, Marissa, Sam H. They were all agreeing with her." Alex pauses for a minute and I brace myself for whatever is coming next.

"And....."

"And the football guys were saying stuff like 'I'd like to kick their asses' and 'They'd better hope they end up in jail.'" This makes me sit up. "That was Chris Johnson," Alex adds. I picture Chris, tall, broad-shouldered and, well, big. He's a senior. Is actually a year older than most of the seniors. Easily twice the size of Rob or Zach.

"Oh my God, Alex, do you think they'll try to beat up Rob and Zach?"

"I shouldn't have told you that," Alex says. "And anyway, you shouldn't care what happens to traitor-boy." That's Alex's new nickname for Zach. Sometimes it annoys me, but sometimes it gives me a strange satisfaction. Now, I just shiver.

"I don't know how I'm going to get through this next week."

"I know...I take it I'm not going to see you at school?"

"Uh—no. Actually...my mom is going to talk to Dr. Finnely about Rob and me finishing the semester at home."

"Oh, do they have a policy about that?"

"I don't know that they actually have a policy about what to do when one of their students is accused of *killing* another student—Oh God..." It sounds even worse when I say the words out loud.

"Hannah."

"Alex," I whisper. "This is what we're talking about, though. Seriously. This is. Just...." I let out a heavy sigh.

"I know. But I'm going to really miss you if you don't come back to school." She pauses, and then quickly adds. "But I totally get it." She's a good friend.

Neither of us says anything for a few moments. Then Alex says, "Hannah, you never know. Maybe some more evidence will come from the car..."

"Yeah, but remember, all of their fingerprints were on the steering wheel..."

"I know, but maybe if they continue to question people they will find someone who saw them leaving the party, who could testify that Rob wasn't driving."

I know Alex is just grasping now, but appreciate that she's trying to find something for me to hang my hopes on. "We'll see," I say. But I'm not optimistic.

"Maybe they're checking traffic cams that we don't even know about as we speak," Alex adds. She sighs. Even she knows how unlikely that is.

"Well," I say, trying to find a bright side. "At least it's staying in juvenile court."

"Yeah, but..." Alex starts. I don't like her tone.

"But what?" I ask cautiously, not really sure if I want to hear the rest of her sentence.

"Well, I did some research."

*Of course you did.* My heart speeds up. I'm starting to think twice about encouraging Alex to turn her reporter's lens on my family.

"And even when someone is convicted of a felony in juvenile court, there is still a chance of a lot of years in jail." Alex pauses for a minute and then changes course. "But of course, there are also a shit ton of cases where teenagers just get community service," she adds quickly.

I try to get my mind off the "a lot of years in jail" part. When I don't say anything, Alex continues talking, fast, her words forming nervous run-on sentences. She often does this when she regrets something she has said and wants to fill the ensuing silence with something else. I would be annoyed if I wasn't so freaked out by the thought of Rob spending the rest of his teenage years in jail.

"I mean, more of the cases ended in community service and I'm sure that's what will happen in this case too. It's just that I can't believe they fell for their lies, the police I mean—of course Zach and his cousin would back each other up—but how can the police not see through that? It's so obvious! It's completely unfair."

"Exactly." This is what I keep coming back to. How is this proof beyond a reasonable doubt? How could they just take Zach and Bryan's word over Rob's? Or is there evidence against Rob that we don't know about? Could Zach actually be telling the truth? My brain hurts.

"I've gotta go."

"K. I'm sorry. I shouldn't have said that about the jail."

"It's okay," I say, though the hitch in my voice as I say it reveals that it really wasn't.

"Oh." Alex says, and then is quiet for a minute. "But Hannah?"

"Yeah?"

"It's not over till it's over."

"Yeah, I know. Bye Lex."

"Bye Han."

I stare at the phone in my lap. I'm so sad. And regretful. Anxious. Overwhelmed. So many thoughts and feelings, questions and doubts, bounce around in my head that I feel like I might explode. And though I know I have Alex, and am so thankful for that, the person I really want to talk to—well, I can't.

I think again of Zach's "I'm sorry," the sound of his voice brushing my ear as we exited the court house. His remorseful expression when he caught Rob's eye—and then mine.

"I'm sorry." They're just words. His actions speak so much louder.

I think of my own words and actions, the "I'm sorry" that I'd thrown Rob's way. My own actions meanwhile—continuing to be with Zach, continuing to believe him over my own brother—showed Rob where my allegiances really lay. Just as my mother's actions revealed her true allegiances. Both of us have risked our family's well-being for some ephemeral pleasure, for some fleeting moments of happiness.

And though I've carried the weight of the boys' secret for far too long—and worried endlessly over the implications of what I'd overheard—I *had* been happy. So happy. The way Zach used to look at me. Nobody had ever looked at me that way.

We were sitting on the front porch one afternoon—only about a month ago, I realize, though it seems now like so much longer—and I was playing something for him on my guitar. I glanced up between strums and was astonished to see the expression on Zach's face as he watched me.

It was a look of… admiration. No, more than that. Devotion. I know that Alex is devoted to me, and my parents. But this was different. It was like devotion mingled with a kind of awe— I recognized it because it was the way I felt when I looked at him sometimes. With awe that—wow—I can't believe this person wants *me*, that *I* am the object of this person's attention, that *I am his person*. That's the way he was looking at me in that moment. And when I think about that look, I can't help wondering: Could Zach have been telling the truth when he said that though it all started out as a plan to get me on his side, he really ended up falling in love with me?

I sigh, a deep, surrendering kind of sigh. With that breath, I release any hopes and expectations for what a future with Zach might have looked like. That chapter of my life is over. Where my story will go from here is a scary unknown. Who knows when I will ever have a person again? I don't even want any other person. I just want my family to be a family again. My parents to stay together. My brother not to go to jail.

# Chapter Fifty-Five

On my way downstairs for dinner, I hear Mom whispering. I pause mid-step. Dad's voice, also low. I move slowly, soundlessly, down the stairs, stopping at the second-to-bottom step, where I know I'm still out of the sightline from the kitchen. I cock my ear in the direction of the kitchen doorway.

"Do you think he's getting back at me?" Mom whispers to Dad. Her voice is wobbly, as if she's been crying. "Maybe I should have waited to end things." She already ended things? With Officer Scarelli? When? And why in the world would she end things with him *before* the trial?

"What do you want me to say here, Julie?"

"I don't know. I just don't want—"

"Look, I'm no fan of his, you know that, but I would hope that even *he* wouldn't sink that low. Anyway, he's not the only officer on this case, and ultimately, it's the judge who will decide, not him..."

I miss the rest of his sentence, because I try to lean slightly further forward, in the hopes of hearing better, but lose my footing and stumble down the last step. My parents abruptly stop talking.

"Hannah?" Dad calls, coming to the doorway.

"Hey," I say, righting myself.

"How're you holding up, honey?"

"Fine."

Before I can formulate my next sentence, he puts his hand on my arm and says, "I'm going to check in on Rob—I'll be right back down for dinner." I nod, and make my way into the kitchen. Mom's putting a rectangular glass container filled with some kind of frozen leftover into the microwave with one hand, and swiping at her eyes with the back of the other.

"Mom, can I ask you something?"

"Sure, Hannah." She closes the microwave and comes toward me so that we're facing one another across the kitchen island. I hope I'd been a better actor with Dad than my mother is being with me. She gives me a calm, fake smile, but her red eyes give her away.

"Did you end things with Officer Scarelli?"

"You heard us talking."

"Mom, why would you end things now, right in the middle of the case?" I can't help wondering if Officer Scarelli had anything to do with the department's decision to pin all the blame on Rob, or the DA's decision to try him as an adult. Mom looks down at the countertop and fidgets with the edge of the granite.

"Because, Hannah, I should have ended things a long time ago." And then more quietly: "I never should have started." She looks up at me. "Because no matter what, family comes first." I feel a stab of guilt. Still, there's so much more I want to ask my mom. Before I can respond, I hear Dad's heavy footsteps on the stairs.

"Why don't you sit down, Hannah?" Mom says. Dad enters the kitchen just as the microwave beeps. *Saved by the bell.*

"Rob's not hungry," he says, taking his seat at the table. *Big surprise there.*

"I'll bring him something after," Mom says. I sit down and Felix, who's been sleeping under the table but has been brought back to consciousness by the aroma of tomatoes, beef and melted mozzarella, stations himself on the floor beside my chair.

*Family comes first.* I know I will think about my mother's words again and again over the next week—and will be consumed by guilt every time. But for now, I have to get through this dinner.

The quiet at the table is only interrupted by the distant sounds of children's voices—it is Halloween, after all—and Felix barking in response. He sporadically jumps up from his usual place under the table to run to the door and yap at people passing on the street. Or news vans that pull up in front of our house, only to be waved away by the patrolman parked in our driveway. We've kept the front lights off to discourage trick-or-treaters from ringing the bell. The patrol car reinforces the message.

I wonder if my friends have dressed up, if they are gathering at one of their houses like we usually do on Halloween. If they're going to make the rounds later in the evening when houses are eager to get rid of their leftover candy. I wonder if they're talking about me and Rob and the case. And what they're saying.

Nobody at the table is saying anything. Silverware clinks against dishes. The refrigerator hums in the background. Every now and then, someone audibly sighs.

Mom interrupts the awkward silence at one point to wonder aloud whether Frankie will try to plea bargain before the hearing.

"No way should he confess to something he didn't do," Dad says firmly. "A plea bargain would be as good as an admission that he was the one driving."

"You're right," Mom says, nodding her head. I can't help but agree. Why should Rob agree to a worse punishment than Zach or Bryan, especially when he was the one who wanted to turn back? When he was just along for the ride? There has to be some kind of proof. There just has to be. How could they just take Zach and Bryan's word for it?

"What makes them so sure that Rob was the one driving, anyway?" Mom adds. So I haven't been the only one wondering about that. Still, I'm surprised Mom voices the question. Because that question inevitably leads to another: Could Rob possibly be lying? Even to them?

Dad shakes his head. "I don't know, I don't get it. I would think anything the other boys say would be considered hearsay. They have as much to lose as Rob..." I feel a twinge of guilt. More than a twinge. I should never have warned Zach.

"Frankie will tell us what's best," Dad concludes. I eat my lasagna as if on auto-pilot, putting fork into pasta, pasta into mouth. Chewing, swallowing. I study my parents. How they speak to one another, how they look at each other.

"Maybe she'll even find some evidence to exonerate Rob," I add. My weak attempt at trying to ease the tension at the table.

"Maybe," Mom and Dad answer at the same time. But neither of them sound convinced. Meanwhile, Rob's empty seat at the table is a constant reminder of what's at stake.

# Chapter Fifty-Six

The days between the arraignment and the hearing move slowly. So slowly. I try to fill the time with homework and catching up on reading for my classes—I'm so behind. But I can't focus. I start reading a chapter and find myself back outside the courthouse, surrounded by reporters and hostile faces and angry voices. I'm sure the hearing will be more of the same.

Often, my mind drifts to Zach. Does he feel guilty? Not just for what he did to Rob. But for what he did to Tyler. He'd *killed* someone. That has to weigh on a person. Does he feel guilty for the pain he caused Tyler's family? Does he feel guilt for pushing the blame onto his best friend—or rather, *former* best friend? Who could end up in jail because of him?

Does he feel guilty for hooking up with me under false pretenses? Just to gain an ally? Was his cousin in on that plan too?

It makes me feel so naive, so stupid, that I fell for it, that I'd thought he was just attracted to me. But confused too, because how could he have faked it so convincingly? There *was* chemistry there, I know there was. But no. I promised myself I would no longer go there. Instead, I will focus on helping Rob. However I can. After all, it's my fault that Zach and Bryan had time to conspire, to plot, to pin everything on my brother.

Frankie agrees that before we consider a plea bargain, she needs to see what evidence the town has against Rob. Do some more investigating with her team. Make sure no stone has gone unturned in terms of getting at the truth of who'd been driving. She drills Rob and me on the names of all the people who might have been at that party, the names of all Rob and Zach's friends. I feel bad naming names, possibly subjecting people we know to questioning. Giving them more reason to gossip. But I double-check with Alex on the sly to make sure I'm not leaving anyone out.

Rob remains adamant that he will not admit to something he didn't do. Which I have to give him credit for. So we just *have* to find more evidence.

"Why can't they take lie detector tests?" I ask during one of our meetings with Frankie. Frankie's worried about the pot. There's no way for the police to prove that the boys had been smoking after all this time—and, more significantly, that one of them had been driving under the influence when they struck and killed Tyler. But what if they're asked that question while hooked up to the lie detector machine? It's too risky. I try not to consider whether they deserve to pay for their recklessness.

So Frankie does her investigating, Rob remains holed up in his room, and I try to work. Check in with Alex daily, in case there's any gossip that might help Rob's case. And continue to watch Mom and Dad.

Our parents have never been ones for PDA—but they used to laugh a lot together, tease one another. Clearly, nobody is laughing now. And it isn't a teasing time. But it seems to me that they are being extra polite around each other. They're no longer snapping at each other, or making sarcastic comments, or giving each other dirty looks. So that's something.

One night, as I'm heading to my room after dinner, I peek inside my mother's office. There are no longer blankets and pillows stacked neatly on the chaise.

Rob and I will finish up the semester at home. I never thought I'd end up being a homeschooled kid, but the school agreed it would be too disruptive for us to continue attending. The crowds of reporters that initially camped outside our house has dwindled to just a few hangers-on. Still, we stay inside. All of us.

Dad's working remotely until the hearing and has set up a makeshift office in the basement, where an old computer desk lives. Mom is meeting with most of her clients via video calls. When I'm in the hallway, I can hear my mother enunciating words, and then her young students trying to echo them back to her. Most of these are kids from other towns. Mom lost many of her local clients, though a handful, she tells me, are more understanding. "They know that what our family is going through is painful too," she says.

Aside from the voices coming out of Mom's office, the house is eerily quiet for most of the day. At night, Mom concocts meals out of whatever we have in the pantry or freezer—pasta, rice and beans, frozen leftover pizza. Nobody really feels like eating anyway.

The week drags on. How can Rob bear it? He meets with Frankie and she practices questioning him. He won't have to testify against himself, she says, but in case she feels it necessary, in the end, to put him on the stand, she wants him to be prepared. She wanted to practice with me too, but I begged Frankie—and my parents—not to make me testify. Not to make me get up in front of everyone, including Zach and Bryan, and say things that could end up landing one of them to jail.

My parents got mad at first.

"You need to do this for your brother," Mom whispered furiously in my ear so that Rob wouldn't hear.

"I hope you're not still trying to protect that boy," Dad added quietly. It annoyed me that he referred to Zach as *that boy*, as if he hadn't been hanging out in our basement for most of his life. "Your brother's future is at stake."

But Frankie said that a defendant's family member is rarely considered a reliable witness, anyway, so they backed off. Privately, Frankie tells me to think about it. Just in case.

Night after night, I sit on my bed and stare at the wall dividing my room from my brother's, wondering what Rob is doing on the other side. He's barely left his bedroom since the arraignment. Hasn't even come to the table for meals.

Mom has gotten into the habit of bringing a tray of food upstairs when the three of us finish a meal. She stays in Rob's room for a while, keeping him company while he eats. Maybe this is her way of apologizing to him, of bridging the distance he'd created between them since he saw her kissing *that man,* of trying to undo the damage she has already done to our family.

I know that I too, owe Rob an apology.

I knock on his door one afternoon when I know our parents are both on work calls.

"Yeah," he answers. His voice sounds flat. It worries me.

I open the door and slide inside, closing the door behind me. He's just sitting there, on his bed. Hasn't even bothered to turn on the light.

"Rob....I'm sorry." I look down at his carpet. "I should have believed you right from the beginning. I was stupid to believe anything Zach told me. You're right—he was just using me." He doesn't say anything at first, so I look up to make sure he's listening.

Rob shrugs. It doesn't really matter anymore, his gesture says. The damage is done. But what comes out of his mouth next is completely unexpected.

"He wasn't just using you. I know Zach. He really liked you. It was annoying." But he says it in a way that's like he's giving me a gift. It's the nicest thing he has ever said to me. I glance up at the carefully-arranged video game boxes and the long-forgotten Lego structures that fill the shelves behind Rob's bed, and think about how he and Zach used to spend hours huddled together on his shaggy blue carpet, piecing together those colorful plastic squares and rectangles. It makes my heart heavy.

I lean my back against the door and regard my brother. "I'm going to testify against him," I hear myself say. Rob looks surprised.

"You are?"

I take a deep breath, to steady my quickening heartbeat. "He initially told me that Bryan was driving. He changed his story. I think the police, the jury, the judge—whoever needs to know this—should know this."

"Hannah, you're my sister. They'll just think you're trying to protect me."

"Well, then, they'll be right."

# Chapter Fifty-Seven

Frankie and I practice for the hearing.

"Did Zachary Kirkland come home with your brother after school on September 24th, the day after the accident?" Frankie asks me.

"Yes," I say, answering the question simply, without elaborating, like Frankie has taught me.

"Did you hear them talking?"

"Yes."

"How did you hear them? Where were you, and where were they?"

"I was in my room, and they were in Rob's room. The two rooms share a wall."

"What did you hear?"

Even though we're alone, just practicing, responding to this question puts me on edge. I kept what I'd heard a secret for so long, that repeating the boys' words out loud—or at least what I'd heard of them—feels wrong, and I stumble on my words.

"This is why we have to practice," Frankie reminds me.

Frankie also repeatedly asks me to try to recall—and recount—exactly what Zach told me about that night. And each time I do, I feel like I'm betraying him all over again. I have to keep reminding myself that *he* betrayed *me.* Not to mention Rob.

Still, I'm petrified to take the stand. Am dreading the idea of spilling his confidences in public, in front of our families and the lawyers and the judge. In front of the court stenographer, who will type out what he told me in private, word for word, to be preserved forever in the public court records.

"Did you find any new evidence?" I ask Frankie over and over. "Anything to prove that Rob is telling the truth?" Most days, Frankie shakes her head.

"But I'm not done trying," she always adds.

"There are no traffic cameras that could show that Rob wasn't driving?" I ask, hopefully, even though I already know the answer.

Frankie shakes her head. "I've heard they've collected some more photos from Ring cameras on people's houses that place the car near the accident scene at the right time," she says. I tense. "But the photos are all too blurry to identify the people inside." I drop my head down on the table.

"I don't think they have enough evidence to pin the felony charges on him," Frankie reassures me. But it doesn't make me feel any better.

The problem, I know, is that Bryan let Rob drive his car *to* the party. This is tricky, Frankie says, because even if people at the party only saw Rob drive into the party and not out, they might just remember it as: Rob was driving that night. Which explains why Rob's fingerprints were on the steering wheel. *But why were Zach's?*

"People were trashed by the time we got there," Rob admits during one of the many family discussions on this topic, causing Frankie to sigh and Dad to shake his head. Frankie also suspects that the police aren't sharing everything they know—I overhear Frankie telling my parents that.

"It's highly unusual," Frankie told them. The police *have* given her a short list of witnesses they are planning to call, kids who'd been at the party, kids who might claim on the stand that they'd seen Rob behind the wheel. I also hear Frankie tell my parents that my testimony might just be my brother's only hope. I'm terrified.

The night before the hearing, I sit at the dinner table with Mom and Dad—Rob's seat empty, as it has been all week. The dread that is now lodged in the pit of my stomach makes it impossible for me to eat. I push around the food on my plate with my fork, pretending every now and again to put it to my mouth and take a bite. When my parents look down at their plates, I slip my fork under the table and feed my food to Felix.

I listen to my parents' silverware tapping against their plates, watch them force themselves to eat. I wish someone would say something, but what is there to say? By this time tomorrow, the judge may have already made her decision. Between now and then, I will have to get up before the court and condemn Zach—or perhaps Bryan?—in front of everyone. Including Zach and Bryan. And what I say could determine Rob's fate.

After dinner, I retreat to my room. A few minutes later, I hear my parents' footsteps on the stairs. I hear them pause in front of Rob's room. Then the light knock, the door opening, even though I don't hear my brother answer, the soft murmur of voices on the other side of my bedroom wall.

I stand to the side of the window, so that I can't be seen by anyone outside. Without touching the closed blinds, I peer through the crack on the side, where the window covering almost meets the wall—but not quite—and try to angle my glance down toward the reporters who, as of this morning, have once again planted themselves on our front lawn.

Some of them are actually broadcasting from the front of our house—telling the world, I imagine, that my brother will be tried tomorrow for committing a felony, telling the world that my brother was responsible for killing Tyler Miller, football prodigy, local hero, would-be NCAA star. *Now the haters know where we live.*

I'm jarred from my thoughts when I recognize Frankie's charcoal gray Prius pulling up the driveway. The reporters are drawn to her car like metal filings to a magnet. They crowd around her door as she emerges. I'm confused—I thought Frankie wasn't coming back until the following morning. She said she would give us some family time tonight, that she would come back bright and early in the morning to go over everything one last time.

Maybe she knows something.

I go immediately to my bedroom door, turn the knob quietly, and tiptoe quickly to the steps. I jet down the stairs and then peer out the peephole in the front door. I wait until right before Frankie's finger reaches the doorbell, and open the door just widely enough to let her in.

"Hi Hannah," Frankie says breathlessly. "Where are your parents?"

"Is everything okay?"

"Yes, more than okay." My eyes widen. *More than okay?* "I assume they're here?"

"Upstairs with Rob. I can get them."

"Okay, please." Frankie holds a yellow manila envelope in her hands.

"MOM, DAD, ROB," I shout as I take the stairs two at a time. "Frankie's here!" Rob's door opens, and Dad, then Mom, and then Rob emerge, one at a time, all with quizzical looks on their faces. Rob's face is red and his eyes are swollen. I look away, so he won't see me notice that he's been crying.

We all join Frankie in the foyer, though Rob remains standing on the bottom step, his hand gripping the railing like a vise. We all look expectantly at the lawyer.

"Zach confessed!" she announces.

"What?" Rob says, as if he is in shock.

"What?" we all echo. Nobody moves.

"Apparently," she says, "he drove himself over to the police station and told them everything. That he had been the one driving. That Rob had wanted to go back, and that he talked him out of it."

My mouth hangs open. He confessed? I won't have to testify? Does this mean Rob won't have to go to jail? I turn to gauge my family's reaction and am shocked to see Dad hugging Mom. My eyes move quickly to Rob. He's sitting, dumfounded, on the bottom step.

Dad sits down on the step and puts his arm around Rob. Mom, teary-eyed, just clutches her hands together and beams at Rob.

"Should we sit?" Frankie asks. "I'll tell you everything I know."

We file into the family room, and sit—collapse, really—onto the couch and chairs. The hearing is cancelled, she tells us. They will have a meeting to discuss a plea bargaining deal. Rob and Bryan will probably still get community service, she explains—"They did leave the scene and withhold information about a crime," she reminds us. *As if we need reminding.* "And removed the car, which was evidence...." Still, she says, she's fairly confident that she can negotiate a deal so that it will not go on Rob's record.

After Frankie tells us what she knows about Zach's confession, she suggests we regroup in the morning. Once she has a chance to speak with the other lawyers. They can discuss the possible terms of a plea bargain deal then.

"Meanwhile," she says, standing up from the couch and straightening the wrinkles out of her pants, "I'm going to make a brief statement to the press—just let them know that the felony charges against Rob have been dropped. That Zach has confessed."

I watch out one side of the blinds, while my parents and Rob peer out the other, as Frankie stands in front of the reporters and makes her announcement. There's a burst of sound as more than a dozen reporters shout out questions at the same time. Rob sinks down in a chair next to the window and lets out a long-held breath.

As I plug in my phone before bed that night, I notice that there's a text. It's from Zach.

*I did it for you.*

# Epilogue

I fiddle with my guitar. I move my fingers around on the frets, experimenting with different chord progressions. *C7, Am7, Dm7, G7.* This is one of the basic jazz cadences, according to Matt, my new guitar teacher. All I have to do is play the chords in a cycle of ascending diatonic fourths, he says, to achieve that jazzy tone.

I love the way jazz sounds on the guitar; love making up different chord combinations, thinking up different ways to riff on the same chord using the pick. Eric connected me with Matt when we moved to Guilford. The two studied at The Hartt School together. Eric would be impressed—and probably surprised—to see how far I've come in the past few months. So would Zach.

I put down my guitar and reach under the cushion of my window seat—my favorite spot in our new house. I glance at my bedroom door to make sure it's closed before drawing out the unopened envelope. It's slightly wrinkled from being pulled out and put back so many times. I smooth the crinkles with my fingers. Stare at my name, written in small block letters on the face of the envelope in Zach's handwriting.

Frankie gave me the letter privately, when she stopped by to check in on us a couple of months after we moved. She had business in a neighboring town, she said when I answered the door.

"Zach asked his lawyer to give it to me," Frankie whispered as she slipped me the letter. I tucked it between the pages of my music book before calling my parents from their offices. I assumed it was an apology of sorts. But couldn't bring myself to read it. I haven't told anyone about it. Not even Alex. Figured I'd revisit it when more time had passed. When it was less painful to think about Zach. But every time I think about reading it, I change my mind. What's the point? I slide it back under the cushion.

Zach didn't end up having to go to jail—instead he was put on probation. The papers said they'd gone a bit easier on him because he'd confessed. And because he was a minor. His license was taken away, according to the articles, and he was only allowed to leave his house to do his community service and to go to school. But he hadn't gone back to school, according to Alex. I didn't blame him.

My family moved to the Connecticut Shoreline to give both me and Rob a fresh start. Mom and Dad too. Dad's company has an office in New Haven, which isn't too far. Mom managed to get a job with a local school district. Rob is volunteering in New London, tutoring kids in computer science. He still has about two months more before he completes his six months of community service, but has started to help out with the high school's e-sports team, and is considering staying on for the rest of the year. I think it gives him a sense of purpose. Or maybe he just likes passing on his gaming knowledge to the kids.

Our parents separated for a few weeks about a month into our move. The case was behind them, so I guess they no longer had that to force them together, and I think the reality of Mom's betrayal finally sunk in for Dad. But the separation was short-lived, thankfully, and they are back together. It isn't exactly what it used to be, but as Mom tells me, small steps.

I'm getting used to our new school, and there's a neighbor my age who seems nice. But I don't really have any friends yet. I talked to Alex multiple times a day when we first moved four months ago. Now we just text a few times a week. I spend a lot of time alone with my guitar.

Most afternoons, I grab my instrument, settle into my little window nook, and play. I like the feeling of the sun on my back, the way the mahogany on the lower bout of the guitar catches the light that comes in through the window. Rob has been going with our parents to visit colleges, and sometimes I go too. I'm thinking I might want to study music theory. For now, though, I just have to get through physics and algebra.

In physics, we're learning about chaos theory and the butterfly effect. The butterfly effect, Mr. Meyers tells us, describes how small things could have "non-linear impacts on entire systems." He shows us a scene from the movie *Jurassic Park* in which Jeff Goldblum's character explains chaos theory to Laura Dern's character. He explains how a butterfly can flap its wings on one side of the world, and cause something to happen – like a change in weather – on the other side of the world.

Reading about the butterfly effect makes me think about Zach's Rube Goldbergs. I think about how the accident was like the flapping of a butterfly wing, or the first drop of a marble in one of Zach's intricate machines. How it set so many things into motion.

But really, I think, it's like there were multiple Rube Goldbergs, all interacting with one another. Each thing that happened set off a series of other things that happened. What if I had never run into Zach at The Music Shoppe? Maybe that whole relationship would not have happened, maybe Zach would never have confessed, and maybe Rob would be in jail. Or if my mother hadn't cheated on my dad? We wouldn't have been warned about the questioning or the arrest and maybe Rob would have said the wrong thing. If I hadn't lied to Alex, I wouldn't have been so alone, wouldn't have had to bear the crushing weight of that secret by myself. And what if the boys had turned back? Every act—or failure to act—had repercussions. So many butterflies. A multitude of wings flapping.

A few weeks ago, my mom and I ran into Tyler's mother and little brother at Trader Joe's, which is halfway between Woodfield and Guilford. They were in the produce aisle. Mom had one hand on our shopping cart, and another reaching for a plastic tub of arugula; I was heading back to the cart with a carton of organic blueberries. I froze when I spotted Tyler's mother coming into the aisle from around the corner, a basket of groceries in one hand, her son's hand in the other. My heart rate quickened, and I watched in horror as the pair approached.

They walked quietly. Unsmiling. They both gazed downward, toward the floor. I didn't remember Tyler's mother being so petite. She looked—diminished, somehow. And he looked way too serious for a little kid. I supposed they had to go through the motions of everyday life just like everyone else, but it made me sad to think of them having to do mundane things like buying food after all that had happened. It had been hard for me and my family, but things would get better for us. Tyler would always be gone. The Millers would always have a hole in their family.

Jared saw us first. Stopped in his tracks. Tugged on his mother's hand as if pulling on the brakes. His mother and my mother looked up at the same time. Mom dropped the carton of arugula. Tyler's mom's eyes filled with tears. Mom swallowed hard.

Mrs. Miller turned around first. "Let's go, Jared," she said, pivoting, and practically dragging her son around the corner. Mom was too flustered to even finish shopping.

"We'll come back another time," she told me, abandoning both our cart and the upside-down carton of arugula, which remained, forgotten, on the ground, in the middle of the aisle. I felt a pang of guilt as we left the store. I didn't look back.

Our new house is only a few blocks from the water. Sometimes I grab my guitar, and walk to a small park that has a few benches facing out toward the Sound. I sit there and play, staring out at the water. It's peaceful.

On this particular afternoon, the sun glitters on the Sound, and I watch a gull swoop down, touch the water, and then sweep back up toward the sky, a spray of twinkling droplets in its wake. My guitar remains in its case, lying on the bench beside me. I look out to the horizon and wonder about what's on the other side. The line between sky and water seems so far away, yet, I know instinctively that there is so much more beyond it —a vast ocean, continents—that I can't even fathom.

It's time to put the past behind me. I reach into my jacket pocket, and pull out the folded envelope. I smooth it out and then carefully run one fingernail along the edge of the seal. I pull out the letter.

*Dear Hannah,*

*I'm so, so sorry. About everything. Sorry doesn't even begin to describe how I feel. I can't stand to think about what I did to you. I should never have lied to you about Rob, never forced you to choose between believing him or believing me. And Bryan told me about the texts he sent you.*

*Confessed that he had found your number in my phone. I had no idea. Please believe me.*

*I've really missed you. I know I can't call or text you. I understand that you need to be loyal to your brother. But I keep wanting to tell you about these kids that I'm working with at Big Brother Big Sister in Waterbury. That's where I'm doing my community service. I ride my bike there—I'm sure you heard that they suspended my license. Sometimes I help them with their homework, and other times we just hang out, shooting hoops or playing computer games. But there's this one kid who's into music, and I'm teaching him how to play guitar.*

*A lot of the kids I work with live in really harsh neighborhoods, and some of them don't have fathers, or have brothers who've been killed or who are in jail. This kid that I'm teaching guitar to—his older brother was killed in a drive-by shooting. He reminds me of Tyler Miller's brother, the one we used to see at the Music Shoppe. He's serious like him, doesn't smile much. But he tries really hard to get his fingers right on the frets, to make the chords sound right. And when he does, he looks at me like he's waiting for my approval. And when I nod at him, give him a thumbs up, he smiles so wide it nearly breaks my heart. Sometimes I think if I can help him, be a person he can look up to...I don't know. I guess this is just my own private way of doing penance.*

*I think a lot about the accident. How we should have turned back, like Rob said. How not doing something is still doing something. And how not saying something—well that's a choice too. So even though it was an accident, I know that I am guilty. I'm not* not *saying something ever again.*

*So let me say this. Hannah, I don't think our meeting was an accident. And however fucked up it was for me to think that I could get you on my side by getting you to like me, the joke was on me. Because I love you. It was real.*

Rob is pissed at me for a while. I know I deserve it. But we're both the new kids now, and often find each other home together, since we don't really have other people to hang out with yet.

He talks to me sometimes, even though he isn't high. In fact, he doesn't smoke anymore at all as far as I can tell. Sometimes he tells me funny stories about the kids on his e-sports team—he seems to spend more and more time with those kids, even though he doesn't have to. He also actually seems to care about his schoolwork now. I get it—he wants to move on with his life. So do I.

We sit on opposite sides of the kitchen table doing our homework one afternoon. We do this more and more often. It's kind of nice.

"Have you talked to Zach lately?" he asks out of nowhere one afternoon. I pause in the middle of doing an algebra equation, my pencil hovering above the page.

"Uh—no," I say slowly. I decide in that moment that reading a letter that Zach had written a couple of months ago doesn't count. "I don't talk to him anymore."

"Oh," he says, shrugging. "Just wondering." And goes back to highlighting the textbook he's been reading.

I don't regret what I did. Being with Zach. Or betraying him. I did what I had to do. For Rob. For my family. And life is moving on. It isn't perfect, but for the first time in a long while, I feel like I'm looking forward instead of backward. Thinking about what lies ahead, instead of worrying about something that already happened, something that can't be undone. I try not to think of all I've sacrificed to get here.

After a few minutes, Rob puts down his highlighter. "I can't focus on chemistry. Want to play a video game with me?"

"Sure," I say, acting chill, as my insides make a tiny jump for joy. Small steps. But I'll take it.

# About the Author

Lori Miller Kase is an award-winning journalist, short story writer, essayist and young adult author. Her work has appeared in a wide range of publications, including *The New York Times, The Atlantic, Vogue* and *Literary Mama*. She studied comparative literature at Brown University and creative writing at Wesleyan University, where she earned a Master's degree. *The Accident*, her debut novel, was the 2024 YA finalist for the Tassy Walden Awards for New Voices in Children's Literature. The mother of two grown children, Lori writes from Simsbury, Connecticut, where she lives with her husband and a bossy dog named Joey. You can visit her at www.lorimillerkase.com.

# Acknowledgments

Ever since I started reading books, I've wanted to write one. You are now holding this novel in your hands thanks to the help and encouragement of so many people.

Thanks, first, to David LeGere, Miranda Heyman, Christopher Madden and the rest of the team at Woodhall Press for turning my manuscript into a book, and for bringing my book into the world. Your insightful editing notes helped to make *The Accident* a better novel, and I so appreciate the time and dedication that everyone at Woodhall put into my project.

To Denise Alfeld, editor extraordinaire, and the best cheerleader: You were the first person to read this manuscript in its entirety and your astute editing feedback was invaluable in setting me on the right course.

To Christine Pakkala, an incredible teacher and editor, for your spot-on critiques, impeccable editing, and inspiring classes: Thank you for helping me to find my teen voice, and for making me a better writer of YA and children's literature.

To my other writing teachers, especially Anne Greene, Jamie Cat Callan, Rachel Basch, Marcelle Soviero and Rahla Xenopoulos: I can't overemphasize how important you have been to me and my development as a writer. You have inspired me and taught me to dig deeper. Shout out to all my teachers over the years for encouraging my love of writing and reading, especially Mrs. Slater (second grade), who actually assigned my suggested creative writing assignments to the class, and who wrote "someday you will be a famous writer" in my writing journal, which I still have; Mr. Pehlke (sixth grade), who nurtured a love for reading in all his students, awarding us "home runs" for every book we completed (my "Most home runs" trophy was the only baseball-related trophy I would ever receive); and Mr. Broza (high school), for being encouraging, supportive, and completely engaging as a teacher of both literature and writing.

To the students in my many Writing Books for Kids classes at Westport Writers' Workshop, especially the core contingent who returned with me session after session, and especially Diana, who went above and beyond: Thank you for offering such amazing, constructive feedback on this novel, five pages at a time.

To the incredible writers I meet with weekly, biweekly, and monthly—and my earliest writing friends, who I still exchange writing with on a less scheduled basis—I can't thank you enough for your writing advice, your insightful feedback, your support and your friendship. Writing can be a lonely endeavor, but not when you are surrounded by a writing community as supportive and inspiring as mine.

To my Beta Readers—Debbie, Stacy, Sara, Karen, Stacey, both Laurens, Caroline and Alex—and all my friends who told me they couldn't wait to read *The Accident* before it was published: Thank you for your unwavering love and support.

To my team of criminal justice experts: Judge Stuart Rosen, Attorney Eric Hard, Judge Barbara Aaron, and Police Chief Paul Hammick: Thank you so much for taking the time to educate me about the ins and outs of hit-and-run accident investigations, for explaining the Connecticut laws pertaining to such accidents, and for walking me through the way the juvenile justice system works. I may have used some creative license when scenes called for added drama, so anything that veers slightly from legal reality is on me. Your patient and thorough explanations were invaluable.

To Jason Mraz and Bluewater Music: Thank you so much for allowing me to include song lyrics from "I'm Yours" and "Hey Love" in this book.

To my parents, who have been reading my stories since I was in first grade: Thank you for your endless encouragement, and for filling my life with books since as far back as I can remember.

To my amazing siblings, those I grew up with and those I've acquired through marriage, along with my mother-in-law and the rest of the Millers and Kases: Thank you for cheering me on, for reading the things that I write, and for your unconditional love and support.

To Brandon and Sara: Your passion for your pursuits inspire me every day. Being your parent and watching you grow up has been the highlight of my life—it's not surprising that family relationships are at the center of almost every piece of fiction that I write.

To Danny: Thank you for encouraging me to do what I love, and what I've always dreamed of doing—writing books. And most of all, thank you for being—as Hannah would put it—my person.

And finally, to you, reader: Thank you for picking up this book, for spending your time reading my words, and for making it all the way through the acknowledgements!